Joyce Stranger is the author of many well-loved novels for both adults and children. She has always been associated with animals and has spent much of her life helping friends who farm or breed horses and dogs, as well as training her own dogs for Obedience shows. All the animal incidents in her books are based on her own experiences.

She and her husband live in Anglesey. They have two sons and a daughter, and many grandchildren. She now has Janus, a Golden Retriever, and Chita, a German Shepherd. Her bitch Puma, who made up the trio in Joyce Stranger's book, THREE'S A PACK, died recently: she won a championship certificate and was well known in the breed ring. They also have a Siamese cat, Chia.

Also by Joyce Stranger

and published by Corgi Books

The Stallion
Joyce Stranger

CORGI BOOKS
A DIVISION OF TRANSWORLD PUBLISHERS LTD

THE STALLION

A CORGI BOOK 0 552 12100 2

Originally published in Great Britain
by Michael Joseph Ltd.

PRINTING HISTORY
Michael Joseph edition published 1981
Corgi edition published 1983

This book is set in 10/11 Plantin

Corgi Books are published by
Transworld Publishers Ltd.,
Century House, 61–63 Uxbridge Road,
Ealing, London W5 5SA

Made and printed in Great Britain by
Hunt Barnard Printing Ltd, Aylesbury, Bucks.

Dedicated
in memory of Anthea Joseph
who has left behind her, for all
of us, a gap that nobody else
can fill.

My thanks are due to Vivienne Kershaw, editor of *Dog Training Weekly*, for allowing me to use the poem 'The Greyhound' by 'Dale', which first appeared in her magazine, and also to 'Dale' herself.

1

Roderick Morland stared at his mother in fury.

'You're mad,' he said. 'Absolutely out of your mind. How could you do such a thing, and with Father not yet cold in his grave?'

The trite and absurd phrase triggered a nerve.

Rhea looked at her son. It was hard to remember that this was the baby she had nursed, the boy she had watched grow up. Rod had become a very hard man. Like his father, he was a lawyer, preferring to prosecute, and the eyes that looked at her now were considering, alien, an interrogator's eyes, with no affection in them at all.

They woke her to anger as nothing else could. He behaved as if he thought she didn't care. The guests had left for home; the remains of the meal were still on the table. The service had ended just over four hours before and she was raw and aching with misery and wanted to be alone with her grief. How dared he speak to her like that?

Mark, her second son, was watching her, knowing her better than Rod. Rod seldom saw beyond his own desires and his own needs. Ambition drove him as mercilessly as it had his father. It had driven his father to death, clawing at his heart as he raced up the steps of the Courthouse to what was to be the most important case of his life.

Rhea hadn't recovered from shock, from the sight of the quiet man who had come to her door, the police car standing outside. They had told her, as gently as one could tell such news, that her husband had died of a heart attack; died at once, with no time for help, as he had been dead even before the ambulance arrived. He had always driven himself too hard, she thought desolately.

The next few days had been a nightmare. She had coasted along, doing all that was needed, in a haze that isolated her from reality. She could barely remember any incident at all, walking, talking, replying to questions from a remoteness that frightened her but that she could not reveal to anyone. Nothing seemed to matter any more. She looked at the food her daughter-in-law set before her without even realising what it was.

The world had stopped for her, but other people went on. Lying on her bed at night, staring into the darkness, she wondered about life without John. She had refused sleeping pills; she hated taking any medicines unless they were unavoidable. Nature healed and Nature killed, and you had to learn to cope.

She had coped once before, long ago, when a speeding car, driven by a drunken driver, had crashed into her as she brought her five-year-old daughter home from a party. Elizabeth had died at once. She could still remember the broken doll that had been her daughter, lying in the ruins of her party dress; she had dressed her with such pride.

That had been over twenty years ago but the memory was as fresh as yesterday. She had never had another daughter and now she wished she had.

Sadie, Rod's wife, was competent and hard, a sophisticated woman who, Rhea sometimes thought, totally despised her. Louise, her other daughter-in-law, was very different. Gentle and pretty, spoiled by adoring parents, Louise had not learned to face reality or take responsibility. Rhea sometimes thought her son found his wife something of a liability, as he had to be father as well as husband, cushioning her and protecting her, and if there was something Louise wanted that he couldn't afford, her mother always bought it for her. Louise, now two months pregnant, was lying down, giving way as always to uncontrollable tears. She hardly knew John, Rhea thought resentfully. Louise needed life and gaiety, constant parties, friends around, visits to expensive restaurants, a house full of flowers. She wondered how Mark could afford it. He was only

8

just starting his career and a wife with such expensive tastes might well prove a liability. He worked for a small advertising agency, having a flair for amusing pictures and zany captions that the advertisers liked. He had a long way to go as yet.

Rod was still intent on making her realise her folly. John would have felt the same way, she thought, yet this time she was sure she was right. She had to learn to live alone. She needed a new direction, needed to get right away. It was impossible to explain to either of her sons.

'Leaving London and all of us is bad enough,' Rod said. 'You'll be on your own; you aren't so young, and you could die as Father died, suddenly, away from us all, with no one to help.'

'It would have made no difference to your father whether we were there or not,' Rhea said. It was one of the unhappiest thoughts in her mind; that he had died alone, without her near him, without her even knowing. She didn't want to be reminded.

'As if that isn't enough,' Rod went on, bearing her down, as if she had never interrupted, intent on finishing what he had to say. 'You buy a stallion . . . a stallion. I never heard anything so crazy, now, when you need money more than ever. It will cost a fortune to keep; you can't ride it; you can't do anything with it and you leave it in the care of a man you knew as a child and haven't even met for how long, thirty years? He could be anything; he could be a crook.'

'I knew him very well,' Rhea said, anger sharpening her voice.

She had looked in the mirror an hour before and been shocked by the face that stared back at her, an old woman's face that she barely recognised as her own, a travesty of herself, hiding the beauty that she had cherished for long enough but knew would pass. Grief had destroyed it, adding another, and yet an absurd sorrow.

It wasn't fair.

She had known Rory well. She had been going to marry him, all those years before meeting John. She had been nineteen and he was twenty-five, managing her father's stables.

He was a born horseman, as dedicated to the horses as her

father, giving up his free time, schooling them, living with the mares when they were foaling, most of the time barely noticing her, yet, when he was aware of her, he had courted her assiduously and the wedding date had been arranged. She had bought her dress and they had been given a cottage in the grounds of the stables.

Ten weeks before the wedding Rory had vanished in the night, leaving a note for her.

'Darling Rhea, I can't do it. It would never work. You're too intense; you worship me and I'm only human. I'm a tomcat, and I'll never settle down. The thought of being married terrifies me. I'm sorry, sorry, sorry, but you'll get over it. Marry someone who wants a secure future. I don't. And you would never accept the kind of life I'll be leading. I'm going to see the world, to learn about horses of all countries and all breeds, and then one day come back and have a fine stables of my own . . . *always the horses*. Rory.'

The words burned in her brain. She had thought she would die, but nobody died of love. And then John had come along, four years later, safe, sensible, wanting all the things she thought she wanted. Suddenly, in the middle of her marriage she had found that she needed something different too; and neither he nor Rory could give it to her.

She had known the stallion for six months, long before John died. She had met Rory again by accident when she had driven north to paint a stallion that he had in his care for the summer. She had no idea who owned the stables when she accepted the commission. They had both changed. He was still the best horseman she had ever met and she admired the stables that he now owned. She had gone there on her own business. He had told her the stallion would have to be sold; he needed the money. Horses cost a fortune to feed and to keep, he had a new young colt that was up and coming and he didn't want both animals. Yet he'd have liked to keep the older beast on the premises. He was very fond of him, which was absurd for a man in business.

'I don't often let my heart rule my head,' Rory had said. There had been silence, both of them remembering.

She had sat, the day that John died, in a limbo of feeling, not

10

realising she was numb with shock. Nothing seemed to matter any more. The family had gone home, on her insistence, leaving her on her own. She would wake up and John would comfort her, more comforting in memory than he had ever been in reality. He had been unaware of her most of the time, she thought. His work was his passion. He had time for little else. Sometimes he talked about it to her, but very rarely. She might read of a case in the newspapers. She knew he had been about to take on the prosecution of a woman who had been involved in something very nasty indeed. He hadn't told her the details, saying it would upset her and better not to know. Now she found herself wondering about it, absurdly latching on to something that could occupy her mind and let her forget that John was dead.

She had phoned Rory on impulse and arranged to buy the stallion. Rory would keep him for her. She had to make a new way of life; her life had changed course within hours, and nothing would be the same again. She had always longed to live in the country, to recapture the peace of her childhood, only enduring city life because John liked the town. He enjoyed urban life and its pleasures. He liked eating out and being recognised by head waiters. He had craved recognition all his life, and sometimes, dressing for an occasion that was alien to her, wearing clothes and jewellery that made her feel guilty when she considered the price, she had wondered what life was really about. There seemed little point to their existence. She had worked hard at the façade, but often she wondered what had happened to the girl who had been engaged to a man who loved horses, the girl who had been brought up with horses, who had intended to breed horses, and who had vanished long ago.

Fifteen years ago she had had to make a decision. It was that decision which had led to her purchase; had led to her son's anger, although he would never know why or how she had taken the course she had followed since then. He would never understand either. John would not have understood, but now she knew her long-kept secret would have to be revealed. She could not go on leading a double life, and there was no longer any need.

11

She had been wife and she had been mother; she had cherished a tiny place of her own, and in recent months she realised that her secret could not be kept much longer. It had been increasingly hard during the past year to hide the truth. She had put off the revelation, afraid that John would never forgive her for her deception. Now she wondered what her two sons would say, and also what her daughters-in-law would think.

When the boys left home, Rod to follow in his father's foot-steps, Mark to follow his own longing to work with words and pictures, she had found her escape had become a challenge.

'Mother . . . you aren't making sense and you haven't answered me. Why hide in a backwood and why waste money in such an insane way? You owe us an explanation.'

He paced the room, a lion in a parlour. He was a big man, bigger even than his father, his dark red hair beautifully cut and groomed to perfection. Rod had always needed to be immaculate even as a small boy. He had been a very trying boy, she realised now, looking back, detached from her family in a way she did not understand. His suit must have cost a fortune; how dared he criticise her?

'You'll have to economise; Father can't have left very much,' Rod said. 'We'll help of course, if you need it.' Rod thought he was being kind and practical, but the patronage infuriated Rhea. They seemed not to understand she was an adult, fully capable of running her own life. They were treating her as if she were ninety, instead of being still a couple of years under sixty. She was young; she could ride again; and above all could live as she chose, and enjoy a freedom she had never known. She had lived at home until she married; always a daughter and then wife and mother and never herself.

'I'll manage,' Rhea said. 'And I'm not really sure that it's your concern.'

'Mother,' Rod said in tones of sweet reasonableness, 'you don't understand. Father cushioned you from reality, he was earning vast sums of money. You won't be able to go on living like that.'

'I sometimes earned more than your father,' Rhea said, wanting to assert herself. All her life she had listened to them;

listened to blow-by-blow accounts of football matches and boxing matches and boyhood triumphs and manhood triumphs. The stallion bragging of his prowess, she thought. At least my stallion can't talk. 'Your father spent far more than he earned. I had to make up the deficit – all our lives.'

'How could you?' Rod asked, disbelief in his face.

'Have you ever heard of Ray Morton?' she asked.

'Everyone has,' Rod said impatiently. 'She's one of the best painters and photographers of horses in the country. Her picture of a stallion earned fifteen thousand guineas at the last auction. It's a magnificent piece of work. I wanted to commission a picture from her, but she wouldn't do it for me. I never met her of course.'

'You're talking to her now,' Rhea said. 'Ray Morton; Rhea Morland. None of you ever asked where I spent my days; or how I spent my days. None of you ever wanted to listen to me; only to yourselves. I listened to you; my God, how I listened to all of you, talk, talk, talk, when there was a picture burning in my brain, when I wanted to rush over to my studio and put down on paper; when I wanted to get it right, the line of the animal, the curve of his neck, the set of his tail, the shape of him, the passion of him, the strength of him. But mostly I couldn't. I had to cook for you and had to help your father; I was never me; I was something you all made me into. I was mother, I was wife; I was hostess, I was cook, I was a zombie, doing your bidding; Now I'll do my own bidding; now I'll live for myself. I bought the stallion I painted. I wanted him – that's all.'

She looked at their astounded faces, at the dawning of interest in Sadie's eyes, and knew that of all of them, Sadie understood, because Sadie was fighting for her own survival, which was something she hadn't thought about before. Sadie had a career and she cared about it. She was a dress designer, designing costumes for some of the big London productions. Sadie's mother wanted grandchildren, but Rhea had never put that as a main priority. She was not a maternal woman herself; something had died in her when her small daughter died. She had begun to paint during long months when she couldn't walk after the crash and had been recognised as having a rare talent by her teacher, who had encouraged her to go on, had later lent her studio space and an address and become her agent.

'I painted that stallion; he earned me fifteen thousand guineas and he was up for sale. He has cost me two-thirds of that. I can have him trained; follow his career, get back among my horses. I have to look forward, not back. You don't need me, any of you.'

'Louise needs you,' Mark said. His wife needed more strength than he had to give her; she drained him of energy; and he wanted to have his mother near. Rhea had always been strong; had comforted them and helped them solve their problems. He hadn't realised it until she talked of moving to a quiet village two hundred miles away, to the north, not very far from Rory.

'Louise needs to learn to cope on her own, not to stand on my feet for the rest of her life,' Rhea said. 'I'm tired; I need to rest. I need time to myself and time to think. I've a lot to do. Tomorrow I'm going down to see Rory and finalise details of Lucifer's transfer. Later I may buy a mare and breed a foal; I've needed horses for the last forty years and I haven't even known it.'

Was it forty years? It couldn't be. She had married at twenty-three and been married for thirty-five years; she was fifty-eight. The same age as John. If she wasn't careful she'd lapse into old age, a sit-by-the-fire-and-dream-of-the-past-person; of what might have been; of what could have been. That had never been her way. She had fought to make a career and had made it; it had been a well-kept secret as no one ever met her. Rachel Dean who had lent her her studio had negotiated always for her; Rhea had gone down to see the horses, taking her camera, posing as Rachel's assistant; no one was sure whether Ray Morton was not a pseudonym for Rachel Dean. It had taken a great deal of connivance, but John would have been furious at the thought that his wife had another identity; he would never have understood. There had been all the fun of an intrigue and none of the risk; her love affair, all her life, had been with horses.

And now Lucifer was hers in fact as well as on canvas, and no

14

one but she would understand what that meant. Maybe Rory did. The association with Rory would be spiced with memories that might re-awaken pain. He was still attractive, a big burly man with a weathered face and dark eyes alight with amusement, and he laughed.

Did her sons ever laugh, she wondered, looking at them now, wishing they would go.

It was Sadie who interpreted her thought. She stood dark, elegant, beautifully dressed, her exotic face for once thoughtful. She walked over to Rhea and lightly kissed her cheek.

'Rest. I'll take them away; and I apologise.'

'For what?' Rhea asked in astonishment.

'For misjudging you. Would you paint a horse for me? One I can treasure and say to my friends with pride: "Yes, it's a Ray Morton; my mother-in-law painted it. Isn't it fabulous?" '

Rhea had never been nearer to tears. She swallowed, and took Sadie's hand and squeezed it and smiled, but dared not speak.

'Come on,' Sadie said, her voice suddenly sharp. 'Your mother needs to be alone. Fetch Louise, Mark, and let's go.'

'I'll bring her in to say goodbye,' Mark said, as he turned towards the door.

'No.' Sadie knew that Rhea had had all she could stand. She went to the cabinet, and poured out a large glass of brandy.

'Drink that; and rest. We'll be in touch, and good luck,' she said.

The room was blissfully silent; she was alone at last, as she had longed to be alone; to collect her wits if she could, to think, to plan. She was taking nothing from here with her; only the furnishings of the studio and the little room above it that Rachel had let to her; a refuge where she had run when the demands of her menfolk grew too strong.

'Vampires, sucking me dry,' she thought, as the front door slammed behind them. She had done everything she could for them: sacrificed her time and her money and her self and grown old looking after them.

She sipped the brandy.

The silence of the house closed round her. She had wanted to be free and now she was free, but she knew she had lost something that could never be replaced; there had been more between herself and John than she had realised. He would never have understood her need to paint; her need for horses; her crazy purchase of a stallion, but he would have recognised the rack the boys put her on now; their comments and their criticisms and the lack of understanding that would only come years later when they in their turn reached this point in life and this experience.

Now they dismissed those nearing sixty as if they were beyond it, past it, incapable of anything but sitting by the fire and doddering round the town. She would prove them wrong; prove all of them wrong.

Tomorrow she would drive into the country and find herself a cottage; and she would claim her stallion, and make sure that Rory understood that this client was on a business footing and there was nothing else between them. She paused, looking back to her nineteen-year-old self, aware for the first time of betrayal; she had thought herself loved and needed and about to be married. He had gone, and for four years she had lived without self-confidence, aware she had been of secondary interest in his life. To her he had been a hero – she had worshipped – and nothing had ever been quite the same again.

So why had she gone to him now? She didn't know. She didn't much care. She was on her own. A widow; it was a word that reminded her of weeds and of spiders; a word she hated as much as she hated the word spinster – spinster of this parish – it sounded dry and eaten up with virginity, repressed and bitter; yet spinsters could be sixteen or twenty and only bachelor girls.

The brandy was making her maudlin.

The silent house oppressed her and she knew she was right to get away. She prayed that the phone wouldn't ring, but maybe it wouldn't because people had no idea what to say.

'How are you?'

What did you answer? Devastated, destroyed, desolate; I'm bereaved. That was a word too. Her eyes hurt and her throat ached and she wanted to scream. Hysteria would claim her if she wasn't careful.

She had bought a stallion.

He was Lucifer, son of the morning. An Arab. She couldn't pronounce his official name. He was the colour of sunlight, and his flosslike mane was spun silk; his tail was long and gleamed as he thrashed it. He had curvetted for her, reared up to show his nobility and mastery, and come to her and nipped her ear. She had fallen in love with him when she painted him – a kind of totally unselfish love that few people would ever understand. He was perfect.

He had nibbled the button delicately off her coat and dropped it into her hand, then had raced up the pasture, and she had watched him move, sweeping over the ground, so that she wanted to catch the moment and hold it, with the sun setting behind him and mountains black against the sky and the woods that grew dark and secret. The sunlit field, the running horse, and the wind soft on her cheek, promised peace if she came here to live. Peace and a place to paint.

Villages were always peaceful.

She went up to bed and undressed in a dream and lay and thought of the future, blotting out the past. Rory would train Lucifer and win with him; make a name for him? Perhaps jump him, but he was a dressage horse. He loved the work; he could have been trained for the ballet of the Austrian Riding School; she had spent a month in Vienna before she was married and watched the training daily, wanting to try it herself.

She would watch him train; and paint and live in peace.

She fell asleep, unaware that the gods were laughing and she was about to enter some of the stormiest months of her life.

2

It was a grey day, the woods damp with moisture from last night's rain. Dave Martin removed the tracking harness and threw his old glove for Venn to fetch. The dog bounded after it. He was delighted with himself, knowing he had just completed a good track. It had been a tough one, through the forest undergrowth, over a wall, along a hard concrete path that held little scent, ending with the glove hidden in a cowfield, where even Dave could smell the reek of the cowpats and where it might have proved almost impossible to find.

But an operational policeman had no choice as to the places in which his dog tracked. He watched the dog. He had matured into a powerful animal, all black, with dense brown eyes that held confidence and wisdom. The dog was now six years old. Six years since Dave had named him Avenger; in memory of his dead wife, killed by a drunken hit-and-run driver; in memory of his dog Royal, killed in a fight.

Time had blunted the misery. Time had changed him. He was now a hard, tough professional, with enough confidence to deal with anything, but with enough compassion to make him a first-class man for the job. The dog was no longer Avenger; he was Venn, which was Norwegian for a friend. The only friend he could trust, never to let him down, never to betray a confidence, never to stab him in the back. People were difficult to handle; difficult to understand, but the dog was never difficult.

Learn his behaviour, know his pattern and he was yours for the whole of his life. Dave watched the dog lope into the bushes and emerge, his tail waving. He raced back, and leaped at his master's face. It wasn't allowed, but it was something

Dave could never resist, when they were alone.

He stroked the hard head, looking into the dark eyes, and then spoke. 'Off.' Venn dropped to his side, watching him, eager for another command, a dog that always wanted to be working, a tireless dog, capable of hard training, of a long track, of going on for ever. A dog in a million. Dave slapped the dog on the rump and grinned. 'Off with you,' he said and the dog bounded ahead of him, down the path, pausing to cock his leg, to sniff on a rabbit trail, but coming at once when Dave flicked a finger, or cracked his knuckles.

He and the dog spent much of their time together and knew one another as few husbands and wives knew one another. The dog read the man like a book; knew anger, knew when his master needed instant unswerving obedience; knew when he could safely play the fool and earn a laugh.

Soon it would be time to return. Susie would be home from school. It was Dave's day off, but he lived in a police house beside the kennels, so that days off, if spent at home, were days on duty, without even realising it. The men came in and out, wanting advice and help. Dave was a sergeant now, and in charge of training.

He thought of almost nothing but training dogs; training them to scale, to hurdle, to long jump; training for tracking; training for searching; training for heeling; training for control. Training for man work, to disarm a man with a gun, to stop a crook in full flight, to bring home the criminal, tracked from the scene of his crime.

Tom, who ran the kennels, was an ex-huntsman, a good man with a dog, and Dave's right hand, having more importance than he realised. Tom's wife, Heather, looked after Dave's home. He had never wanted to re-marry. Susie, now ten, had come home to live with him. She was a solemn girl, who had spent too long with her grandparents, but Dave had had no choice when she was small. Here, she was never alone, as Reg, in the house next door, was married, with two young children, and Susie went in there for her tea if Dave were out on duty, accepting her father's job as part of her life. She never complained, even when a promised treat had to be foregone because he had urgent duty. People were lost, or injured, or killed, all the time, and his life was unpredictable.

He had bought Susie a dog of her own; a little collie cross, and she was learning to train him, going out solemnly with any man off-duty prepared to give her time, learning to manage a dog, to handle a dog, and able to join in some of her father's conversation about dogs, as she watched a dog track, and knew he had lost the urge to go on. Her dog, like Venn, would track for ever.

Dave sat on a fallen tree and ate the sandwiches that Heather had made him. She was always convinced that any man who went without food for more than four hours would die of starvation. She was a round plump jolly woman, very good for the child, feeding her up, making her her favourite dishes, teaching her how to cook, having no children of her own, and a long stifled desire to have a daughter.

Tom enjoyed talking to Susie, too, and she helped him swab out the kennels, helped him move the dogs, took some of them for exercise, feeling needed and important and a big help to her father. She looked after the babies next door and played with them, so that she did not feel the lack of brothers or sisters. Heather, and Mair, Reg's wife, were always there by day to mother her and comfort her, and both had time to listen to her and talk to her. It was a good place to live; there was always someone around.

Heather's idea of a sandwich was a round of beef with lettuce and pickle; a large pasty and a piece of fruit cake. At this rate, he'd be needing to go on a diet.

Dave stood and folded the paper, and put it in his raincoat pocket. He whistled the dog to heel and set off down the ride towards the cottage. This was his favourite walk; the last part of his day off, a routine he had kept for the past five years.

The cottage stood at the end of the ride; it was old and had a beaten-up look, and had been empty for as long as he could remember. One day, he would buy it and renovate it, and he and Susie would live here, out in the air, away from the town, away from the job, away from the constant reminder of pressures to bear, of work to be done, of the ringing phone that summoned him to duty.

He would make a garden; grow his own vegetables. Susie

could keep a goat and learn to look after it and milk it. It was an idyll, as unreal as a child's fairy story, but it sometimes served to keep him sane. They would build the cottage again together, would choose furnishings and Susie would be old enough to sew curtains. He refused to contemplate the thought of her growing up, of her marriage, of her leaving him entirely alone again except for the dog.

He could see the cottage, restored and attractive, its roof repaired, chintzy curtains bright in the old leaded windows; walls whitewashed and his own furniture there. It had become a part of his life, a dream so real that when he saw the garden littered with ladders and a man re-thatching the roof, as he turned out of the ride, he felt as if someone had thumped him in the midriff, and taken away his wind.

Someone else had bought his cottage. Incredibly he felt cheated and angry so that the thatcher, looking down, saw a tall man – dark haired, dark eyed, his mouth grim – surveying him, and felt uneasy, as if he was committing a crime.

'Good-day,' he called, trying to erase the feeling, which was absurd.

Dave suddenly realised what he was doing. He had his business face on; a face that made even Susie anxious so that she said, 'Daddy, where have you gone?' and brought him back to his senses.

The man came down the ladder, and walked towards the gate.

'Someone bought the cottage?' Dave asked, knowing that someone must have done but hoping against hope it might be bought as an investment, to rent; he could move there then.

'A widow lady; she's spending a fortune on having it done up. Comes over to my place to give instructions. No expense spared. Her husband was a barrister, they say. John Morland. Died sudden of a heart attack, not so long ago. A few weeks back.'

He nodded, and went back to his work.

Dave thought back. John Morland. He'd met him once when he'd worked in London. He'd seen the obituary and remembered the name, He'd been a good man, very good at his job. He'd died only recently, so his widow must have moved

21

fast. So far as Dave knew he had never seen her, though he had known her husband by sight. He guessed at the motive behind the move. He had wanted to throw up everything when Donna had been killed; to move away from memory, to a place he had never known with her. But he had Susie to think of and he couldn't abandon his job. He wondered if John Morland's widow had been happily married; or had merely endured. It wouldn't be an easy life; and it wouldn't be easy here, isolated in the woods, away from people. He wondered why she had decided to live here. There was an old barn behind the cottage. He walked round the back to look at it, wondering if she would have it knocked down, but workmen were busy restoring its fabric, and re-roofing it.

He whistled the dog. The van was parked at the other end of the ride and he was now late. He had promised Susie he would he home early for tea and he was going to be hard put to it to keep his promise. He ran, the dog bounding joyously beside him, sure this was for his benefit.

The van was almost a second home for both of them. Venn leaped into his compartment and settled down, and Dave drove fast, covering the miles, bringing the van in to the yard where three other vans were parked, the men washing them. Susie was with them, laughing as she dodged the hose. Two of the men were new recruits, both young enough to make Susie feel as if they were older brothers; both ready to kick a football with her, or throw a tennis ball or help her with her homework.

'I wrote a poem at school about dogs,' she said, when Dave had hugged her and taken off his raincoat. Venn was in his kennel, with Tom feeding him. They were late.

'A poem?' Dave's mind was on the cottage.

'Can I read it to you?' Susie asked, trying to bring him back to her. So often when she spoke to her father he seemed to be thinking of something else, but she was a persistent child.

'Yes, read it,' Dave said. Susie had made him a pot of tea and cut a slice of cake. He didn't want either but he couldn't refuse. He poured himself tea, hot and strong, and added milk and sugar, and perched on the edge of the battered armchair that was as comfortable as a second skin.

'Dogs,' Susie read. 'It was my English homework; we had to write about an animal. Miss Holland read Blake's "Tiger" to us. "Tiger, tiger, burning bright." Mine isn't as good as that,' she ended anxiously and Dave tried hard not to grin.

'They're a lot of work
And they make a mess
And they don't do what they ought to do
But all they ask is a quick caress
And a moment's thought from you.
In return they give you an ocean of unstinted lifelong undying devotion.
Don't you think you owe them a minute or two?'

'That's very good,' Dave said, and meant it. She had said a great deal in her own way, and he thought it worth copying and putting on the wall of the pre-fabricated hut they used as an office, with the training charts and the duty rosters.

'I couldn't write one as good,' Dave said truthfully. He yawned. He had been up since six, when he took three dog handlers out for an early morning practice track; two of the dogs had been half hearted on the last training session, and flagging enthusiasm helped no one. Besides they were due to hold the Area Trials soon, when men would compete to see who would work in the National Trials for best man and dog of the year. It was a coveted place and no one from his section had ever won. One day he and Venn might have won; but not now. He had too much to do and wasn't competing.

Tom came into the room carrying a large pasty in a pie-dish.

'Heather can't come tomorrow; our next-door neighbour's broken her ankle and Heather's going with her to hospital to have the plaster off. So she sent this so you wouldn't be put out.'

Heather provided them with more food than they paid her for, Dave thought, but she would never take extra money. She worked for interest and she loved feeling in the centre of things, keeping Dave's home going well so that he was freed for what she felt was one of the most important jobs in the world. Heather had her own views on life; a good day's work for a good day's pay, she told Susie often enough. No work, no

23

food, was another of her sayings, and if Susie didn't do her homework well, it was Heather who rebuked her for bad marks.

'Got to grow up clever; can't earn wages unless you're clever,' Heather told her. 'I earn because I'm a good house-keeper; just as well; not every woman makes a good housewife. Some are born sluts.'

Heather had no time for sluts; every room shone under her care; dishes were washed as soon as the food was eaten and she would have made an excellent candidate for all the whiter-than-white advertisements, as her idea of a decent washing line was to have everything so clean it would be a matter of pride when worn. She kept Dave's uniforms immaculate, taking them off to the cleaners, pressing his trousers, brushing dog hairs off his suits.

Susie had gone off to her room, which Dave had fitted out as a little bedsitter, with a divan bed, an armchair, wall cupboards for her books and clothes, and a large desk, big enough to paint on, or do a jigsaw on. It was her private room, and he only went in by invitation. The walls were hung with posters of animals; with a wall chart she had begged from the vet, of all the breeds of dogs in the world, and a bird chart she had bought by collecting tokens off a breakfast cereal packet.

The wall above her desk was a portrait gallery, of all the dogs she knew; of any publicity that the press gave the dog handlers; pictures from the daily or evening papers of one of the dogs in her father's section.

One day it would be a wall on which her rosettes were hung as she was determined to win competitions with her dog and had just persuaded Dave to let her join the dog club, where one of the men helped with the teaching on Wednesday nights. As a result Dave found himself with a motley collection of children and dogs sometimes on Sunday mornings, all wanting to teach their pets to jump, so that the police jumps were lowered and any men around watched with amusement at the rabble of animals that were, rather to Dave's surprise, slowly coming under control and doing rather well.

Susie's collie could jump as well as any police dog and she put it over the scale daily, handling him like a veteran. Trot thought it great fun and co-operated willingly.

Len, the handler who took the class, was toying with the idea of a children's display team. He had some promising youngsters and Susie was the star of them, handling her dog better than many adults, able to get the most out of him, perhaps, Len sometimes thought, because children and animals were on the same wavelength, uncomplicated by adult woes and worries, living for the moment and concentrating on the job in hand.

Susie was unaware of his thoughts; he made sure she had no favours from him and was often harder on her than on the other children because he knew she could do more than they and had a future they did not. She also had a major advantage in that she was always around at weekends and in the holidays when they were training, and was learning fast, fascinated by all the dog lore that came her way.

Talk of tracks; of failed tracks and successful tracks; talk of different dogs and different dog natures. There was Matt, who was slow and solid and had to be played with and excited before he would work; and there was Chuff, who was so excitable that he had to be handled with extreme care, or he was out of hand, and so enthusiastic he turned on his handler and nipped his leg playfully in frustration at being held back when he wanted to track.

There was old steady Tammas, who was soon to be retired; and Venn who was tireless, and could go on when the other dogs needed to rest; and Solly who was splendid at tracking but useless at criminal work, and hated running out at a man with a gun, though he did it, out of bravery and love for his handler, rather than of his own will.

Len sometimes thought Susie was exactly like her father, and not only in looks. Both had a way with a dog. It was lucky for Dave that he had a daughter who could share his enthusiasms. They had great fun together when there was time.

Time. It vanished. Dave sat long after Susie had gone to bed, working out the plans for the next course; they always had a test at the end of it and he needed a judge; someone from a distance who wouldn't know any of the men; nor know what standard to expect, so that he got a good idea of how they compared with other Forces.

There were notes for him. Len's radio was on the blink. One of the vans had a puncture and the tyre was wrecked; needed a new tyre. Tammas had a lump on his back which the vet said needed removing as the dog was in pain; so he would be laid off for at least a fortnight. There was always something.

He switched on the television set and lay back, his mind roaming freely as the soap-opera detective series was well below standard and did not hold his attention.

Venn had tracked well, but had been slow on the search, apparently tiring of hunting for small objects that might be clues. He needed to brighten the dog up; life had been too serious recently. He needed also to get that searching right as he used his dog to show the others what to do. He had been hampered when Venn was young by not having a dog of his own; now he was hampered because he and Venn were rarely operational. The dog needed his interest revived.

He needed his own interest revived. He was bone tired; aching with weariness, his brain for ever busy, planning, thinking, seeking for reasons for things that had gone wrong.

The search a week before for an old lady, who had wandered in her nightdress from her daughter's home. They had nearly been too late and the dogs had had problems that he couldn't fathom. They had searched the main area four times without finding her and it was only by chance in the end that one of the dogs had come upon her lying in the undergrowth, soaked to the skin, suffering from exposure. She was recovering in hospital now.

He went across the yard to the office and looked at the large map that occupied the whole of one wall, pin-pointing the area. He knew the man who farmed most of the fields. He picked up the telephone.

'Joe?'

The voice in his ear was sleepy; a man preparing for bed, up early for milking. Dave cursed himself for forgetting farmers had different hours to the rest of the world. He asked his question.

'A week ago?' Joe was rousing himself to think. 'Had the

fields sprayed by air the day before, didn't I? The whole area was saturated at about ten o'clock that morning.'

And the old lady had gone missing at about six in the morning. They had had the call at eleven that day; after the fields were sprayed; after all scent had been destroyed. What was worse, he wondered what harm the spray would have done to his dogs' noses. You never could tell what had happened; the dog couldn't tell you. If only they could talk.

He had his answer and that itch was stilled. It wasn't his men or his dogs; it was circumstances beyond his control. Sound well on a report, he thought sourly, writing it mentally. The victim died because of circumstances beyond our control. Trouble was, only people who understood about dogs would understand they weren't foolproof and a fouled trail or a very old trail was impossible for the dog to follow.

The poor brutes tried, and half the time you didn't know how hard they were trying because you couldn't do it for them.

He went over and switched off the television set. He had forgotten to lock the office or check that the garages were locked. He went out again. His neighbour was just about to go out in his wife's car.

'Mair wants fish and chips. Like some?' Reg called, and Dave handed over the money.

'Makes a change,' he said. He yawned. 'Hang on, I'll come with you. I'll just ask Mair to keep an ear open for Susie.'

It was an old routine. There was a bell by Susie's bed that rang in Reg's bedroom, so that if Dave were out on duty, Mair would hear her. Susie never worried when she was alone in the house. The doors were locked and her dog was by her bed; he'd guard her from here to hell and back. Two of the police dogs were kennelled by the back door for extra protection; Mair listened for them barking.

A dog was howling in the kennels. A new dog, handed over by a member of the public who couldn't manage it. It was totally out of control and at the moment a major nuisance, needing a very firm hand to remedy the damage done by a year of doing as it chose, with no one bothering to check it. It didn't like being alone. It had been bought for an old lady, to protect her, and had had no exercise and no training and had finally

27

got free and killed a sheep. It was death or the police. Dave doubted it would make a good dog; too nervous and too stupid, but they could re-train it and find it a decent home where it would behave itself; preferably well away from sheep country.

'Want a quick one before we go back?' Reg asked.

There was just time. The Jester and Bells was packed, men gathered round a darts match; the air was steamy with heat and cigarette and pipe smoke, and the place was noisy with talk and laughter and the sound of a juke box that someone had just fed. The music pumped out, drowning voices. Dave whistled the tune as they fought their way to the bar. Just time for a bitter before going down to the chippie. The froth spilled on the polished wood. He turned to look round the room, dim from red lampshades. There was nobody he knew.

'Remember John Morland?' Dave asked.

'The barrister? He died, didn't he. You pointed out the obituary, said you'd met him. Good bloke.' Reg was watching the dartboard. Someone had just scored a bull and there was a flurry of congratulations. There was barely room to lift an elbow.

'His widow has bought the cottage in the wood; down at the end of the fire break,' Dave said.

'It's a lonely place to live. I wouldn't like it.' Reg led the way to the door. He'd promised Mair they wouldn't be too long. He was on duty often enough; it was a rare night when they could settle peacefully as the baby was so fretful, crying often, and a worry to both of them, though the doctor assured them there was nothing at all wrong.

The chip shop was empty. Dave chose curry; Reg took fish for his wife and a pie for himself and double chips for everyone. Driving back the smell of the chips dominated everything. There was a full moon; a cat raced across the road, and somewhere, as the car drew into the yard and Reg killed the engine, an owl hooted.

The light was on in Susie's room and Dave went in.

'Have you got chips?' she asked. 'Can I have some?'

'No,' Dave said and laughed. 'Put your dressing-gown on and don't tell Heather. She'll be giving me the wrong side of her tongue for giving you a bad night. Did you hear us go?'

'I heard Reg ask you and I got to thinking about chips and my mouth watered so much I couldn't go back to sleep,' Susie said, perched on the arm of her father's chair, helping herself liberally. 'Can I have some curry too?'

'No.' Dave watched her. She grew more and more like her mother every day, reminding him with a movement of her head, a laugh, or a look in her eyes of times long ago, never forgotten. He had never met another woman like Donna; never wanted to marry again. Perhaps he had romanticised her in his memory. He didn't know. But he needed a woman who would help with Susie and those he had met had been impatient at sharing him with a child. He pulled her hair gently.

'Bed, chicken, and no more wandering.'

She kissed him, and went out of the room, knowing better than to argue. Tomorrow he would take Venn out and try to get him searching eagerly again; tomorrow he had to take four of the men tracking in the park; tomorrow he had three reports to write and he needed to see the Inspector. Tomorrow he would be too busy to worry about the cottage and regret the loss of a dream. He would never think of it again.

He made himself a cup of cocoa and went up to bed, to lie and wish the dream hadn't ended. He would have to find another place to think about; it was good, sometimes, to dream.

He fell asleep to dream of the cottage, as he had wanted it to be and suddenly he was watching it burning, standing helpless, unable to do anything at all to stop the inferno. A voice cried out from the inside, but he was still rooted to the ground.

He woke, drenched in sweat, thankful to find he had been dreaming; it had been a very vivid dream.

He would not train near the cottage again for a long time. He need not even see it again. He fell asleep, and dreamed of nothing, unaware that the cottage was going to form a major part of his life and that from that day on, everything would be quite different.

Beyond him, in the woods, a bitch gave birth to five pedigree pups. Her owner lay dead in his car, only half a mile from her. They had been on the way to the vet when the car skidded and

29

went out of control and rolled over. The bitch jumped free as the door opened. Her need to get away was great; the first pup was almost born and the noise of the crash had terrified her.

She was all instinct, needing to find sanctuary, which she found in a deserted shepherd's hut in a big field. The policeman who came on the scene of the crash never thought of a dog, and the man's wife, badly shocked, mentioned it, but thought the bitch must have been left with the vet. She was not very attached to it anyway. Her husband had bred and shown the dogs. She sold those that were left.

It was only a week later that she realised the bitch had gone free, and that somewhere she was lying up with her puppies. By then they were talking of a sheep killer on the loose and men with guns were hunting her.

Dave heard of her the day that the new owner moved into the cottage.

The pups were then about five weeks old.

3

Moving away, at least for the present, had been a very good idea. The builders hadn't finished, but Rhea didn't care. She had to get away from memory; had to be busy. The barn was finished first, with new wood flooring, newly rendered white-washed walls, and a vast skylight that let in the day. She had all the room in the world and until the cottage was ready she could sleep here on a camp bed, using a sleeping bag; could picnic, and be free. No one to consider but herself.

It was a startlingly rare luxury.

She watched the cottage take shape; the men liked her and worked willingly. There was a great deal to do. The old plaster was rotten and had to come away; the wood work had to be replaced; the roof beams were new under the new thatching. The cottage needed re-wiring and she was installing central heating.

The oil tank was beside the barn. She would plant shrubs in front to hide it. She would make a garden and build a rockery; she would lead the little stream in falls through a woodland path.

Meanwhile she painted as if she were possessed. The men, coming into the barn, looked at the horse that sprang from the canvas. He was proud headed, arrogant, and very male. He was for Sadie, who had surprised her by her consideration and patience, by keeping both Rod and Mark from nagging at her, from demanding more of her than she had to give. Sadie recognised her need to be alone; to come to terms with a new way of life; and never to forget John.

She wanted to talk about him but other people told her not to dwell on the past. No one could blot out the past. The past had

31

happened and the past was important. Without even knowing it, John and the boys had shaped her; had driven her to her own private refuge, so that in painting she had come near to fulfilling some of her dreams.

Once she had wanted to ride; to showjump; to gain a place in the Olympic team; to train her horse to surmount all obstacles. That was one dream that would never now be fulfilled, though it might in part by proxy as Lucifer was proving that he could jump.

'You got a bargain there,' Rory said, looking at her with the dark eyes she once had thought so wonderful. She smiled at him. The world had taught her a lot, she thought, as she stood back and looked consideringly at the picture, of the people she had known so few had troubled to write; only two had bothered to phone. Rory had offered to take her out and get her drunk.

'Anaesthetic,' he said. 'Do you good.' He was being kind in the only way he could think of, but that wasn't Rhea's method of forgetting.

She put down her brush and took up a pencil and began to draw; she drew John in court, looking at her; considering, assessing, testing, as if she were a witness. He had needed everyone about him to be totally accurate; had corrected her exaggerations; had been angry when she wanted to be frivolous. Life was real. Life was earnest. Life, she thought suddenly and bitterly, was mostly a pain in the neck.

She put down the pad and went out into the garden. It was wild and overgrown, long neglected and she attacked it as if she could change the world by her energy.

The thatcher had just finished his job. He came over to her.

'You haven't got a bitch, Mrs?' he asked, in his soft alien burr, an accent that Rhea had never identified.

'No. Why?'

'There was an Alsatian bitch at your dustbin, foraging; she's in milk; pups somewhere around, I'd say, and not too old at that. She's bone thin, and cagey. Ran off when she saw me.'

Rhea thought of a bitch alone in the forest, keeping pups. On what? Dustbin leavings and maybe rabbits and mice; and she'd be a runaway pet at that. She watched and listened and once

32

glimpsed the bitch, grey and wolf lean in the darkness of a moony night, trying desperately to suck nourishment from an old bone. Rhea went out and called at her but she raced through the garden and leaped the wall, no longer a pet dog but a wild animal, lean and hungry, savagely defending her pups. The loose teats swung against the rocks, and in the morning there were traces of blood where she'd cut herself.

No one saw the bitch again until four weeks later when a farmer shot her as she raced among his sheep, trying to bring one down, desperate with the hunger that now savaged her and the need to provide meat for the pups.

Rhea heard of her death and went out into the forest to see if she could locate the litter.

Dave heard about the bitch's death and knew that wild pups growing up would cause immense problems. He took Venn and tracked back from the dead bitch; along the forest ride, to an enlarged rabbit hole, where five pups played roughly, trotting up to one another, growling and biting and worrying.

Rhea came up from the other side of the ride.

He was watching the litter, and his first knowledge of her was Venn's head butting his leg, a signal that meant 'strangers about'.

'What will happen to them?' Rhea asked.

Dave was frowning. He looked at her, seeing a neat woman with greying hair and unhappy brown eyes.

'God knows. I'll take them over to the RSPCA and see if they can rear and find homes for them. They won't trust people; they've been reared wild. About eight weeks old, I'd guess, and in pretty bad shape.'

'Pure bred or crossbred?' Rhea asked.

'Look like pure bred to me. Someone lost a bitch in a car accident round here a few weeks back, the times are right and she was a good bitch. Anyone having a pup could probably get its papers. The owner is coming to identify her; her husband was killed in the crash. Double trouble.'

Always trouble, Rhea thought. She knelt and held a hand out to one of the little bitch puppies, and was promptly and savagely bitten.

'They'll be a handful,' Dave said. 'Anyone taking one of

those on has to be someone who wants a job and a challenge. They'd probably make excellent guard dogs, but they'll need taming first. Wild as any fox cub.' He looked at Rhea, seeing a face that he liked, and eyes that looked back at him wearily.

'You'll be Mrs Morland,' he said.

Rhea nodded.

Dave ceased to regret the loss of his cottage.

'I used to daydream about the cottage; I was going to buy it when I won the pools and live there with my small daughter; peacefully, away from people,' he said. He laughed. 'One never is too old to dream.'

'Never,' Rhea said, from a vantage point of nearly twenty years. 'Sometimes dreams come true, though never quite in the way you expect.'

She looked down at the pups, who were keeping a safe distance, steadily backing away, wary of people.

'How are you going to catch them?'

'Offhand, I can't imagine,' Dave said. They were waiting for the mother who would never come back to them, unaware as yet of desertion, playing together happily, but whenever Dave or Rhea moved, or Venn shifted his position, they growled like small wild creatures, snarling angrily at these people who threatened their solitude.

'Can you stay with them while I get some food?' Rhea asked.

Dave seated himself on the stump of a tree trunk and watched her walk swiftly down the ride. She moved as if she were forty or less; yet she had to be almost sixty, remembering the newspaper reports that couldn't report on any person without revealing their age, as if age made any difference at all to a report. He still felt as young as he had at twenty – and as old.

The pups curled to sleep, weary from exercise, secure in the knowledge that their mother would come soon and bring food for them. There were the remains of rabbits, and feathers that told their own tale around the den.

Rhea returned with a bowl full of chopped-up cold meat; she had nothing else. These pups had fed on anything the mother could bring; so maybe it wouldn't matter. She put down the plate.

She backed away.

None of the pups moved.

They lay, watchful, eyes now open, the wind bringing them news of meat, but they distrusted the bowl; distrusted the scent of humans, distrusted these two people who were watching them.

Rhea tipped the meat on to the ground and removed the bowl.

She looked at Dave, who understood the look. They moved away, taking care to stand so that the wind blew their scent in the opposite direction to the pups. Dave stood behind a tree trunk and Rhea crouched down behind a bush, watching through the branches.

One by one the pups moved suspiciously to the food, sniffing it. They were ravenous, and presently small fights broke out, as first one and then another tried to take it all for itself.

Rhea watched the little bitch that had bitten her. She was almost coal black, her tiny eyes beady and suspicious, but she was the first at the food and the quickest to retaliate if any of the others came too near while she was eating. Her flop ears looked odd; one day they would stand erect, but just now they looked unnaturally large and gave her a comical expression.

She trotted off to lie by the rock beside the den and licked her front paws thoughtfully.

Rhea, watching, saw sunlight flicker across the dark back; saw the pattern of light and shade on the grass, saw the boulder towering above the bitch, and a picture was born, a picture she had to get on to paper and get there fast. It was an urgent drive, a need beyond any need she had known, and this little creature had triggered it. She was immensely drawable.

'I'll try and get that one, and keep her,' Rhea said.

Dave turned and looked at her with considering eyes.

'Know anything about dogs?'

'Only to draw,' Rhea said. She had had many commissions in the past for other people's pets. She preferred drawing horses, but sometimes went to dog shows, to get the set of a head, or try to capture movement; movement fascinated her. She had watched her stallion train only the day before, seeing his proud head, his arched neck, his neatly stepping hooves as he practised in the training school. Rory was a good horseman; he had looked down at her.

'Well?'

She had nodded. He didn't need her to boost his ego.

'You'll be in for a hard time,' Dave said, bringing her back to the present. Her thoughts seemed to wander against her will.

'It will do me good; if I fail, the dog will have had a chance at life,' Rhea said. 'And I'm not too old . . . or too proud . . . to learn.'

She had all the time in the world. Endless days and endless nights, spent alone. Already, in only a week at the cottage, the isolation had begun to daunt her; she did not care over much for people; too many people spoke fair words to her face and maligned or mocked her behind her back. She knew too much about them. Gossip was not a pastime that she cared for one little bit.

Animals were kinder, and safer; they never gossiped or indulged in vicious lies; they liked you or they hated you and you knew where you were with them.

Dave, watching her, was reminded of his own mother, now dead. She had died when Susie was six. His father lived alone and visited but had not been able to manage the child. Life changed; all the time. It might be good to have an excuse to come and talk, and if she had the bitch he had a ready-made excuse; a common interest and a knowledge of the breed. She might join the dog club; and here was he building up on a short acquaintance with a woman he had only met that day, simply because he felt that anyone who loved his cottage must be someone he would like to know.

It would be good to visit the cottage; get away from the police house briefly. Susie was alone so much and a proxy grandmother might help her.

Rhea would have been surprised if she could have read his thoughts. Her own were concentrated on the pup, on the need to tame her, to make her a dog to keep and own and be proud of, a dog that would give her company in the lonely hours; another living being that she could talk to; could trust as she trusted no human now. John had been safe, she thought with a

36

sudden ache of longing; he did understand some things, though never all.

The sense of being forsaken was almost too strong to bear. She didn't know how she could think of John here, in this woodland ride, with five wild puppies within a few yards of her; with a man she had never seen before in her life standing in police uniform with what was obviously a trained police dog, a world so divorced from London and her patterned days of routine that never varied, except for her escape, while everyone was at work, to her studio and her secret world.

To paint all day . . . her fingers suddenly itched and her eyes looked at the shape of the trees, at the smoky background sky, at the curve and bend of the hills, at the sweep upwards of the land beyond the pups, at the tiny scene in which they were the most important figures, tiny creatures dwarfed by the immensity of everything around them, yet totally at home, aware, distrustful, watchful.

'If I bring food for a few days they will survive; they must be fairly strong,' Rhea said. 'And if I paint them, setting up my easel, becoming part of their landscape, do you think they'd learn to trust?'

Dave didn't know. He thought back to Venn's first days, long ago. He had been a rescued dog; a dog that didn't like people.

'You'll have problems if you go for that little bitch,' Dave said. 'She's litter boss; pack leader; and she will try and be your boss. Could you manage to convince her you are stronger than she is?'

'I used to ride horses that thought I could be fooled, but I beat them,' Rhea said. It had been a long time ago. She was much older now; some of the strength had gone from her arms, but she was still powerful compared with some of her own contemporaries, who led far less active lives.

'It would be a change to try and dominate a dog,' Rhea said. Dave looked at her, puzzled by the exultation in her tone. He tried to remember his first dog; that was long ago. Luckily Susie kept him at a sensible level, as he had to teach her and her need to understand something difficult ensured that he remembered some of the problems of those first days; the first time you tried to make a dog sit, or come when called, or even teach it house manners.

He watched the little bitch trot up to a large stick and take it back to her side of the den to chew. That was her territory, her own small space, and when another pup stepped towards her to challenge she snarled viciously. She was not going to be any milk-and-water madam; she was going to be one hell of a pup.

'We'll get some tranquillisers from the vet and put it in their food,' Dave was more concerned with getting them out of harm's way. The farmers would not take kindly to dogs growing up near their sheep fields; wild dogs that could kill more ruthlessly than a fox, because these pups would form a pack. Also there were three bitches and two dogs; and in time there would be more wild pups. A whole pack.

It was unthinkable.

A thin rain began to fall.

Within seconds the pups had vanished; all that was left of them was the debris of their meals and the sound of squabbling as they tried to settle inside the den. Rhea wondered if they would miss their mother overmuch. They seemed able to eat; the bitch had still had milk. It was difficult to tell how old they were.

Dave, looking at the builders' stocks in Rhea's garden, had an idea. He took several large pieces of wood, and built a small enclosure round the den. When the pups came out they would be contained; he used cut logs to back it up, hoping they couldn't climb. The rain was falling steadily now, soaking the ground.

Rhea, watching, thought of dog food; she did not know what to buy and asked Dave diffidently what he would suggest.

'I can give you enough for today; perhaps you could put down food for them during today and part of tomorrow; and we can lace their last meal with tranquillisers. It's only a couple of miles to my home. You'll be too late for the shops in town. It's early closing.'

Rhea, to her surprise, found herself passenger in a police van, Venn lying quietly behind the wire partition. She was divorced completely from the life she had known, venturing into new worlds. She looked around her when they reached the

38

yard; at the long line of kennels, where dogs stood against the wire, barking, as the van drew in; at the offices and the two houses and the vans parked neatly side by side, dark blue, trim and clean.

Susie ran to greet Dave, her dog at her side and stopped when she saw Rhea.

'Mrs Morland and I have found some puppies living wild in the wood,' Dave said. 'Their mother is dead. She's come for some food for them. Can you spare some of Trot's, or are we short?'

'Heather stocked up yesterday; we've lots,' Susie said. 'Are they collies?'

'No. Baby police dogs and fiercer already than any of ours,' Dave said, leading the way indoors to a comfortable untidy room where Susie had her homework books spread over the table, a sandwich half eaten and a glass of milk beside them. 'I was waiting for you to come home before I had supper, but I got hungry.' Susie looked at her father anxiously.

Rhea had a sudden vision of duty rosters, of a child left alone at night, of meals that waited endlessly, of a loneliness that a child should never know. Susie, unaware of any other life, forgetting the years of her babyhood with her mother and then with her grandparents, went out into the kitchen and returned with a packet of biscuit meal and several tins of dog food.

'They ought to have milk and they'll need vitamins when we get them; they probably have worms, rickets and heaven knows what besides,' Dave said. 'And after such a start they might not even live.'

'I can only try,' Rhea said.

Dave drove her back and she did not invite him in; the child needed company. She took the dog food and went into the studio. It was dark outside, but she switched on the lights and began to paint from memory, painting the woodland glade and five little pups that curled up close; the wood was wild, and the trees brooded over them, and there was wariness and fear in the tiny tense bodies.

She looked at what she had done. There was an air of waiting, of longing, of guarding, about the pups that she hadn't known she could convey. She had been thinking of them lying alone, no bitch to warm or comfort them, but without even meaning to, had managed to put her own thoughts into the picture.

It was a good picture; it might well make her a good deal of money. She would need money with rising prices, and everything costing so much and there wouldn't be so much left from John. The renovation of the cottage would take all she had got from the sale of her old home, and more.

She lay awake listening to the rain on the studio roof. She would be glad when the cottage was fit to live in and the men had finished and she had furnished it and could move in to comfort. Meanwhile maybe she could house-train the pup before she moved on to carpeted floors.

She needed a name for her.

Distance had lent the tiny creature a glamour that she certainly hadn't had in the wood; she wanted a name that was unusual; a name to remember; a name that came easily off the tongue. She had been a little wild woodland animal; belonging in her den; a creature of the forest and of the night.

Dryad. That wasn't right for her. Rhea got up from her bed and looked in her dictionary. Her books were all here in the studio. She filled a hot water bottle and took down Gilbert White's *Selborne*; sleep was going to elude her tonight. She would find a name first and then read herself to sleep. She put on the electric heater and slipped a stole round her shoulders and propped herself up in bed.

Dryad . . . a nymph inhabiting woods or trees; a wood nymph. From the Greek Drus for tree. Drus. Drusilla. How did Drus become dryad? Thoughts spun round and round, out of hand.

Drusa. Drya; Dadyra; she thought of the pup lying against the rock. Ink black; Inka? Not Blackie; that was too trite.

Nymph?

No, that was wrong too. How absurd to spend so much time trying to name a pup; moreover a pup that as yet she hadn't even got and might never get.

She thought of the stallion and took his stud card from the bedside table. Whispering Corn. Whisp? Whisper? Wish?

She was falling asleep at last. Outside the moon shone brilliantly through the skylight and patterned the floor. The pups would be hidden and secret in the enclosure Dave had made for them. Tomorrow she would go out early and take them food. He had given her a tub of vitamin tablets. She must remember to pay.

Maybe the pup should be titled Debt.

She yawned and settled the pillows. The bed was narrow; but it did not remind her at all of the big bed she had shared with John; of the loneliness there was when she stretched out, the space beside her so empty that she had gone, before she moved to sleep in the spare room, not wanting to face the fact that now she would always be entirely and utterly alone.

Venn, a friend.

Until the pup had a name she had no identity; no reality. She was part of the wild world, and always would be unless she were named quickly. Rhea was too tired to be rational.

She sat up again and picked up the dictionary, riffling through the pages. That did not give her any ideas at all. It only seemed to reveal the absurdity of words and what stupid words there were. She paused in amazement at some she had never heard of. Soutache; an embroidery braid. It sounded more like a kind of peculiar moustache.

Immixture. How on earth could you have such a word?

The thesaurus would be better. She fetched it, and it brought John back vividly as it had been his. He hated to have the wrong word. When he prepared a speech or a brief every word had to be exact; had to mean exactly what he intended it to mean without possibility of misinterpretation.

Black.

Ebony. Jet. Sloe.

The right name wouldn't come.

Venn, a friend. She liked that and turned to companion. Chum, pal, gossip, crony, bully, sidekick.

Lovely names, Rhea thought, and turned the light out again, sliding in to the warm luxury of bedding.

Names went round and round in her head. She'd never think of one that was right.

Black. White.

Ebony. Snowball.

41

She drifted off to sleep.

Morning dawned bright and clear. She sat up and looked out at a deer, standing poised, ready for flight, staring at her. It was an elegant little roe hind, pretty as any Bambi deer, wild eyes watching. A flirt of its body and it was gone.

She dressed, still busy with names. It had to be right; it had to be more than right, it had to be perfect.

It was an absurd worry; it dominated breakfast and it dominated her walk into the woods, but it prevented her remembering John.

4

It was another grey day with rain in the air. The ground was wet from the downpour the night before and the wind sighed constantly in the trees. It was a noisy morning; a slightly uncanny morning, with a feeling about it that Rhea was unable to identify. Nothing felt right. She was a stranger in a strange place; she didn't belong; maybe she never would belong. Her life with John had lasted for over thirty years and old ways died very hard. She must not dwell on the past. She had wanted to break away from everything familiar and she had. If it went wrong, there was no one to blame but herself.

Maybe that was the story of everyone's life.

Sow and ye shall reap.

She was trying to sow a new life and all she appeared to be reaping at the moment was a total desolate loneliness. There was no one to phone; the phone was not yet connected anyway. There was no one to visit. She didn't miss John's friends, but how she missed Rachel; Rachel who laughed and who shared her appreciation of painting; Rachel to whom she had fled the day after John died, and there in the studio she had painted in a frenzy that blocked out suffering, and there, until early in the dawn, she and Rachel had sat drinking coffee, not talking of John, but having a furious argument about the illustrations for a children's book that Rachel had been commissioned to do.

The story was a fantasy and Rhea felt the drawings should fit it; Rachel was trying to invent a new style; a style that was outrageously fantastic; elaborate patterned pen drawings of twisted and convoluted lines that made more of an anagram than a picture.

They had argued so angrily that she had dropped on to the

43

little camp bed that she kept in the studio, where she sometimes spent the night when John was away, and slept until almost lunchtime, waking able to deal with the multitude of aggravating and hurtful details that a death in a civilised country incurred.

Now she was beginning to heal, but she had not found the solace she expected alone in the cottage in the woods. Instead, this morning, the world was inimical, and her footsteps, thudding softly on the bare ground, were an echo of misery.

She had to think of other things; had to plan, had to finish the picture on her easel, which had gone wrong in the last hours of the evening.

She would collect the puppy and go and see Rory. Rory was part of the past from the days before she knew John.

Even now fingers were itching to draw. The soft patterned moss at her feet, the curve of the petal of a single forlorn flower on a gorse bush; the towering arch of a tree above her, sweeping to the sky, majestic and awe inspiring, so that she stood beneath it wondering how it looked to an ant, high as a mountain if you were as small as a pinpoint.

It was a new thought and she began to wonder if she could write an ant's eye-view children's book, a world of fearsome ogres, of enormous towering plants, of mountaineering up a thistle stalk. It had probably been done before.

The rain began again and she drew her collar closer round her throat.

Raindrops were wet on her cheek, and a long forgotten poem came into her mind:

'When I went to thy grave, broken with tears,
When I crouched in the grass, dumb in despair . . . '

She hurried on. She had to think of other things and the sound of three shots, one after another, brought her up short, but grateful for the unexpected interruption.

The puppies!

There was no thought of danger to herself in her mind as she ran. She was aware of the thump of her feet on the ground, loud and clear, aware of the thudding of her heart, and the breath that caught in her throat.

She came into the clearing.

Dave's small protection had been flung away and a man stood over three dead bodies, firing into a fourth. The fifth pup, the black bitch puppy, was racing for her life, running towards Rhea, who bent and scooped her into her arms and stood still as the man fired the fourth shot and turned, swinging the gun towards her.

'Put that vermin down,' he said.

'I planned to keep her. We are going to find homes for them,' Rhea said.

'Homes. What kind of sentimental fool are you? The bitch was running the sheep and killing when Wilde shot her; these things are worse than fox cubs, worst breed of dog there is and bred out here, wilder than any wild beast and near my pheasants. Got to protect myself. Put that pup down and let me shoot it.'

'I'm keeping it,' Rhea said. The gun pointing at her frightened her and so did the man facing her. He wore corduroy breeches tucked into boots, and an army camouflage jacket. The cap on his head was pulled down over a thatch of iron-grey hair; iron-grey eyebrows, straight as rulers, bristled over grey eyes that glared at her unnervingly, as unwinking and unmoving as a hawk's eyes. The tanned hand that held the gun steady, pointing at the pup in her arms, was strong and mottled with darker brown spots. A man who lived out of doors; a man whose mouth was as uncompromising as his body, a man to fear, and Rhea was suddenly and desperately afraid, alone in the silent ride, the dead pups behind him, the gun seeking for the pup that had forgotten its terror of her in the terror of death and in the recognised knowledge of a deadlier enemy than the woman who held her tightly.

The sound of an engine cut through the silence.

Rhea turned her head and felt overwhelming relief as Dave's blue van drove up the ride. Dave, seeing the two figures and recognising Thorpe, accelerated, then braked sharply, wheels skidding on the soft turf.

He strode up to the man and turned the gun away.

'What the hell do you think you're doing? I've warned you, Thorpe. Want my dog at your throat? Want to know what it feels like to be the wrong end of a threat for a change? How dare you threaten a lady?'

'I want those pups dead.'

'They're young enough and were doing no harm. We'd have had them away by this evening. You had no need to kill; and they're not going up on your gallows to make the kids cry on their way home from school.' Dave was angry. Thorpe had strung the corpses of dead moles along the roadside and Susie had come home crying her heart out.

'I'm keeping this one,' Rhea said. 'She'll be taught and trained and kept in and she won't harm your pheasants.'

She had never trained a dog in her life, let alone one of this breed and at that a pup born wild. She must be crazy, but no way was she going to let the man triumph or take this last small life. Maybe it wasn't an important life but it had an importance to her. Life was life, no matter where or what.

'Get out,' Dave said, and Thorpe, after looking at him from under his level terrifying brows, turned and walked off. He whistled and a pointer came from the side of the ride. Rhea had not noticed the dog. It joined its master. 'His dogs love him – I don't know why,' Dave said.

He glanced at her.

'Your hands are bleeding. Has the pup bitten you?'

She hadn't even noticed. She watched the stocky back disappear into the woods, and discovered that her legs were trembling so much that she longed to sit down.

'Are you all right?' Dave asked with some concern. Rhea's face was so white that he thought she was about to faint.

She shivered.

'I'm just scared silly. I've never had a gun pointed at me before,' she said. She managed a faint grin. 'I suppose it happens to you daily?'

'Fortunately not,' Dave said. 'Our villains aren't all that wild yet. Thorpe can be a mean one; nasty when he's sober and a devil when he's drunk. Luckily his way home doesn't lie past your house. All the same, I hope you have good bolts and bars.'

Rhea looked at him.

'I came here for sanctuary,' she said. 'I thought it would be more peaceful and safer than a town.'

'Better to be safe,' Dave said. 'The woods are lonely at night and you're pretty isolated. And no man around. It might be a good idea to train that pup of yours fast. Nothing like a good noisy German Shepherd to make people think again, but for God's sake don't let her wander, or Thorpe will have her and legitimately too. Anywhere near his pheasant pens and he's a right; and so has Wilde, the farmer who shot the bitch; she was killing sheep.'

He glanced at his watch. 'Lucky you were up early. Another few minutes and they'd all have been dead.'

'Would you like coffee?' Rhea asked. Her voice betrayed the fact that she not only needed coffee, but she also needed company. He was not on duty this morning. He had dropped Susie at school, on his way to buy the morning paper, and obeyed an impulse to come back through the woods and have a look at the pups. He was very glad he had.

'A quick one.' He looked at the studio. 'Are the men due to work on the cottage today?' he asked.

Rhea nodded. 'They have the decorating to do; and some of the wiring, and I'm waiting for the telephone engineer.' She wished it was already connected. The barn was huge, and at the far end there were shadows and a man might lurk there unseen. She had not been nervous before.

'I'll see if we can speed up your telephone connection,' Dave said. 'You never know, you might feel ill, out here alone . . . '

That was something else she hadn't considered. She was so rarely ill. She hadn't time. Every moment away from household chores was filled with painting and the need grew as her skill grew, so that she turned to her easel and looked at the picture she was painting of Lucifer. She had decided that Sadie would have a portrait of her own stallion.

She was not happy with the head.

Everything else was right; the powerful curve of his rump; the arch of his plumed tail, the turn of the neck and the softly lying gleaming mane that was so perfect, that lifted from him and fell again as he galloped in his paddock, that she had combed herself for the first time only the day before, a little afraid of his exuberance. All the power of him was in the body but the head wasn't Lucifer's head.

47

She wanted to alter the mouth and nostrils; they had more flare, she had given him a mean expression that was quite wrong, as, though he was mischievous and boisterous, though he pushed and shoved and loved with all his heart, pinning her against the stable wall, rubbing his enormous head up and down her shoulder in an ecstacy of pleasure at her nearness, he was far from mean. If she moved the eye; if she brought the mane down a little more between his ears; if she curved the cheek outwards; and softened the mouth and opened the lips very slightly . . . that was what was wrong.

Dave, watching her, knew she had forgotten him and he took the pup outside and watched her puddle, praised her and brought her in. He filled the two cups that stood on the little draining board, a spoonful of coffee in each. He found milk and poured it, and touched Rhea on the shoulder.

She jumped, and then laughed.

'I'm sorry. I was miles away. I'm trying to paint him for my daughter-in-law; and he's not right.'

'He looks magnificent to me,' Dave said truthfully. He had been admiring the painting ever since he came in. The horse was ready to spring off the canvas, to leap into the room, to race away, every muscle betraying his power. He was tense with pride, with the knowledge of his maleness. Dave only knew geldings. None of them looked like this.

There was arrogance as well as pride.

'Where is he?' Dave asked. It had to be a living horse, not a memory or a copy of a photograph.

'He's mine; in training with Rory Deane,' Rhea said.

'Rory Deane? He's well known round here – a very rich stables,' Dave said.

'I've known Rory a long time. I was engaged to him when I was nineteen. He couldn't face being tied down and went off to see the world. He was too adventurous for marriage. It wouldn't have worked.'

Dave said nothing. He had long ago learned to keep his eyes open and his mouth shut.

He looked at the painting again. The stallion stood in a field. Behind him were twisted trees that gave extra point to his perfection; he was beautiful but his background was distorted, was odd, so that only he was right. The fencing was broken down; the buildings behind him were tumble-down but he was God's creation. Man's work was crumbling all around him and he showed man up for the paltry thing he was, incapable of making anything as wonderful as this beast that dominated the foreground.

Dave drank his coffee, startled at his own thoughts.

He had never thought much about painting before, though Susie loved to draw and they said at school that she had flair.

'He has to be perfect and I can't make him perfect,' Rhea said. 'I try and try and there's always something lacking. Only Allah makes a flawless creation they say, so I suppose I have to go on being satisfied with being human and far from perfect.' She finished her coffee and looked down at the pup.

'She's like my painting; I don't know what to do with her. I've never had a dog before. Where do I start?' She was almost regretting her impulse. She seemed to be living by impulse now; John would never have approved. He had to think out every action, every thought, every word; had to weigh and consider, not only the present, but the future, so that often she felt as if she were held back by chains, prevented from doing something because of the effect it might have in five years' time, or ten years' time.

In ten years' time she would be almost seventy and the owner of a stallion and of a large powerful bitch, who would be ten years old. If she gave up now she could go back to her studio, which Rachel had not yet let, and could continue as she had while John was alive, only openly, admitting to being Ray Morton, building a reputation second to none. A person in her own right, no longer Rod and Mark's mother; no longer John's wife, who had to be careful of everything she did or said in case it affected John's career.

Now that career was over; ended by his own enthusiasm for doing his job beyond the call of duty; he had worked day and night, long into the night, had travelled and come home so briefly. She hadn't known him at all. Maybe one day, she used to think, he will retire and we will learn one another again. Life wasn't like that. It had a habit of knocking you on the head.

She had planned retirement with John and that would never

happen. She had come here for peace and almost within days of moving had been threatened by a man with a gun who was about to be a part of her life and who she would have to consider with every move she made if she kept this small pup.

The pup had been exploring busily. The death of her brothers and sisters in front of her eyes seemed to have caused her to change her attitude to people. These two were friendly. She did not care much for being handled but she endured it and Dave had been very careful to caress her and fuss her and talk to her when he picked her up.

He flicked his fingers now and held out a piece of chicken that Rhea had taken from the cupboard.

'Pupppppupppppupppppupppppuppp; hooo hooo hooo,' he said, making the puppy noises that all professional dog trainers used to attract attention and the puppy responded at once, trotting over to him, her head held high, her eyes on the titbit in his fingers.

He stroked her all over before giving it to her. She was flea ridden and filthy, and she stank, but that would have to wait. There was flea powder in his van, kept there in case his dog came up against the wretched creatures. He fetched it and rubbed it into the thick fluffy coat.

She growled and bit his hand.

'You'll have to tame her and woo her to get her confidence,' Dave said. If he wasn't careful he'd be late.

'She needs to be taught to trust; she needs a bath; she needs consideration and care and careful training. Once she's inoculated she can go to the dog club and you can learn there how to treat her. We've a good club. My daughter goes to it. It's run by three people who really know what they're doing; one of my men teaches the advanced people. You won't go wrong there.'

He went to the door.

'Watch for Thorpe and watch for Ted Wilde; he deserves his name. He's a young man and he's farming in a big way up there; full of ambition. His last ram lamb sold for nearly a thousand guineas so he's not going to be understanding about dogs near his flock. And don't walk her through his corn either; he's as likely to shoot you as the dog and then say it was an accident.'

Rhea could think of nothing whatever to say. She seemed to have moved on to a battle ground. Peace? Someone had to be joking.

'I'll call over tonight and see how you're getting on with the pup. I've a cage I used as an indoor kennel for Susie's dog till he was house clean and safe with the furnishings. I'll bring it over. Sorry, I've got to rush.'

Rhea stood at the door, the pup in her arms again, watching the van drive away. The sound of the engine died in the distance, and she stood looking at the woods, which had become frighteningly alien. Thorpe was out there with his gun; and little creatures that died were strung up to remind all who walked in the woods that he was their relentless enemy.

She turned to go indoors and thought she saw something move beyond the garden. She walked round the barn and stared at her fence.

The four dead puppies were strung along it, their tiny bodies a monstrous reminder to her that Thorpe had marked her, and that he would not leave her alone. He had declared war.

She shut the puppy in her car, and turned her head as one of the workmen came round the corner.

He stared at the fence, shocked.

'That's nasty,' he said. 'You go indoors, Missis, and I'll see to them for you. Whatever made Thorpe do a thing like that?'

'You know him?' Rhea asked.

'Everyone knows him. Doesn't do to get on his wrong side. What did you do?'

Rhea went to the car and lifted out the puppy; which growled at the man.

'I'm keeping her; I need a dog,' she said.

'You do that, here. You'd be as well getting one that's grown as well as this one; it's lonely down here.'

She could do without being told that, over and over again.

She left the man removing the dead bodies and went in to the barn. She mixed a little biscuit meal and dog food and fed it to the pup. She was ravenous, and gulped greedily. Rhea lifted the plate to add a little more food and was rewarded by a ferocious growl and small teeth sunk into her hand.

She stood, sucking the injury. The pup had meant that bite. Her food was sacred and humans had to learn not to touch. Puppies had to learn too, Rhea decided.

She took meat and biscuit and mashed it into a paste with her hands, and then sat on the floor and held out her hands, the food cupped in the palms. The pup eyed her, head on one side, distrustful of this human smell. Hunger was paramount and a few minutes later she was feeding from Rhea's hands. She licked the palms clean. Rhea was food. Rhea was obviously now her mother substitute; Rhea was safety. Without even thinking, Rhea had obeyed the right instinct.

Rhea took her outside into a tiny enclosure that had once held chickens and was still secure, and then lifted the pup and took her indoors.

The puppy relaxed. She had been fed by this woman and knew her smell; it was a smell of dog food; and of safety; of secure arms that held her tightly. She lifted her small head and licked the face that was so close to hers.

The feeling that swept over Rhea was magical; it was something she hadn't known since the long-ago days when the horse she was riding learned its lesson, and behaved as she wanted it to behave; when every movement became perfection, and the long months of training paid off.

She could train this pup as she had once trained a horse. She would have to find her old books on animal behaviour; have to buy dog books. She would prove to herself and to the world that she could train, that she would train and to hell with Ted Wilde and to hell with gamekeeper Thorpe and to hell with everything.

Magical puppy.

Little witch.

Little witch!

She put her down on the ground and knelt and waggled her handkerchief at the tiny animal.

'Witch, good puppy, come on Witch,' she said softly.

The puppy had a name at last.

'I've buried those pups for you, Missis,' the electrician said. He was a young man with a thatch of tow-coloured hair and he had been shocked by the viciousness that hung the bodies on

Rhea's fence. It wasn't at all nice. People like that. He'd seen Thorpe once or twice when the man was more than half way drunk; a man to watch for.

'Coffee?' Rhea asked.

It seemed the only thing she could offer, as she dared not voice the thoughts that were milling in her head.

5

Rhea tried to paint, but nothing she could do would get the stallion's head right. He leered at her, and she tried again, only to give him a ferocious expression that was totally alien to him. She would go over and visit Rory.

She found a large box and lined it with newspaper and put the puppy inside. The bitch looked up at her, considering. She had begun to trust; it was a far quicker response than Rhea had expected, but even at that age the little creature had recognised death when it came; had run in terror and had also recognised sanctuary.

Her mother had taught her well, even in those few short weeks.

Rhea needed food. She drove into the village and stopped at the local shop. It was a tiny village, a single street of attractive houses, built of local stone. Small bright gardens were neat and trim, waiting for spring. Eyes watched her from the windows. She was a newcomer, someone to be weighed and considered, someone from a long way away. Some of the villagers had never been more than forty miles from home, over to the Beast Sales in the country town.

Rhea parked her car, and looked down at the pup. Witch was fast asleep, tired out by her own fears. Windows and doors checked, Rhea went into the shop. There were two women at the counter, and a third was serving. A man stood beside a display of books, turning the stand as he tried to find a title that he hadn't already read.

There had been a sound of laughter and chatter, but all talk died as Rhea went in. She felt as if she were intruding, breaking into an established routine, unwanted. She thought of the four tiny corpses hung on her fence and shivered.

She was being absurd and fanciful. She was a newcomer and of course she couldn't expect to be greeted as she had been at home, where she had been a customer for nearly thirty years, familiar as the posters on the wall opposite her grocer's shop.

'Can I help you?' the shopkeeper asked.

'I'm not in a hurry,' Rhea said, not wanting to go out of turn.

'It's all right. Did you want something?'

Of course I want something, Rhea thought. Would I be in here if I didn't? She bought sugar and tea and butter; tinned foods and fresh apples and bananas; and a case of Long Life milk, as the milkman did not come to her cottage. Nor did the newspaper boy; and nor did the dustmen. She would have to learn a different way of life. She bought dog food.

She paid for the goods, and went out. Nobody but the shop-keeper had spoken to her. She felt as if she had been examined from head to foot; her clothes assessed and priced; the ring on her finger noticed; it was a large topaz that John had bought her on a rare holiday in Paris. Her car was almost new; a medium-sized estate that she had thought would be useful in a country place where she had to carry all her shopping for several miles. She would need to work out how to shop economically and infrequently; the price of petrol appalled her afresh every time she filled up.

The talk began before she had closed the door. The bag was heavy and she had to balance on one leg to fight the door handle.

'So many newcomers,' a voice said loudly and clearly. 'They'll soon take over the village and drive the rest of us out.'

She stood, the door shut safely behind her, shutting away enmity. She had not expected to be welcomed, but she had not expected hate. The feeling of aloneness grew as she drove away. No one to talk to; only Rory to visit, and that only because her stallion was with him. What did Rory say behind her back?

She liked people when she met them; took them at face value, rarely searching below the skin for the hidden self inside them; assuming that if she liked someone they would like her. Jealousy had never been one of her vices.

It was hard to understand others; hard to realise that they nourished grudge and hatred, that bitter envy might make them resent her and her car and her way of life; she had bought the cottage and spent money on it and everyone would know. It was a tiny place and little happened; every event was a nine-days' wonder to speculate about, to elaborate, to build on.

The puppy whimpered and Rhea drew up and comforted the tiny animal. She could see the roof of Rory's stables beyond the hedge. There, among the horses, she would be understood, surely; a simpler world where animals were paramount. Even so, as she drew into the yard, she looked for signs of dislike behind the greeting of the stable girl who came over to her.

'Rory's out; have you come to see Lucifer? He's looking wonderful today but he's full of himself; he pinned me against the stable wall, just loving me with his head. He doesn't know how bony he is; it's like being loved by a two-ton rock! I had to speak sharply to make him behave.'

The girl was small and fair and pretty, with laughter in her eyes. Rhea relaxed, and for a little while stood at the stable door, watching the stallion as he came forward and took carrots from her fingers, his lips soft against her hand.

'I'm trying to paint him,' she told the girl. 'I can't get his head right; or the arch of his neck. Could he possibly be led out?'

'No problem.' The bright young voice was happy. The girl haltered the animal and brought him into the sunlight. He stood, posing, aware of his beauty, proud of his strength, aware also of a mare in the next enclosure flirting with him, so that he preened himself for her benefit.

Two horses trotted into the yard. Rory swung himself from the saddle, handing the reins to a lad who ran forward as if jet-propelled.

'Come to see your boyfriend?' Rory asked. He looked larger than ever in his riding outfit, the high boots polished so that they reflected the ground. Rory had always been a dandy.

'I wanted to see him out,' Rhea said.

'Come into the office. I've something that will interest you,'

Rory said. 'I didn't show you before – didn't know how you'd react to it.'

She had not been into the office before. He had taken her into the house, and plied her with sherry. She looked about her now; it was as businesslike as that in any factory. Filing cabinets stood against white walls on which were pinned photographs of horses that he had trained, or had now in his stables, being trained.

Over the desk was a tiny painting of a pony, not yet framed.

'Trudi. I couldn't forget your childhood love,' Rory said. 'You painted her for me as a birthday present. Too many years ago. I've never parted with that. I knew your style as soon as I saw your pictures on the market.'

Rhea had forgotten the painting. She had adored Trudi; had learned to ride on her; had competed with her in the Hunter pony trials; had won cups on her. Had lavished time and love and energy on her, grooming her until she was immaculate, always careful to see that Trudi's needs were met before her own.

'A dead giveaway,' Rory said. 'But I kept your secret. How much will you pay me to go on keeping it? I knew your friend wasn't Ray Morton – it had to be you. And then you bought Lucifer. That clinched it.'

'It doesn't need keeping any more,' Rhea said furiously and then laughed at his expression. 'Don't pull my leg. I'm too raw.'

'I'm sorry, Rhea,' Rory said. 'I wasn't thinking; time slipped back. You haven't changed much; not put on weight; that's what alters a woman most. You and that pony; you used to make a lovely sight.'

He walked over to the little painting, and patted it almost as if it were a real horse, and not a picture on canvas.

'Come over to the house and have a coffee. I'm thirsty. I haven't had lunch yet.'

Rhea glanced at the clock on the wall. It was after three. She looked into the car. The pup was still sleeping. Rory glanced inside, wondering what she was looking at.

'Good idea. Where did you get it?' he asked.

She sat on the kitchen table, watching him work at the

cooker, frying bacon and eggs, slicing bread deftly for toast; pouring water on the coffee and setting it to percolate.

'Do you live alone?' she asked.

'It's easier. Mona walked out ten years ago; she had looks and she had money and she had a name that suited her to a T. She enjoyed ill health, migraines and aches and pains, and being waited on. I ought to have stayed and married you, Rhea. We'd have made a good team.'

'You wanted freedom more than me.' Rhea put her cup down. It was too hot to drink from.

'No,' Rory said. 'It was the horses; it's always been horses. I wanted the best; I wanted beauties, I wanted to train them, to race them; that was a laugh. Look at the size of me. I need the big heavy hunters; so I decided to train. When I came home . . .' he was looking back to the start of his present life, nearly twenty years ago. By then Rhea had had three children.

'How did you start?' Rhea asked.

She had often wondered. He had had nothing but what he took from her, and that had been returned.

'Your father staked me. I went to him and told him why I behaved as I did and he lent me the money to begin. Didn't you know?'

'We never talked about you,' Rhea said, thinking back to her nineteen-year-old self, broken, she had thought, beyond ever mending again. Time had given her back her confidence; time had changed her. Nothing had ever again been like that nineteen-year-old adoration of a man who had existed only in her mind.

'I was ambitious,' Rory said. 'It drives a man. And I hate being tied – I was never fair to Mona.'

Rhea didn't want to consider that.

'You asked about the puppy.' She told him about Thorpe; about the dead puppies hung on her fence; about his threat to shoot her little pup if he found her wandering.

Rory listened as he ate. He had always been a good listener. It was odd how the years rolled away. She could almost think herself back to nineteen again, or even younger, to riding Trudi in the local gymkhana; to training for Badminton, for three-day events, discussing everything excitedly with Rory.

58

She could taste the flavour of excitement she had known then, all those years ago, the tiny flutter of unease inside her, the fear she might make a fool of herself and let her pony down by bad riding; the awareness of the training needed and of time against her. In the long years that followed she had come to terms with time.

She had learned to use it to her advantage, to control it as she wished, to expand the days by working during the nights when the boys were sound asleep. She had often painted all night after Elizabeth died, once she had recovered from the injuries she sustained.

'Do you still ride?' Rory asked, bringing her back to reality; to the knowledge that she hadn't seen him for nearly forty years until six months previously, that he knew little about her yet he knew enough to recognise her painting.

She shook her head.

'I'm lucky to be able to walk. My car was crashed into; my daughter died.'

'I read about it,' Rory said. 'She was five, wasn't she?'

Rhea nodded. It was a long time ago; and yet it still hurt.

'I read about your marriage. I kick myself sometimes for being such a fool; if I'd waited, we might have built something like this together; you would have had horses on the doorstep to paint; it would have been very different.' He was looking back to another world, a might-have-been, that sometimes haunted him in dreams.

'How did it feel to be married to a barrister?' Rory asked. 'Did he prosecute his family?'

'Sometimes,' Rhea said. It was not a part of her life that she wanted to remember; John's frequent cross-examinations, making her think and re-think everything she said. Gossip, if repeated, had to be true, and gossip, she had learned in a long lifetime of listening to women's tittle-tattle, had sometimes not even a grain of truth in it; just a hope of proving other people were nastier and unkinder and meaner than yourself so that you could bask in your own superiority. You were the virtuous goodie – they were the baddies.

'Rhea . . .' Rory had walked across to the window, where he bulked large and dark, blotting out the light. 'Be careful.

Thorpe's a strange man and you've come up against him almost as soon as you've arrived. Don't let that puppy out of your sight; not for a moment, not day or night. Put her on her lead when she goes into the garden; a stray shot can easily go through fencing, shooting at a target perhaps, shooting at vermin; and he kills cats. Nothing must interfere with Thorpe's pheasants. One of my dogs got loose, on the scent of a bitch. He's buried out there. Thorpe saw him and shot him and threw his body into my stable yard one morning. I couldn't say a thing. He was wandering. I wouldn't have thought he'd gone that far, but I don't know. I was fond of that dog.'

Rhea sat, her thoughts bleak. Never a moment's carelessness; never a moment's relaxation with the pup off her lead running free through the woods. Never a moment when she could open the door and send her into the garden alone, even if no one were about. Even if the fencing were secure. Thorpe loomed menacingly, his stocky angry figure stalking like an ogre beyond her domain.

Up on the hills behind her the sheep bred, and the farmer Wilde also kept vigil with his gun.

'Thorpe and Wilde between them have accounted for something like forty dogs and any number of cats,' Rory said. 'Don't get a cat, whatever you do.'

'Suppose I have mice? There are signs of them in the cottage.' A cat had been high on her list of priorities.

'Then you get a cat and remember its life will be a short one; some of the villagers keep a constant flow in and flow out of youngsters. They don't survive if they venture far. They vanish.'

Outside the window the yard was busy. Young voices called to one another. A girl walked a horse past the window. Buckets clattered; a horse neighed and another answered. A mare with a foal at foot was led past. The foal was young and leggy; born at the wrong time of year for the racing calendar. Its immaturity called to her, demanding to be put on paper; she needed to go home and to draw; to smooth out the fears that were beginning to daunt her. She should have stayed where she belonged.

Where did she belong?

Back in time, before the last war; before life had grown so complex and so gruesome, before people had become so aggressive. Or were they always like that and she sheltered from them, first by her father and then by John? Maybe he should have told her more about his cases; about the crooks and the villains, the murderers and the embezzlers. Would it have helped her now?

Fear was a tiny prick of worry that, if she let it, would grow, and she trusted no one. Not even Rory, not for a moment. He had let her down too badly when she relied on him – long ago.

'I must go. The pup needs feeding.' The pup would be her only solace, and it would also be something she had to cherish and protect, in a way she had never imagined when she first thought of having a dog. Maybe she could call on Dave – he at least seemed straightforward, and would understand her fears. She would have to train this puppy in a way she had never dreamed likely; to be one hundred per cent reliable, a dog in a million, unlike the lucky dogs that could do much as they chose and venture out where there was no danger.

There was danger everywhere. From traffic in the towns; from other dogs running wild and free; her thoughts threatened to overwhelm her with worries of a kind she had never envisaged.

She drove fast, speeding away from her anxieties. The pup roused and sat up, and pawed at her leg. She pushed her down again, keeping her invisible, away from eyes that might see her and note her and threaten her life.

She had imagined living in the country would be simple; among simple kindly people, with no complexities in their nature. She couldn't have been more wrong. She stopped in the village to buy a newspaper and was aware again of the silence that fell as she entered the little newsagents.

'You're living out at Fawn's Keep?' the man said, as he handed her her change. 'Do you want a paper saved every day? We don't go that far.'

'I'll buy whatever you have when I come in to shop,' Rhea said. 'I may not come every day. Petrol's so expensive.'

'Bit wild out there. I'd hate to be there at night,' he said, as she turned to go.

Thank you very much, she thought, changing gear so savagely that the engine shrieked a protest and she took a deep breath to calm herself down.

The men were just finished as she drew up at the door.

'The cottage will be ready for you within the week,' the decorator said. 'I'd get good strong bolts on those doors, Missis. You never know who's about these days.'

Rhea thanked him and went into her studio, wondering if everyone was conspiring to drive her away. Or was it just thoughtlessness? She didn't know.

She had bought a lead and collar and a disc for the pup. The little bitch did not like the constriction round her throat and, the second she felt it, lay flat upon the ground, her eyes wild. It was a threat to her security. Rhea looked at her helplessly. How did you make a dog like being on a lead? She had no idea. Suppose she tried a piece of chicken in her hand? Would the pup follow that?

She left the lead dangling, the pup lying as if welded to the floor. She had cooked a chicken the night before and she cut a piece from the breast. The scent of food was tempting; the pup stood to sniff it; and as Rhea dangled the titbit enticingly in front of her, she walked towards the door. Within a few minutes she had forgotten about the lead; little bits of chicken were too much to resist.

Rhea took her into the garden. One of the men had fenced a tiny enclosure so that it was absolutely secure, but after Rory's warning she would never dare let the pup come out by herself. She glanced around her, half afraid that she might see Thorpe walking past, or lurking among the trees.

The light was going and she had never felt so alone.

The wind was whispering softly in the bushes; an animal, or was it a man, rustled in the undergrowth. She had a vision of an enemy lurking out there, willing her to go, to leave the woods in peace. She had disturbed a long silence by rousing the cottage to life again. It had been very cheap after years of neglect; cheap enough for her to be able to buy it and spend on it and restore it, bring it back to use again. She had thought that the woods would be peaceful, places of solitude where she could paint.

She had been living a fool's dream; nowhere was safe these days; there were vandals in the towns; there was danger in the countryside; there was threat of war, and ruthless men everywhere wielded power to make others suffer.

She lifted the puppy and walked indoors, drawing the long curtains, and shutting out the night. The studio was too big for comfort, but she had made a recess at the end, with a bed-settee, and an easy chair, a low table, and screens that shut out the large emptiness behind her. She built a fire in the wood stove, and prepared food for herself and the pup.

The pup looked into the blaze, mesmerised; she stretched herself, basking in warmth, experiencing bliss. Her flop ears gave her a quaint look, and her eyes never left Rhea, watching her as she moved about the room, watching her as she settled herself with her tray to eat. The small head shifted, pressing against her owner's leg. The pup had accepted that this was now her place.

Overhead the moon shone through the large rooflight.

Rhea switched on the radio, not thinking. As music welled into the room the pup sat up, amazement on her small face. She cocked her head, listening, and tried to identify the place from which the sound came. Puzzled, she went to the radio, and nosed it. She decided that it had nothing to do with her and stretched out again to the blaze.

The news bulletin that followed the music was far from reassuring. Death in Ulster. A kidnapped ambassador; an attempt at assassination of another ambassador; a student rebellion in another part of the world; a threatened strike in a major industry; another price rise by the oil companies which would make petrol go up by twopence a gallon. Didn't anything good ever happen anywhere, Rhea wondered forlornly.

There was no one to come home; no one to talk to; no need to make a meal for John. He would never come home again. He had given a framework to her life.

The total dreadful finality had not felt so absolute before. Now, in an alien home that was not a home, but a place to sleep and no more, and that threatened to become a prison for herself and her pup, with alien noises in an alien wood and the few friends she had more than two hundred miles away, she found she dared not sleep.

She took up her sketch pad and began to draw the foal. His tiny angular body came to life under her quick skilful hands – the small hooves; the long bony legs; the knobs on his legs; the swell of his hind-quarters and the ribbiness of his chest; the stretch of his neck as he lifted his head to nuzzle his dam, the promise of a mane, now short and erect, like that on a toy horse; the bony ridge above the eyes, and the softness of the eyes as they looked up at the mare, the flare of his nostrils; the lines on his cheeks; the baby look about him, and the tiny white star on his forehead. It was all there, and it was almost perfect. She began to sketch in the solidity and comfort of the mare against him; the mare had to be there, the baby looking up at her, adoring her.

When at last she stopped drawing, the pup was sound asleep, and the moon had vanished, hidden by thick cloud. Rhea undressed and turned out the lamp that had given her light. Sleep, even then, was a long time coming and she had a nightmare, and woke drenched in sweat. The pup whimpered. She needed to go out.

Rhea put on her slacks and a thick jersey and put the pup on her lead. Outside in the dark there was no security at all; the wind had risen and the trees were whipped to sullen protesting shapes. The night was dark, rain just beginning, whispering through the branches, falling on the ground; damp against her face. The pup was entranced by the darkness – wanting to play with a stick, wanting to dig at a molehill, wanting to be off the lead, running free.

Get on, get on, Rhea whispered into the night, wanting to be indoors, locked away from danger which seemed to press in on every side. She thought she heard footsteps and was not reassured when the pup growled. The sound grew louder, and she turned, only to see a hedgehog outlined by the light that shone through the half open door. It vanished, moving purposefully across the garden.

The pup emptied herself at last and Rhea lifted her.

Far away, she heard a shot, and she ran indoors and slammed

the door shut, and stood panting, leaning against it, wondering what went on out there in the night.

It couldn't have been a shot. She had imagined it. It might have been a stick breaking under an animal's paw; or a car backfiring on the road, within a few hundred yards of the wood; she had to stop imagining things.

She had to make plans. She would finish the picture for Sadie and she would paint the foal and the mare and send it to Rachel to sell for her; she would paint the pup, in a thousand different poses. She would buy a deep freeze and cook meals that she could take out when she was too busy to bother.

She would start looking for furniture for the cottage. She had never liked the furniture she and John had owned. They had inherited it from his mother and John had loved it and would never replace it. Vast, ugly Victorian furniture that might well fetch high prices when Rod sold it for her. She wasn't going back for the auction; she couldn't bear to see the past broken up into lots and sold as if she were dead as well as John.

She had to plan and not remember.

She threw down one of her socks and the pup trotted to it, picked it up and brought it back to her, its small body proud. Amused, she took the sock and patted the little animal. She removed her outer clothing and curled up on her bed.

A few minutes later she was aware she had company. A small soft nose pushed against her cheek. The tiny animal was comforting, and she was sure that she belonged here, in the warmth with Rhea. The fire had gone out and she did not like being cold. She had huddled nightly against her mother and her litter mates; she had had the company of bodies against her and this was right.

Rhea tucked her down and fell asleep, lulled by the soft rhythmic breathing.

6

Rhea had not been sleeping well. She hated taking drugs of any kind, and fought the terrors of night-time in her own way, by reading, or by painting, by trying to exhaust herself and distract herself. The puppy by her side helped her to sleep and she slept late, waking to a frenzied hammering on the door.

She woke, startled, thoughts of Thorpe and his gun in her mind. Witch, alarmed, jumped from the bed and puddled on the floor, which was all Rhea needed to make her waking completely unpleasant. She shook herself, took her dressing-grown and fastened the belt, found slippers, put the puppy in the little room off the studio and shut the door.

The hammering continued.

The puppy, left alone for the first time since Rhea had brought her home, howled for company.

'All right, I'm coming,' Rhea said to the angry summons.

She opened the door to face a small woman who glared at her from hostile eyes. She was dressed, rather improbably, in a long shirt and a poncho. Straight black hair lay thick and long about her shoulders, and green eyes glared implacably from a thin angry face that held no trace of softness or humour.

'I want compensation,' she said.

Rhea, barely awake, wondered if she was hearing right.

'Compensation for what?' Had she heard properly, and who was this woman, anyway, who reminded her so much of a harpy that she longed to draw her in that disguise.

'For the death of my bitch and the puppies you shot. And I want the last puppy back. She's mine, not yours.' The voice was strident, and the woman appeared to be so worked up that Rhea was a little afraid she might be attacked. The whole thing

66

was insane. Where on earth had she got such an idea? Rhea glanced at her little clock. It was just after eight. The decorators wouldn't be here for almost an hour. She was alone in the woods with a gamekeeper who shot on sight and a mad woman.

Behind her the puppy yelled in despair.

'Look,' Rhea tried to say reasonably. 'I don't know what you're talking about. I haven't shot any puppies. The gamekeeper shot four yesterday. The farmer shot their mother. I rescued the last pup.'

'You shot them. Someone saw them hanging on your fence; flaunting your crime. What kind of woman are you?'

Please God, Rhea thought, save me from this lunatic.

'I haven't got a gun; I've never had a gun. I can't use a gun,' Rhea said desperately. 'I couldn't shoot them; I didn't shoot them or their mother. I don't know what you've heard, but it isn't true.'

The woman was so obsessed that she wasn't even listening.

'As if it wasn't bad enough to lose my husband. He died in the crash, you know. The bitch couldn't help escaping. She was a lovely bitch; she wasn't doing any harm. She was worth two thousand pounds and I want compensation.'

Rhea stifled an impulse to slap the woman's face. You had to humour lunatics. Presumably her husband had died in a car crash recently. That was enough to unsettle anyone's mind.

'I've only just woken up,' Rhea said. 'I need some coffee. Would you like to come in and have a cup and talk this over? You have got it all wrong, you know.'

'I wouldn't trust you not to put poison in the coffee. Everyone knows what kind of person you are. Taking an isolated place like this for your own purposes. I wouldn't wonder if you were in with the vivisectionists; killing innocent little pups that haven't done you any harm. And then hanging them on the fence. People like you ought to be put down; not the dogs, poor creatures. What harm had my bitch done you except have pups on your land?'

'Look,' Rhea said. 'I don't know what you're talking about; honestly I don't. The puppy is safe here. I'll pay for her if you like; I only took her because I had intended to get a dog and I couldn't bear to see her killed too.'

'It's no use talking to some one like you.' Rhea wondered if her visitor had actually heard a word that had been said. She appeared to wait for a gap in the conversation and then twist everything until it bore no resemblance at all to reality.

The harpy expression was even stronger.

'I'm coming back with the police. There's a police dog-handler down in the town who'll know what to do about you. We don't want your sort here. Coming in to a decent community with your nasty London ways. Harming innocent animals . . . that bitch was all I have left. You wouldn't care about that, would you? You wouldn't know what it's like to lose a husband. Nobody would even marry a woman like you. A monster, that's what you are. A monster. They know all about you round here and why you came. Had to leave the place you lived in before because you'd been banned for life from having a dog so you thought you'd come where nobody knew you but you forgot about the newspapers, didn't you? I'll tell the RSPCA about you; they'll get that poor puppy back from you. What are you doing to her? Just listen. I'll save her from you . . .'

She began to move forward.

Rhea, terrified of attack from someone who could only have escaped from a mental hospital, slammed the door shut, and bolted it. The woman, yelling at her, ran round the house, trying to find another entry. Rhea went in and picked the pup up and held her tight. She couldn't stop shaking. Her teeth were chattering and she felt sick.

The door shook again, as if the woman were trying to shake it off its hinges and for a moment Rhea wondered if she would hurl a stone through the window and get in that way. She stood against the wall behind the door, wishing she were back with Rachel; wishing John were alive to laugh at her fears and reassure her; wishing that the boys were with her; or even Sadie or Louise. She had never felt so isolated in her life.

What on earth had people been saying about her and why?

She felt as if she had come into an alien place where everyone hated her. Thorpe, who wanted to kill her pup; Wilde who would also kill her pup if it were anywhere near his sheep; and now this woman who claimed the pup was hers and was apparently going to do her best to take it back.

Rhea knelt on the floor with the tiny animal held closely against her, wishing she had never tried to find a new place to live. One thing, the police dog-handler knew what had happened, so if the woman went to him at least he'd put her straight, if he could. Could he?

Was she deluded or did she genuinely believe that Rhea was some kind of psychopath fleeing from the place where she had become notorious for her misdeeds?

She dressed, and made a meal for the pup. She put newspaper down in the tiny store-room that was as yet empty of everything except a few paintings brought from home, and a few tins of food. She was afraid to go outside, afraid to let the puppy outside, feeling as if the world were suddenly leagued against her; as if John's death had upset the natural order of things, where people were accepted and liked, and not condemned without even being known.

She made toast but couldn't eat it. She felt sick, the taste of bile as bitter as fear in her mouth. She sweetened her coffee with about five spoonsful of sugar although she never took sugar, and sat, afraid even to think, longing for the men to arrive.

Nine o'clock came at last and the little familiar van drove up and stopped. When Brian knocked on her door she stood to open it and flooded again with fear. Suppose he thought as the rest did? Suppose he thought she had come here with mysterious needs of her own to harm animals and people? Suppose he were as afraid of her as she was of Thorpe? Had there been someone like her in the news recently, or was the woman fantasising?

'You all right, Missis?' the rough voice asked, and Rhea nerved herself to open the door. Brian stared at her, brown eyes under the tow head suddenly concerned.

'Hey, are you ill?'

'I've had a scare,' Rhea said. It was remarkably difficult to talk.

'Not that Thorpe again? The man's a menace, but I don't think he'd harm you; only the pup,' Brian said. It wasn't much comfort. The pup and the stallion had assumed roles in her life

69

that were important to her. She could trust them. They were reality. She didn't know what went on behind other people's eyes; she wasn't sure she even trusted Brian, but she had to tell him what had happened.

He listened quietly, watching her. Poor woman looked awful, he thought, and small wonder, just woken up and faced with nonsense like that. There had been talk in the village. What they didn't know they invented, but he hadn't realised it had gone that far. Always did invent things about newcomers. Like a herd of cows attacking the new member of the herd; people weren't that much different from animals, Brian reckoned, having farmed until the high cost of living and of feedstuffs and repairs had bankrupted him.

'I'll make you coffee. Sit down and rest, there's no one about now. I'll just tell Jim what I'm up to. Maybe he could come and have some coffee too; bit of company might help.'

She nodded.

Jim was an older man, small and grey haired. He listened to Brian and was angry. 'Bloody fool woman; she's half out of her mind since her husband was killed. Didn't she know that Mrs Morland was a new widow too? Husband only died a few weeks back.'

He walked into the studio.

'You want to get out of here and with people for a bit, Ma'am,' he said. 'They're not all like Mrs Redpath; she was never very sensible when her man was alive and she's got a screw loose now, I reckon. Dave'll sort it out for you down at the police kennels; he knows the truth and so do we. Don't be fretting. It's a nasty shock. Haven't you anyone who could come down for a few days and keep you company? You'd be better not alone.'

She couldn't think of anyone. The last thing she wanted to do was to confess to her sons that she had been wrong to move; wrong to choose such an isolated place to live; wrong to even consider that she would find peace in a small community. They seemed, as far as she could see, all to live at one another's throats.

'I'll be all right,' she said.

There was no one to run to.

'I'd go out for the day; we'll be finished with the cottage by the end of next week; measure up for your carpets and curtains and then you can move your furniture in.' Jim, who was a fair man, would speed the job, and get the lady settled. He was an incomer too; he had lived in the area for fifteen years and yet he was not part of it. People accepted him, but they had never been friendly. Just polite.

He didn't tell her that. It was going to be difficult enough for the next few months; maybe years. He inspired Brian to work equally hard and they watched with relief when Rhea drove off, the puppy standing on the seat beside her.

She drove into the town. Here she was anonymous, part of a scene in which nobody and everybody belonged. The shop-keepers made conversation; she was not an object of mistrust or speculation; just a customer. Towns were totally different, Rhea thought, having never considered the matter before. Here she was one of many; nobody noticed her. In the village she stood out. She wondered again just what had triggered the morning's attack.

She drove back, arriving just before the men packed up for the day.

'Better now, Ma'am?' Jim asked, his eyes concerned. He liked Rhea; she was undemanding, and fair, and she knew what she wanted. She didn't get up his nose, the way some people did. And she always said please, which was a word that not many people used these days.

It would soon be dark. Darkness was an enemy, especially if the pup had to be taken outside. Her torch was a target; she cooked a quick meal, and had just finished washing the dishes when there came a knock on the door.

She looked at the door. Dusk hid the trees beyond the garden. Dusk masked the woods, veiling them, and as she looked outside, she felt menace. She picked up the pup in her arms and found she couldn't speak.

'Mrs Morland? It's Dave Martin.'

She ran to the door.

'I'm sorry. I thought . . .' she flung it open. It was raining and his coat was wet. The little blue van was parked at her gate. The dog inside barked once and Dave called to him.

71

'Pack it in, Venn.'

'Come in.' Rhea was thankful to see him and then quite suddenly afraid. He also lived here; he would know the woman; suppose he too was an enemy?

'Jim called in as I was coming off duty. He told me what had happened. Why didn't you come down and see me? There's no need to stay here, being afraid. You'll be welcome whenever you like. There's always someone about, even if I'm on duty. There's Tom, and the other men; people to talk to. It's not good for you, being alone out here, and you've been unlucky. Thorpe . . . we all have to watch for him. Wilde; well, he'll only shoot if the dog's killing, so as long as you keep the pup in there's no need to worry. And as for Agnes Redpath; we all know her, but she must have terrified you, coming at you like that.'

'She accused me of harming animals; of shooting the pups.' Rhea felt sick at the memory. She had just made herself a cup of coffee; she made another for Dave. He looked at the picture of the stallion. The expression was still wrong; he reminded Dave of a man he had just arrested; a mean man with a wicked look in his eyes.

'I couldn't paint today,' Rhea said.

'Agnes Redpath. She's one of the people who protest against anything to do with animals; and get it all wrong,' Dave said, adding two spoonsful of sugar to his coffee and accepting a homemade scone that Rhea had just buttered for him.

'Hunting – she's there. They damage the dogs and horses, and fuss about the fox, never seeing that laying tintacks and hunting the hounds is as bad if not worse than chasing the fox. I don't much like hunting, but I don't like violence used against it. That's as bad. I've had to arrest Mrs Redpath twice, once for throwing pepper in a horse's eyes, and once for assaulting one of the police handlers who was trying to break up the protest and let people get on with their lives.'

'That doesn't account for her opinion of me,' Rhea said.

'Did your husband talk about his cases to you?' Dave asked.

'Very rarely; some of them were horrible and I used to get upset when we were first married; especially after Elizabeth died. If a child was hurt . . .' she paused, and wished she

72

hadn't remembered. John had talked to her once; about a case of child murder. The details were suddenly vivid and horrible.

'It's a rough world,' Dave said. He saw too much and he was sometimes bone weary at the things he saw.

He was here to help Rhea and he needed help himself. He hadn't realised how lonely he was, for someone to talk to who would understand. Susie was only a baby. The other men had their own lives. He had no one. Only the dog and a child whom he had to protect and teach to live in a world he found increasingly sordid.

'All I can give her is self-respect,' he said, and Rhea stared at him.

'I'm sorry; I was wondering what sort of world Susie was going to grow up into,' he said. 'I don't know what to teach her. To be tough and fight; to be gentle and think of others; they don't go together. If I teach her to be tough she'll be insensitive, and she isn't.' It was impossible to explain.

'Why did you ask if John talked to me about his cases?' Rhea asked.

'Because I think I know what triggered Agnés Redpath. She did lose her husband a few weeks ago in a car crash. The bitch was in the car and got loose, and she was the bitch that Wilde shot. But Agnes Redpath had little to do with her. Tommie, her husband, bred the dogs; he had a wife so busy with her protests and her boyfriends that he never saw her. She isn't grieving for him; she saw a chance of easy money, if she could con you into pretending the bitch was worth a fortune. She sold the rest of the stock at once. What did she say she was worth?'

'Two thousand pounds,' Rhea said.

'That's putting it steep, even for Agnes. But the rest of the story . . . I rang up a friend in the Smoke when Jim told me. Your husband was due to prosecute a woman who had been banned once for having dogs because she tormented them and didn't look after them properly. Then she managed to move, change her name and get another bitch and she had puppies; I don't want to talk about it; it hasn't come to court yet, and it was pretty horrible. Enough to make anyone who thought she had met the woman act oddly, and with someone like Agnes

73

Redpath it was a foregone conclusion. She must have heard a bit of some conversation about the case due to come up and your name mentioned and put two and two together and made nine hundred; you aren't the prosecuting counsel's widow, but the woman he was due to prosecute.'

It didn't make it much better.

'What about the puppy?' Rhea asked. 'I'll pay for her; after all she does have a pedigree; and I was going to buy a pup.'

I would have bought one, Rhea thought. She would never have been able to live here without; it was too lonely. Darkness had come while they talked. The woods stretched beyond her, and were haunted by unknown men, and by Thorpe, prowling endlessly with his gun.

'Give me a cheque and I'll take it round to Agnes now and get that silly nonsense out of her head,' Dave said. 'Trouble is, you can't make people actually listen to what you say and lots of them only hear what they want to hear, or they mishear, or they don't listen to a single word. I'll warn her anyway.'

He looked at the pup and flicked his fingers. She came to him and sniffed him. He smelled of Venn; someone who smelled of dog had to be safe. She relaxed and rested her small head on his foot, looking up at him trustingly. She lived in a very bewildering world. Her eyes considered him now, as he towered above her, a giant of a man to a small creature only just a few inches off the ground. His hand was as big as her whole head. He tickled her tummy, and she leaked in ecstasy.

'Little bitches always do that,' Dave said, looking down at her in amusement. He had forgotten how endearing a puppy could be. Venn was a sober fellow, conscious of his own importance, and his training days were so far away that it was sometimes hard for Dave to realise the problems some of his men had with a new brash dog that had been so ruined by a thoughtless or careless owner or simply someone not strong enough to own the breed, that it had been handed over as out of control.

It never had been in control. No one had taught it anything. People expected dogs to learn by magic. They had to be taught and trained; had to be shown what to do, and had to understand what was wanted of them.

Rhea signed the cheque and handed it over to him.

'Fifty pounds would have been enough; especially as you don't know what harm being reared in the wild has done,' Dave said. The cheque was made out for a hundred pounds.

'Perhaps I'm trying to buy peace,' Rhea said. 'I suppose the whole village has heard that story now?'

It was no use trying to pretend.

'Pretty well, I should imagine,' Dave said. 'Rumours spread quicker than weeds here. No one has anything to interest them; it's a bit remote, and so the only thing to do is discuss the neighbours. Go into a bar round here and in no time at all it'll be put about that you're a raving alcoholic. And if I stay any longer . . .' He laughed and went to the door.

Rhea was sorry to see him go. The darkness closed round the cottage and she was once more alone. Witch was restless and began to bark, a surprisingly sharp sound for such a baby. The pup was as surprised as Rhea by the sound she had made and repeated it, off and on, for the next few hours. Rhea quieted her, but every time the pup started again.

Fortunately she tired herself out and slept all night.

Rhea woke to the sound of knocking.

It couldn't be happening again.

She sat up and looked at the clock. Eight o'clock. It was Saturday and Brian and Jim wouldn't be coming. Surely it couldn't be Dave? She called out and was startled when Rod answered her.

'Mother, it's me.'

She opened the door.

'Sorry it's so early. Sadie and I were worried about you; I wanted to see the set-up.' He sounded as if he thought she had fled to some sort of love nest, Rhea thought irritably. Her son was as much a born prosecutor as his father, maybe a better one, and certainly his conversations with her sometimes smacked of the third degree.

'Let me get dressed. Are you breakfasting here?' She was only half awake, and the pup had already wet the floor.

'Honestly Mother, if you must have a dog, you might at least train it to be clean,' Rod said. He disliked animals. Machines were much more predictable.

'I've only had her a couple of days.' Rhea spoke from the little shower room. She dressed herself hastily, and mopped the floor. Witch was hungry and followed her around, so that she almost fell over the pup.

'This is a crazy way to live. Why don't you buy a nice modern bungalow somewhere near us? It's not as if you were a young woman. In a year or two your health will give out, and who's going to look after you?' Rod made her sound as if she were over ninety, and on the way to total senile decay, Rhea thought irritably.

'I'm not yet sixty; not till next year, and since half the doctors, vets, and politicians in this country are considerably older than sixty I don't think I'm likely to dodder into my grave just yet,' Rhea said irritably.

'That's what Father thought,' Rod pointed out, somewhat unwisely.

'My heart's strong,' Rhea said. 'And I don't overwork.' She was angry. She didn't want to be protected by her own children as if she were incapable of making any life for herself. 'Is Sadie with you?'

'Yes. I'm partly here on business. She was tired so didn't get up early; she'll come over for lunch.'

'And will you be having lunch?' Rhea asked.

'No. I'm lunching with Richard Stoke. Do you remember him?'

She did remember him. He had been a singularly boring and pedantic young man and was probably now even more boring and pedantic as an older man.

'I suppose he's acting for some woman who tortured dogs,' Rhea said.

Her son stared at her.

'Mother, are you all right?'

'Prefectly. Why?' Rhea was becoming increasing by irritated. Now he would probably cast doubts on her sanity.

'I just can't see what torturing dogs has to do with anything. He's prosecuting a man accused of fraud. I've had contacts with some aspects of the case and came down as consultant.'

Rod was wandering round the studio as if trying to memorise it to describe in court. He stood looking at the stallion painting for a long time.

'It's crazy,' he said finally.

'My picture?'

'No, Mother. That you should get the prices you do just for a painting. I can't think why people pay.'

It was as unflattering as anyone could get, Rhea thought. Why did families have to be so forthright? You either lived your life among strangers who hid their thoughts and their dislikes and criticised you when you weren't there, unless their emotions got out of hand, or you suffered from your own family, who never seemed to think you had any brains at all.

'I hope Sadie can talk some sense into you,' Rod said. 'I just wanted to let you know she was coming. I didn't mean to stay.'

He went out, slamming the door behind him. It took Rhea back to a thousand arguments; schoolboy arguments; arguments when he was briefly home when he was qualifying; arguments that seemed to have gone on ever since. Rod and she had always sparked one another; had always seen opposite views, and she supposed they always would. Rod was like John's family; downright and, like his father, often domineering. She wondered how Sadie coped with him.

She looked in her small pantry. She had only bought enough food for the next few days. The freezer which had arrived only yesterday, needed stocking up; and Sadie was a perfectionist cook. She put Witch on her lead and took her outside. The woods were damp from overnight rain, the wind rustling softly in bare branches. A kestrel hovered almost overhead. It should have been peaceful, but it wasn't.

She looked down the ride, to the distant horizon where banked clouds promised more rain. Her garden looked out on to a boggy field at the back, and across that to a tiny river that flowed some twenty feet below her. The slope of the land was clothed with shrubs that in summer must be beautiful. Now they were bare and scraggy, except for the gorse which was thick still with spiny leaves and showed a few bright yellow blossoms.

Love is not in season when the gorse is not in bloom.

Who had said that?

There wasn't a house in sight. There wasn't a person in sight; there wasn't a sign of life anywhere. Once there must have been rabbits and hares and foxes, stoats and weasels and bird life everywhere; now the place seemed barren, a wasteland, instead of a place in which animals lived and small lives thrived, with busy personal dramas. There wasn't even a squirrel in sight and she had had squirrels in her town garden. More birds there too. Maybe they took the soft option and went where food was put for them, instead of trying to hunt for it.

She went indoors to comtemplate her larder.

She was good at making pastry. A cheese and onion quiche; she had enough herbs to give it a savoury taste of its own. She had stocked up with fruit and could make fresh fruit salad. It would take everything she had bought. Apples, oranges, bananas, grapes and bright red out-of-season plums that had attracted her not to eat, but to paint, trying to portray the rich colour and the sheen on the skin. It was always a challenge.

She looked at the stallion's head and suddenly knew what was wrong. She took up her brush and the hours sped by. The knock on the door made her jump and Witch barked.

Witch had puddled in the corner.

She hadn't even started to cook lunch, but the head was right; the stallion looked at her with a glowing eye and a kind expression; his muzzle was velvety, his nostrils were perfect. Satisfaction flooded through her. It was the best thing she had ever done. And Sadie could take it home with her.

She opened the door.

Sadie was dressed in cream slacks and a matching blouse, the scarlet blazer showing up her dark eyes and creamy skin and blue-black hair. A jade pendant, carved in the shape of a bull, hung round her neck. She looked very expensive and totally out of place.

Rhea was conscious of the untidy room; of the lunch she had forgotten to cook. Sadie often made her feel incompetent.

'Is that my picture?' Sadie walked over to the easel and looked at it. 'Is that your stallion? No wonder you wanted him, he's heaven.' She walked over and kissed her mother-in-law, an unexpected gesture that surprised Rhea, who found Sadie cool in manner and often daunting as well as sarcastic at times.

'Rod told me he gave you a piece of his mind,' Sadie said. 'Let's have coffee; do you mind if I make it? And I hope you haven't prepared anything for lunch. I've booked a table for two in town; there's a lovely little Italian restaurant there and Rod hates foreign food; I thought you might like a change of air.'

'I'd love it,' Rhea said. 'Can we take my car? I don't want to leave the pup. And she might spoil yours.'

'Fine, but she'll have to get used to being alone,' Sadie said. She spooned coffee into two mugs. 'These are pretty. Where did you get them?'

'There's a small local pottery in Chersey,' Rhea said. 'I'll show you. She makes some unusual things.'

She couldn't take her eyes off the stallion. He was ready to leap from the picture; ready to nuzzle her hands; ready to rub against her shoulder; he was alive and vital and full of his own importance, from the arch of his head to the way he stood. A regal animal. A king among horses. She didn't want to part with him, but she had promised Sadie.

Sadie had brought in a document case with her. She opened it, and very hesitantly, took out some sketches. She handed them to Rhea.

'I thought you might be interested. They're costumes for a new ballet; it's an exciting commission. I've never had the whole thing to do on my own before.'

The colours were vibrant; the costumes medieval; blacks slashed with brilliant orange; deep purple contrasting vividly with yellow and white; feathered caps and pointed shoes; doublets and breeches; long dresses falling in elegant folds, the women with innocent headdresses, under which eyes looked shyly, their expressions contrasting with the bold daring of the men.

'They're lovely,' Rhea said with sincerity. The colours blended and swirled together; when the scene was moving it would be a fantastic kaleidoscope of whirling shades.

'I'm glad you like them. Rod said they were garish.'

'Rod's a Puritan at heart, like his father,' Rhea said. 'Very like his father.' She suddenly wondered how Sadie coped with her son. She found it hard to imagine him as a husband and a lover. He had never been easy, even as a boy. He had John's pernickety demanding mind; an urgent desire for the truth, the whole truth and nothing but the truth. It made conversation unexpectedly full of pitfalls. Do you mean that? Exactly that?

Often, day-to-day conversation meant nothing at all; at other times it masked things that were better not said.

'John never understood my passion for animals,' Rhea said. She was holding a glove, teasing the puppy with it, watching the play of expression on the small determined face, yearning to put the stance of the body down on paper; the backwards pull from the shoulder; the half-crouched hind legs, the urgency of the posture; the light in the dark brown eyes, that were shining with excitement. Witch was in love with being alive.

It was a long time since she had lived with an animal. She had forgotten the joy of tiny things, the absurd self-importance, the total vitality. The abrupt change from joy to fear, the terror of unknown things that would never be explained. The animal world entranced her.

'They live in their own world,' Sadie said. 'I don't want to be with animals; I haven't the time or the patience, but their worlds do fascinate me too. The world of an eagle, high in the sky, everything remote from him, the sudden swoop as he sees the grass move and knows that there is food down there. Your stallion's world; power without responsibility for anything but himself; nobility that demands nothing from anyone around him; the supreme self-absorption that we can never have.'

'You do understand,' Rhea said. She looked at the sketches again. 'That would be more striking if you changed the scarlet to black; more of a contrast; the man has a sombre face.'

'I used to think you a nonentity, for ever in Father's shadow,' Sadie said. 'Someone who didn't know how to fight for what she wanted.'

'I didn't fight,' Rhea said. 'I hate fights; I hate argument; I hate being criticised constantly and wrongly; so I intrigued instead. It was more difficult than having a lover, but much more exciting. Only one person ever found out my secret; I was afraid that others would or that someone would find sketches I had made and put two and two together. Suddenly I'm free of the need to hide away. John would never have come to terms with a successful wife. I pretended I had inherited the money, as I only began to earn well just after my mother died. He was never a curious man, not about me.'

'I fight,' Sadie said. 'I can't pretend to be something I'm not. I don't even know if Rod and I will make it; he resents my work, and I can't give it up. It's a passion, but it's not yours; my obsession is with clothes and with people; with colour and with shape.'

She looked out at the woodland, now dappled with light.

'That makes me think of a pageant of the seasons: spring, with everyone dressed in shades of green and of yellow; summer, blazing with colour – bird colour and flower colour – a peacock parade; autumn in reds and golds and bronze; auburn and rich browns, the dark and sombre wintry death of light and colour. Poets, painters, all obsessed by it; by light and shade, by shadow and by the sun's rays through cloud. Skies, grey and gold and apricot, yet people always paint them blue.'

Sadie stopped talking and looked out at the woods. 'I'm drivelling. What do you see when you look out of the window?'

Fear, Rhea thought. Thorpe walking with his gun. Wilde, a shadowy person as yet unknown, lying waiting for dogs among his sheep; a harpy with black hair and red talons, striking at my eyes.

She shook off absurdity.

A woodland ride; quiet, innocent, the sun shining through. A backdrop for a picture.

'A stallion, walking slowly towards me, his eyes blazing with light; behind him, sketched on the hill, a herd of deer grazing; and in the trees, under the shadows, a hunter waiting, while the animals graze on, unaware.'

Sadie laughed.

'You and I, we see everything differently, yet reflect each other and we married the same man; Rod and his father are totally alike; maybe they needed us in contrast. It's helped me, coming here. I didn't think it would.'

'It's helped me too,' Rhea said.

She looked up and lifted the pup. Witch licked her face. The brown eyes watched Rhea all the time, eagerly accepting that this woman was now the pup's whole life. She provided food and comfort and warmth; even in the few days she had had her, the pup had learned the rules of the house; they were few and they were understandable.

It was good to get away, even briefly. Rhea told Sadie of her fears as she drove; of Thorpe and his vindictiveness; of the pup's extraodinary breeder; of Wilde, out on the hill.

'They'll get used to you,' Sadie said. 'Stories go round all the time. Everyone in London thought you had a lover.' She laughed. 'I didn't believe it. It never mattered and Father never heard. Though I wondered, even . . . Those weekends away; the days off, when you didn't answer the phone and the house empty. Did you imagine we never wondered?'

'I never thought about it,' Rhea said, negotiating a narrow lane and drawing in to the side to allow a milk lorry to pass. The pup was sitting between her and Sadie, leaning her head against Rhea's thigh. 'I was too busy. Ideas never come when you're free to work them out; they come when you are too busy to have time and they surge in your head. I didn't see anything but the picture in my head; light would fall on a scene; horses would race across a field, and one would stand out, above the rest, beautiful beyond imagining. He would speed in my head for weeks, and I had to walk and talk and hide the maddening need to get away, to put him on paper. John was too busy with his own affairs ever to notice.'

'I know,' Sadie said. She translated everything she saw into texture. The rough feel of stone; the smoothness of velvet, the slide of silk; the soft rustle of leaves made her think of draperies gliding over grass; the brown hide of a horse was deep rich velvet, glowing with its own light; the whirling patterns made by colours in the sky entranced her, so that even while Rhea was driving, Sadie had left her in thought and was weaving a stage pattern of grey and silver and sudden flashing brilliant yellow where the sun shone through a cloud.

82

'Where did you get your name?' Sadie asked suddenly, in the middle of eating lasagne.

Rhea laughed.

'My grandfather was a professor at Cambridge,' she said. 'You'd have liked him. He was the absolute typical professor; absent minded, head in the air, busy with his own affairs. He was Professor of Zoology and his speciality was birds. He was brilliant; he also painted. His pictures ought to have been collected, but they never were. That was relaxation. His mother was named Maria and she wanted me named after her. Mother couldn't stand the name, but agreed to Ria. And how would a professor who knew more about birds than any living man, spell Ria on a birth certificate? The name stuck; Mother called me Ray. Father sometimes called me Ostrich and maybe I am. Grandfather registered me. Father was abroad at the time.'

'Let's have some wine,' Sadie said. 'I feel like celebrating, though I don't know what. We'll drink to Fawn's Keep and your future; and mine.'

Rhea, looking at her daughter-in-law, knew that Sadie's future would never be easy. Not with Rod. His prosaic mind, obsessed with accurate detail, would never understand the urgent need to paint; the vibrant world of massed colour, of effects created on a stage very different from his courtroom, where everything was sombre, and the judge in his robes and wig reminded Rhea of a figure of doom.

He was the hunter out in the woods; she and Sadie the running deer, needing to live out their own lives.

She was getting fanciful. She was living too much in her own head without people to talk to, and she had gone high with delight at finding someone to share her thoughts. She had never shared them with John so why did she need to now? Then she remembered Rachel and the long hours they had spent in deep discussion over something so trivial that no one but another painter would understand. Even then, it had to be the right kind of painter; they all had different visions.

Back at the cottage, Sadie looked again at the painted stallion.

'I can't take him; you'd get a fortune for him if you sold him.'

'He was painted for you; because you'd value him,' Rhea said. 'Money doesn't matter between friends.'

She wrapped the painting carefully. The easel was blank, demanding another picture at once; and she saw it, in her mind, almost before Sadie had driven away. A poem in the middle about a pup (she would have to find the right one), and all around the edge of the poem pictures of Witch; Witch feeding, her small body intent on food; Witch scratching, an expression of bliss on her face as the itch was allayed; Witch sleeping, curled in a small ball; Witch bouncing on the paper ball she had rolled across the floor.

She took Witch outside, watching the shadows. The cottage felt very empty now that Sadie had gone. She had enjoyed the day. She had never thought to like her daughter-in-law, but now they had found a common interest she knew they would understand one another and be friends for all their lives.

She wondered about Louise. A grandchild would be fun; but Louise herself was not yet mature; and she wondered what kind of a mother she would make. She doubted if there would ever be room in Sadie's life for a child and perhaps that was just as well, as John had been a very aloof father, finding the boys intrusive and noisy when young, and impatient with teenage passions when Rod was briefly a dedicated revolutionary, a phase that had only lasted a few weeks and would have died sooner if John had learned to hold his tongue. He was too fond of lecturing the boys.

It was odd to look back. They had been agonising years, those teenage years, when the boys were growing up and John was so often furious with them, and her own desire to paint had overwhelmed her, so that she was torn between all of them and often felt as if she would fly apart, with no part of her belonging to herself.

Now she was on her own. Twenty years a daughter; almost forty years a wife; and for the first time she owned herself, and could do as she chose.

She looked into the future, and found it remarkably bleak.

7

Rhea was painting when the knocking came on the door. It reminded her of her morning wakening and the woman who stood there on that day. She was uneasy as she went to the door and even more uneasy when she realised that Agnes Redpath had come back.

The woman was dressed in a flounced, long petticoat-like affair, a shawl draped round her shoulders, looking like a refugee from a Victorian poorhouse. Sandalled feet were bare, the toe nails bright scarlet, rimmed with black. Her hands were equally dirty.

She walked in.

'I've brought your pedigree form; and the agreement my husband and I always insist on when we sell a puppy; and a diet sheet for her. Dear little thing, she's growing, isn't she?'

The change in attitude was nearly as unnerving as her hostility had been.

The bright glittering eyes were looking around the room, checking on the prices of the furniture, on the bareness, on the lack of curtains and the picture on the easel, on which Witch appeared in several poses.

'Oh, you paint. How nice. It will give you something to do. Dave tells me you lost your hubby too. I thought you were someone else.'

Rhea restrained a desire to throttle her visitor. She had come in unasked, and was behaving as if the pup had been reared in the best of homes, instead of found wild and rescued when about to be shot.

'Her mother won a great many first prizes,' the ingratiating voice said. 'She was very well known to everyone round here.

Anyone will tell you what a lovely bitch she was. This is her third litter. Two of her first litter at Cruft's last year; and one of the second is a police dog; another is a Guide dog. We always concentrate on temperament. It's so important in a Shepherd.'

Rhea listened blankly. She had had little to do with dogs or dog people. Her passion was always horses. She had never owned a dog in her life, not even as a child, though her parents had kept several. Her father insisted they stayed in kennels and, as he trained them, no one else was allowed near them in case they ruined his work by ignorant handling.

'Here is your receipt. This is the diet sheet. I sell the food, and I can let you have a slight discount on it. You'll have to collect it of course; I can't afford transport costs and this is too far out. I live on the other side of the village, towards Merchent Leavers. And here is the agreement. She's lovely breeding. The whole of the first litter of puppies will belong to me, as you've paid so little for her.'

Rhea looked at her in astonishment.

'How much will you sell the puppies for?'

'That depends on the stud dog. If it's a good one, they'll be worth around £200 each.'

'I see.' Rhea was doing frantic calculations in her head. £100 for a bitch puppy, badly reared and suffering from dietary deficiencies; and if she had eight puppies, or even six, that would be another £1200; and if the bitch weren't mated till two and cost £3 a week to feed, she would have spent another £300 at least on food; and then there were extras and vet bills as well.

'Do you have this kind of agreement with everyone?' Rhea asked.

'Of course. It's the only way you can make money out of dogs; the puppies cost a fortune to rear.'

Rhea restrained an impulse to say that this one didn't cost anything; and the profit had been total, but after all they had reared the bitch and had lost the other pups which would have been a source of income.

She looked at the receipt, which was in perfect order.

The pedigree meant nothing. The mother had been called

Glittering Glory; the father's name was long, involved and very German, full of vons, and totally unpronounceable, as were all his ancestors.

Rhea wanted to draw. She did not want to indulge in long discussion with a woman she felt was bordering on lunacy. She was edgy, unwilling to talk, and wanted nothing more than to push her visitor out. She had no intention of offering coffee or anything else to drink.

'I'd like to add a few words to that agreement,' she said, looking down at it. She needed to protect herself. Anything could happen to the bitch and if she guaranteed to hand over a whole litter, what else might not be implicit in the deal? John's caution had taught her something after all.

The agreement was short and to the point.

'I hereby promise that all the first litter of the bitch puppy Angerson Smiler will be the sole property of her breeder, Agnes Redpath. Also all dog food will be purchased from Mrs Redpath, as well as necessary vitamin supplements.'

She took pen and paper and sat down to think. The puppy was sitting by her feet. Witch made no move whatever towards the visitor, but seemed to regard her with acute suspicion.

How would John have worded the agreement? It had to look right but had to tie her to nothing. There was no way she intended to hand over £1300 or more for a bitch puppy bought at eight weeks old. She might have all kinds of things wrong with her as she grew up. Rhea knew enough about dog and horse breeding to know there were no guarantees with a baby animal.

'What's wrong with the agreement?' the sharp voice was suspicious.

'I'd rather write my own; so that we know exactly how we stand.' Rhea was a little afraid that the sharp tongue might launch out into further accusations of cruelty and shooting the puppies, but Dave seemed at least to have convinced the woman she had been wrong about that.

She thought deeply and then began to write.

'I am paying £100 for the bitch puppy Angerson Smiler.' She looked down at the name; she wondered how it had come about, and then wondered how the woman had dared name her at all, with the history of the pups. But they had to be registered and she needed to establish ownership. She looked at the papers on the table. A Kennel Club form transferring ownership was among them.

She wrote on.

'If she proves fit to breed from, and if the mating is successful, the puppies will be the property of her breeder. She will not be mated before she is two years old, and only then if circumstances permit. She is being kept as a companion and guard and is primarily a pet, and not intended to be used as a brood bitch for profit.'

'You've not said anything about dog food,' the woman said.

'She's doing well on what she's having and I don't want to change.' Rhea was feeding her on meat and biscuit, having bought a book which told her about feeding Alsatian puppies and about their general care and management. Dave had recommended it to her, and she found it extremely useful.

'Everyone who buys a puppy from me buys the food from me; it's my living,' the woman said.

Rhea began to wonder if she had wandered into Never-Never land where everyone thought differently and all the rules were made up as people went along. Maybe she should insist that everyone who came to her door bought a picture because that was her living. John had never been a thrifty man and the insurance he had taken out had not been increased to keep up with inflation. That would have been impossible. She had to earn now to keep herself and keep her home. No one realised the vast inroads tax made into her income. It was something she hadn't realised fully before.

'I'm sorry, I don't,' Rhea said. 'I'm very busy. Will you please go? But sign this before you go. I've signed it.'

'It's not what I said.'

'It's very similar; there are two sides to every deal, and I want to make sure I agree with the deal. Supposing the bitch is barren? What would you do then?'

The woman shrugged and signed. Rhea closed the door behind her. She hadn't even smelled clean. She had an aerosol spray in the little kitchen annexe and sprayed the room. Even that didn't drown the traces of her visitor. She opened the window at the top, and went back to her picture, but the urge to draw had gone. She was edgy and unhappy and began to wonder if she had been wise to insist on keeping the pup.

Witch nosed her leg. Rhea was already very fond of the little animal. She was gentle and playful and affectionate. The puppy sensed distress. She ran into the middle of the room and tried to chase her tail, and flopped to one side; she picked up the sock that Rhea had left for her and teased and tossed it, growling at it in puppy anger, and then trotted up to Rhea and pushed the sock against her leg.

The small tail wagged furiously, circling oddly, more like a windmill than a tail.

The knock sounded on the door again.

Damn the woman. Couldn't she leave her alone?

Rhea opened the door.

'If you don't buy food from me, I'll sue you,' Agnes Redpath said. 'You have to buy it when it's one of my puppies. Everyone knows that.'

Rhea looked at her.

'My husband was a lawyer. There's very little I don't know about consumer rights,' Rhea was so angry that she unconsciously lapsed into John's legal way of phrasing sentences. 'You can't impose conditions of sale. It's against the law. Also through my husband I know the best lawyers in the country. I wouldn't advise you to try anything so absurd.'

She slammed the door shut.

She could see John's face looking at her, registering amazement. It was totally unlike her to flare up and defend herself. It was about time she learned. She wished she hadn't been brought up to be kind and considerate. It was a big drawback in the real world.

She cooked herself an omelette and fed Witch. She would take advantage of Dave's invitation and go and visit the kennels. She needed company; human company. Maybe later she would dare to walk in the woods, but the woods were Thorpe's territory and she couldn't do with meeting any more enemies. She knew, as well as if she had been told, that she had not made progress with the puppy's breeder. The woman was mildly deranged; she had to be to be so demanding, and so certain of rights that no person could own.

It was almost four o'clock before Rhea was free to drive away from the cottage. She had more to do there than she realised, and the pup took time.

Susie was training her own dog in the yard, and she looked up as Rhea drove in. Two blue vans were parked outside the big double garage. Two tiny children, warmly dressed, were playing in a sandpit in one of the gardens. Dave, hatless, but in uniform, raised a hand to her through the office window, where he was talking to two of the men.

Rhea smiled as she stepped out of the car. Susie was standing by the office door.

'Dad won't be finished for another hour. Would you like to come in and have some coffee? Then I can have tea a bit early; I'm starving.'

'I'd love coffee,' Rhea said.

Dave came through the office door into the yard.

'I'm tied up for a bit, but stay and eat with us,' he said. 'Did Mrs Redpath bring your receipt?'

'Yes. I had a very odd interview with her,' Rhea said. 'I'd love to stay and ask you about it . . .'

Dave grinned.

'I can imagine. She's well known round here. OK, Susie, love. Give Mrs Morland something to tide her over till I come in and make supper. Done your homework?'

'Nearly all,' Susie said. She skipped into the house in front of Rhea. She was a slender child, her face solemn under a fringe of straight, very dark hair. Vivid blue eyes gave her face an appeal of its own. She was far from pretty but it was a good face with a strong jaw like her father's. A child who knew her own mind, Rhea thought.

The house was cosy, the sitting-room, with its deep chintz-covered settee and chairs, was very warm. A budgerigar whistled to them from his cage in the corner. A large ginger cat was sprawled on the hearthrug, his tummy to the blaze. It was a long time since Rhea had seen a real coal fire; it lent more comfort to the room than she had believed possible. She would get logs for the cottage fire; it would be lovely to bask in the blaze and watch the glow and the leaping flames. Modern life lacked warmth in every direction.

Susie was totally at home in the little neat kitchen. She made coffee and brought scones and made herself a teacake sandwich, of ham dripping with mustard.

She settled herself beside the cat. The collie stretched out on the far side of the settee, obviously going to an accustomed place.

'That's Trot,' Susie said. 'He's all mine; Dad has Venn.'

'I've met Venn,' Rhea said. She was totally at ease for the first time since she had moved. The room was relaxed, the child was uncomplicated; there was no overtone of unfriendliness here; no secret thoughts or hidden envies. Susie was simply and unaffectedly delighted to have a visitor.

Witch needed inoculating. There was always the risk of distemper. And there was now the new parvo-virus to contend with. Jim had warned her.

Dave, coming into the room an hour later, suggested she drove to the vet with Susie and got the first injection done now. He would make a meal. Susie chattered happily, about school and about the children next door. Tony was two and Maxie was four, a monkey of a child with a mind of her own who needed a great deal of watching over as she had an urge to explore. There was a new baby coming.

'I'm teaching Trot to track,' Susie said. 'He's good but not nearly as good as Venn. I can go out with Dad then, when he's training and I won't get in the way.'

By the time the visit to the vet was over and the puppy had had her inoculation, Rhea had realised that training a dog was as demanding as training a dressage horse; if you took the job seriously.

'Some people think it's cruel to train dogs,' Susie said. 'You have to be careful where you go; people are so silly. They don't realise the dogs love it; they get excited and scream with impatience because they can't wait to have the tracking harness on, and people who don't know about dogs think they're screaming in terror. I wish people would understand. Trot gets so crazy if he thinks we're going out to train that he jumps up and down and chases his tail and sometimes bites my leg because he just can't wait. It's the most terrific thing he knows. Lots of people won't let their dogs do anything that's fun; and when we do they think we're the ones that are cruel, not them.'

Rhea referred to the conversation during the meal. Dave was an experienced cook and had made the two chops he had bought for himself and Susie into part of a mixed grill, with bacon and egg and sausage. He listened quietly; Rhea suddenly realised that, unlike John, he did listen, with all his mind. John had only listened to business conversations. Everything else went into his head and out again as swiftly as it was spoken.

'There's something about the dog world that is very odd,' Dave said. 'It's composed of fanatics in some parts. Fanatics about breeding; they disapprove of everyone else such as pet owners, or those who train for working trials or obedience – they're all wrong. Very few people take part in more than one aspect of it. Those are the ones who get the worst part of the deal, as whichever world they move in is against them, because they take part in the others.'

'The obedience people hate the working-trials people; the working-trials people think obedience is a series of circus tricks; nobody ever seems to think anyone else might have a point,' Susie said. It was obviously a conversation she had heard before, but it was all new to Rhea.

'In Breed, they do what?' she asked.

'Breed is a beauty show. There are standard pictures drawn up of each dog; its shape, the way it moves, the size of its head, the way the ears are set; the proportions of each part of the body to the rest; the coat, and in some breeds the coat colour. White German Shepherds aren't showable, nor are those with long coats. They can be all black or black and gold, but even there nowadays there's a split. There are almost two totally different types. The old-fashioned dog, which is long in the body, and big built and solid; and the newer type which is being bought in from Germany. The dogs are shorter in body; and are harder and leaner; and sometimes smaller, although the breed size is definitely stated and still observed, so no one has done anything about that yet. Those that make the ring have to be a certain height, not over or not under, in all breeds. And then of course judges vary in their opinions. One judge may think a dog as perfect as it can be and another dislike everything about the dog, so it wins one day and the next show it's down at the bottom.'

Rhea looked at him in astonishment.

'It sounds a total gamble,' she said. 'And it's very hard on the dogs that aren't born beautiful. What happens to them?'

'We get them. You get them. The breeders keep the best, obviously, and sell the others, so you get another faction still. The pet owners who may land up with the kind of dog no one should have bred or sold. We get some of those, though most of the dogs that are passed on to us are passed on because no one has understood how to train and control them and because in pet circles training is often a dirty word.'

Rhea thought of the old rivalries and factions from the days of her pony-club riding; the people who were supposed to have broken the rules; those said to train cruelly; those said to use unpleasant methods on a horse. She had known too much about horses to believe most of them. There was no way a badly treated horse would appear happy when ridden in competition; you could tell at once. Presumably you could also tell with a dog.

She helped with the dishes and sat by the fire, grateful for company. She couldn't talk to her sons; they lectured her. John had either lectured her or ignored her. Only with Rachel could she talk for ever; and they had always discussed pictures; the techniques used by different artists; the play of light in a painting, the way that the Old Masters had used their methods to give drama, to highlight a feature, to show the world a different point of view. It was impossible to explain to an outsider, and the dog world sounded almost as involved.

'What is the difference between obedience and working-trials?' Rhea asked.

'Obedience is more like dressage in horses; trials more like show-jumping in some ways, I suppose. It's impossible to equate them. The Obedience dog has to work accurately, sitting straight, walking close at heel, echoing every stride of his handler, paying total attention. Each class is built on the class below; in the first class, the nursery class, the dog has to walk at heel, on the lead, with right, left and about-turns and has to sit when the handler stops still. The same routine is repeated off the lead; then the dog has to come to the owner when called, sit in front, and when the judge commands it, go round the back of the handler and sit at heel. He does the same thing picking up a dumbbell, the retrieve, and then has to sit for one minute without moving and lie down for two minutes without moving. They lose the points, as horses do in show-jumping.'

'It sounds difficult,' Rhea said. 'And that's just the nursery class?'

Susie laughed.

'It isn't really difficult. Come on, Trot, let's show her.'

The collie leaped up, tail waving so fast that it fanned Rhea's face. Susie whistled the dog to heel and danced round the room, the dog following every movement. Child and dog were totally absorbed, enjoying every second. The dog's tail never stopped waving for a moment and his eyes never left her face.

'You're clever,' Susie told him and the tail thudded against the table leg.

She called him to her, and then threw a wooden dumbbell; the dog appeared to Rhea to do everything faultlessly.

'Not bad, but it wouldn't win her any prizes,' Dave commented. 'It does the dog good, though, if you do it the right way; Trot enjoys every moment of his training, as he's a working breed, like the German Shepherd, and it's a substitute for work.'

'Working Trials is more like police work,' Susie said. 'It's marvellous for pet Alsatians as they can use their brains and then they aren't naughty. They do the Obedience the same way but it doesn't have to be so accurate; and they track, search for hidden objects and have to jump; nine-foot-long jump, six-foot scale, and a hurdle; if there's nothing physically wrong with them they adore that part of it. Trot jumps for fun every morning. My problem is to keep him steady till I tell him to go, or he's off; he can't wait.'

Dave, pouring coffee, laughed. 'Susie never remembers that the proper name for an Alsatian is now the German Shepherd.

I'm lucky to have a daughter that likes my work,' he said. 'I probably load her with more information than she can take at times; she loves every minute she spends with the dogs, though. And she can practise with him in the garden when I'm busy. You'll have to train your pup. It would make a new interest; you aren't going to ride your stallion, are you?'

'Can I see your stallion?' Susie asked. 'Is he beautiful?'

'He's gorgeous,' Rhea said. The stallion had become a symbol of her new life; and he at least was perfect; she was back to her old love, to something she had almost forgotten, but the yearning had never been killed. All those years . . .

'Did your husband share your animal interest?' Dave asked. He had met John Morland on several occasions; had been cross-examined by him twice.

'No,' Rhea said. 'He had nothing to do with animals. We didn't even have a cat.'

She sighed, remembering.

'I'd have loved an animal. John was often remote, and he had a total passion for accuracy. I drove him mad – I'm so vague. Our conversations were often ludicrous. Are you certain? What time was it? How many people were there? Even if I was only telling him about a coffee party. In the end it was easier to live within my head, and paint, because I couldn't bear to be cross-examined and if I had much to do with people it always ended up like that. I was brought up to tell the truth and shame the devil and it's not always a good idea.'

Dave laughed.

'If I thought that, I'd have to change my job. As I was walking along Wellington Road at seven-fifteen precisely . . . I can't change the rules of truth when I'm writing down evidence. Your husband and I had a lot in common in that way.'

'Dad does it to me,' Susie said and grinned at Rhea. In that moment a small conspiracy was born between them. Life wasn't easy for Susie either.

'It's not always tough,' Dave said. 'I was walking home the other day when I came upon the most immaculately dressed gentleman I have ever seen. Beautiful city suit; tie that had cost about fifty pounds, of hand-made silk; gold cigarette case, diamond ring on his finger that would probably pay my salary for a couple of years; handmade shoes; tailored shirt, custom made; beautiful hat at a slight angle. Grey moustache and thick white hair that also cost a fortune to cut; and he was walking along, as drunk as any drunk I've ever seen. He stopped and looked at me. He was on the canal bank, and I was just coming along in the other direction. He teetered in front of me and said,

"Officer, if you think I'm drunk, you're quite wrong," and with extreme dignity toppled backwards into the water.'

'Daddy fished him out and took him home and couldn't stop laughing for a week,' Susie said. She laughed too. 'It must have been very funny.'

Rhea had a wild picture enter her mind; a cartoon or a caricature, which would make a companion to the one she had dreamed of, with the harpy clutching her puppy, trying to run off. Memory was still painful. She had spent the evening free from fear, but she didn't want to go back to the cottage. She wished she had never bought it.

Time was running away and Dave needed time with Susie, and the child would have to go to bed. She had intruded long enough. It was time to go. She drove home, the pup lying beside her fast asleep. She wished she had left a light on. She wished she had a companion; she wished that John hadn't died. If he had lived to retire they would have found common interests; maybe he would have enjoyed having a dog.

She sat in her car, not wanting to get out. The woods enclosed her. Somewhere out there Thorpe walked with his loaded gun. And somewhere out there was Agnes Redpath with her twisted ideas. There were others who had heard stories of her and might never believe the truth. Why were people always ready to believe the worst of everyone; to turn against a newcomer?

The herd protecting itself against change. People hated change. She hated change herself; yet she had gone far away from everything she knew and everyone she knew.

She thought of Louise. For the first time she thought she understood her daughter-in-law, grown up as a petted and much-loved only daughter, who had never been asked to do

96

anything she didn't wish to do. She had never had to face reality and now she was about to face the ultimate reality and give birth to a child, and learn to be responsible for that child. If only people would let her grow up, and not rush to help her every time she cried out for help; Louise had learned to cry out a lot.

She put the puppy on her lead and took her into the little enclosure. She fitted her key in the lock a few minutes later, holding the pup close to her, as if the pup would banish the dark. A small wet tongue licked her face, saying, 'I'm here, it's all right.'

The place was darker than she had believed possible. She switched on the light.

The window was broken. A pool of rain lay on the floor, and a knife had slashed brutally through every one of her paintings. The pieces lay on the floor, none bigger than a post card. The same knife had slashed her bed; had ripped the chair; had damaged the rugs. She thought of the knife; sharp as a razor blade, and stood looking at the little door to the shower room wondering if an enemy stood there, ready to slash at her and the pup.

Outside the window, rain pattered softly. Somewhere far away an owl hooted.

The pup whimpered.

Rhea was holding her as if she were a talisman against terror.

She ran from the house, leaving the door open, the light streaming out across the garden, and got into her car and drove fast, away from whatever demon waited there in the garden, reaching the police house just as Dave was switching off the light to go to bed.

He sighed and dressed again and spoke on his communicator to the men on duty.

Rhea couldn't stop shaking. Her knees shook and her teeth chattered and she felt sick. Dave went next door for Mair. Reg was off duty. He could stay with the children. Mair, who was small and blonde and far tougher than she looked, made tea, and hid her own anger. She had been a woman police constable before she married. She knew the feeling; she knew the outrage; but anger didn't help.

97

Susie, sound asleep, heard nothing and Rhea was glad. She couldn't have faced the child.

She couldn't talk, her throat had closed up tightly. She could never go back there again.

And then resolve tightened. She wouldn't be driven away. She had as much right there as anybody else. What was the matter with these people?

'It's insane,' she said, looking into the fire, hugging herself to keep warm. The puppy was in the corner of the room in a wire pen that Mair had bought for their own dog when she was small. Their police dog slept in the kennels, but they had a second German Shepherd, a bitch they hoped to use for breeding police dogs from. Nan wasn't yet old enough to be mated. Another year . . .

'There are a lot of odd folk about,' Mair said. 'You're getting more than your share. The cottage has been empty a long time and it's lonely down there.'

'Who'd want to drive me away? What harm am I doing?' Rhea asked.

The question was unanswerable.

8

Rhea slept in Mair's spare room. She slept late, totally exhausted, and woke to wonder for the first moments where she was. Memory flooded back. She did not want to return to the studio. She hadn't even looked at the cottage. That had been almost ready for occupation; as soon as the furniture arrived.

She wanted to run away but there was nowhere now to run.

She was alone, totally alone, surrounded by people whose hatred was so great that they were combining to remove her. Suppose the cottage had been a headquarters for some gang? She dismissed the thought irritably as fantasy, and dressed and went downstairs.

Tony was sitting in the middle of the floor, his small face totally absorbed, playing with a toy farm. He set the animals in tidy rows, at if they were soldiers on parade. His tow hair drooped over his forehead. He looked up at Rhea with brilliant brown eyes, smiled at her confidingly, told her she was a naughty boy and returned to his own affairs. He was lost in his own world, ignoring her.

Mair came in from the kitchen with a cup of coffee.

'I didn't want to wake you. Pup's fine; she's out with the kennel man who's having the time of his life, teaching her to sit. He adores pups. He has designs on ours when Nan's old enough to mate.'

The bitch came into the room and barked. She was a dainty bitch for her breed, not yet adult in body. She was slender and immature, just growing the thick fur under her tail and on her rump. Witch would look like that one day, not so far ahead;

99

and would be old enough to mount guard, and maybe keep away intruders.

Rhea shivered.

'I'll cook you something in a few seconds. I've just got back from taking Maxie to nursery school. I can relax a bit now. That child will grow up to be a mountaineer or an explorer. She always has to find out what's at the other end of the road; and after turning one corner there's always another to turn. She takes a lot of looking after.'

Mair plumped up the cushions and poked the fire.

'Dave's in the office. He said not to hurry. He got Jim and Brian. They're cleaning up for you. No need to go back till it's shipshape again.'

'They can't restore my pictures,' Rhea said. They had been ready for sale. Two commissions and three pictures she had done on impulse and hoped to sell. She was thankful that Sadie had taken away her painting of the stallion. She would have hated to have had that destroyed too. It was so senseless; so vindictive; so impossible to understand.

'You're a newcomer,' Mair said. 'So everyone's aware of you. In a year or two you'll have merged into the background and they'll start on someone else.'

'Who are "they"?' Rhea asked. 'People known to the police?'

'There are always some, in every community. You aren't the only one it's happened to. The new vicar had all the hassocks slashed; and the new prayer books were torn apart and thrown down in the graveyard. Flowers were taken off the graves and headstones painted over. There's nothing for the youngsters to do around here; so they make their own fun and it's often not very nice fun. Broken shop windows; smashed phone kiosks. Dave will put a patrol on for you; the sight of police vans passing every few hours will have a deterrent effect. And come and see us whenever you want. It's quiet out there.'

She put bacon and egg and fried bread in front of Rhea.

'Eat. It'll do you good. Come on, Tony love. Time for sleep.'

He smiled at Rhea, a brilliant trusting smile, and went to her and kissed her.

'I like you,' he announced gravely, before following his mother out of the room. The warm feeling of pleasure stayed with Rhea all through her meal.

Mair, sitting relaxed for a few minutes over a cup of coffee, talked of the children. The police house was a good place to live, as there was always someone around to babysit briefly for her; one of the men, off duty, Tom in the kennels with time on his hands, with some wonderful stories to tell of dogs he had known and with a store of nursery rhymes that were not printed in any books. The children adored him. He kept Maxie busy round the kennels, carrying bowls of food for him, fetching grooming brushes, and helping to groom the big dogs, which all loved the children and could be allowed to play with them when they were off duty.

There was no question as to whether the police dogs enjoyed their work. Two vans drove into the yard and instantly dogs began to bark. The men went into the office, and Tom brought out their dogs, pulling to get to the vans, bounding in, watching eagerly through the wired windows for the men to come back, tails waving the whole time. Another man in uniform brought his dog out of kennels, laughing as it leaped around him. Going out, going out, the dog said with every muscle in its body, its mouth open, tongue lolling, eyes bright with excitement.

'Must get on,' Mair said. 'I do Dave and Susie's washing as well as my own, though that's not specially arduous with a machine. Heather does the ironing for both of us. Dave buys the soap powder; it works out very well. Dave's office is through the left-hand door. They'll be having coffee, I expect, now, so you won't be interrupting anything if you go across.'

The yard was swept clean. Two dogs looked at her from the kennels and barked and leaped at the wire. Tom appeared, with Witch on a cord, following him trustingly.

'Nice pup,' Tom said. He was a comfortable-looking man with a kind face that was full of creases, the laughter lines from lips to nose deep, and often used. He grinned at her now.

'Nothing like a pup to make you laugh. She's a caution. Tried her carrying things yet?'

'Only socks,' Rhea said. 'She pinches those.'

'Watch this.'

Tom took a large stick, almost as big as the pup and threw it a few inches from him. Witch pounced and tried to lift it. It was too heavy, and she pawed at it in frustration, then, eyeing it with extreme consideration, dragged it a few inches back to Tom, who took it and petted her.

'Clever baby.'

He looked at Rhea.

'You see you train her, missis. She's a cracker. A little genius. Brighter than any we've got here; be a crime to leave her just as a pet. Come over when you're not busy and we'll help you. Be fun to have one that doesn't have to work for a living and learn it the quick way. And I've time on me hands here, during the day. Go on in. I'll look after the little 'un. Long time since we had a pup this young round here.' He flicked his fingers and Witch trotted after him, and then turned to pull back to Rhea. She had felt a brief moment of jealousy, but it was appeased. The pup wanted her most; she went into the office.

The big desk was covered in papers. Dave, his long legs stretched out, was reading a letter thoughtfully. He smiled up at her and pointed to the other chair. The room was bare; wood walls, on which were pinned posters of wanted men. They looked like anybody esle; she would have trusted them once, but now she wasn't at all sure she trusted anyone.

'We went over your place with a toothcomb,' Dave said. 'We know who did it; they're sitting in the cells now. It wasn't malice directed at you; it was purblind stupid drunken louts. There was a disco in town last night; they come out of there punch drunk. You weren't the only place attacked; they got into Thorpe's place too; made a right old mess of that. They drew him out by bursting paper bags down in the copse; he thought there were poachers and went off after them. One lot led him a right old dance; the other lot went in and did the job. Let his ferrets out too; that annoyed him more than anything as he thinks he's lost the lot.'

Rhea looked at him. Tom came in with another cup of coffee. She was floating on coffee, but she managed to smile as she thanked him. Witch was tied outside, looking remarkably tiny after so many full-grown police dogs. Behind her a dog in a kennel was trying to sniff at her tail. She turned to face him and lifted her small nose to his and licked him through the wire.

'No malice?' she said.

'I didn't mean that, exactly. Just that it wasn't directed especially at you; they managed to do a considerable amount of damage around the place and broke down the fences round Wilde's farm; there are sheep all over the place this morning. Wilde and Thorpe are both swearing vengeance, and so is an old lady down the other end of the wood. She'd gone to a WI meeting and they got into her place. I think once you've got over the shock you'll find the village has more sympathy. They don't like it any more than we do. It's been getting worse over the years. Too much lenience; too little discipline.'

It brought John back vividly.

The ache got worse instead of better; she had been numb for weeks; numb while she went through the motions of living, doing all that had to be done, finding brief comfort in planning a different life, in being on her own.

Being on her own was no fun at all.

'I thought it was so peaceful here,' Rhea said.

'Peace? I don't think you'll find that anywhere in the world,' Dave said.

'Peace in the grave,' a man said, coming into the room at the tag end of Rhea's remark. ' "The grave's a fine and private place, but none, methinks, do there embrace." '

'Stan's showing off his A-level English,' Dave said, his face amused. 'He never can resist a quote. One day we'll do him for it.'

'I only quote what others wrote,' Stan said. 'Look, Sarge, if you don't want us down here, George and I'll go up and help Wilde get those fences safe again and the sheep back. He's in a right old pickle up there. His ram's missing too; the fellow he paid near on a thousand pounds for. Only hope he's still alive. It's not much fun trying to farm up there these days. Too near the town now.'

'Carry on,' Dave said. 'Tracking tomorrow morning, before school: Susie wants to join in. Do you good to be up early and put in some extra work for a change. That chap of yours is getting bored; he's not had a track for real for some time, has he?'

'No, and the last one ended in the road because they took to wheels,' Stan said. 'OK. See yer.'

'He's a good lad. Best tracking dog of the lot, but somehow he's always off duty when there's need to track. Mair says you can sleep at her place again if you'd like to, tonight.'

'Lightning doesn't strike twice,' Rhea said. 'Or does it?'

'We'll watch out for you,' Dave said. 'I'll send a van past you every hour tonight; but not on the hour; so if you see head-lights on the ceiling, don't worry, it's only us.'

It could be someone else, Rhea thought. She was becoming edgy and nervy. She'd soon be a total neurotic.

'I got the receipt for the puppy,' Rhea said. 'She wants me to have a litter from her and give her all the pups; and to buy puppy food from her and then dog food.'

'That's an old trick,' Dave said. 'Nothing so green as a new owner. Some of them fall for it too. I'd have that pup spayed if I were you; she won't ever body up enough to be a good brood bitch. She's had too rough a start. As for dog food, you buy it where you like.'

'She said she'd sue me,' Rhea said, and laughed. 'I don't know a lot about the law, but I do know my rights consumer-wise; John made sure I knew that.'

The phone rang.

She was in the way and Dave was on duty. She thanked him and went, collecting Witch from Tom.

'Don't forget now,' he said, as she put the puppy in the car. 'Come over whenever you want. It's lonesome down there in the woods.'

Jim's dirty little grey van was drawn up by the studio and the windows were whole again. It was a relief to see it there; a relief to greet the men as she went in. They had tidied up and cleaned up and the studio looked as it had before she moved in. The ruined bed and the chair were outside in the garden.

'I've a camp bed you can have, and an old chair you can borrow till you get sorted,' Jim said. 'Eh, if I'd got my hands on them lads . . .'

'Were they lads?' Rhea asked.

'The oldest was fifteen. Devils, the lot of them. They rampaged all along the line last night; we heard them, but never thought. You were unlucky, missis.'

Suppose I'd been at home, Rhea thought. What then? She wanted to shutter the windows, to armour the doors; she wanted Witch to grow up. She wished she had never come; may be she'd be safer going back to Rachel's little spare flat, but that was already let. Rachel needed the money. Rachel would be the loser on this, too, as bang went her commission on the sales. She would have to start again and the second time round was never as good as the first. She needed working sketches again, it was a bigger nuisance than she'd realised as one of the horses was over three hundred miles away. She'd have to write to the owner and tell him what had happened; make arrangements to stay, as it would take her several days to get what she needed and she didn't want to leave the place empty for so long.

'You go and get your shopping done and I'll stay on,' Jim said. 'I've nothing to go home for. Live alone. Luckily I was in last night; they only went for empty places. They're safe under lock and key and we're safe enough for a bit now. Brian can take the van and come back for me. I can get on with tidying up here for you. Don't like being idle. It'll give me something to do.'

Rhea was grateful. She needed more food; eggs had been smashed and flour emptied all over the floor; nothing was left to eat. She made a list and whistled Witch, thinking of what she'd need. She glanced at her watch. If she shopped quickly she could call in on Rory. She could look at Lucifer; he was the reason for her being here; he was going to be the subject of most of her paintings; she wanted every pose, as he went through his paces. She needed to get back into her own world; but her world had vanished, nearly forty years before, when she married.

Bleakness assailed her as she drove.

She shopped in the town in the supermarket where no one knew her and no one cared about her. She chose what she needed, loading the trolley with extras, yearning for comfort in the shape of food; smoked salmon, which was an absurd extra-vagance; fillet steak and frozen asparagus. Tomorrow she'd come down to earth; to bread and cheese and pickles. She hadn't been bothering much with food. It seemed pointless cooking for herself, but if she were to stay fit and sane and active she must learn to make more effort. She had been drifting along, getting through the days as best she could.

The cottage was almost ready; the studio needed refurnishing; the garden needed to be tidied and she could start on that, though she knew little about gardening. They had had a tiny patio and a few hanging baskets in their town home. Very little space around them; only houses, all the way down the street, with a tiny slit of sky. Here she could look out to wide horizons.

She was glad of the brief anonymity of the town. Confidence had gone; she drove slowly down the lane and looked at the stables. The sun shone faintly, and Rory was in the yard, putting Lucifer through his paces. She sat watching, overwhelmed as she always was by the majesty of the stallion, by his grace, by the gleam on his hide.

She got out of the car.

Rory saw her, waved and dismounted, throwing the reins to a girl who ran out as he snapped his fingers. He grinned at her.

'Hear you had trouble,' he said. 'You're OK?'

'News flies fast,' Rhea said.

'One of my lads is nephew to Wilde's next-door neighbour; he had to cycle past your place this morning; it was crawling with policemen and police dogs. One of the dogs found a trail that led straight to another of his neighbours. It's a small world, Rhea. Want a nice stiff drink?'

'I haven't had lunch and I'm driving. Trouble is I lost some of my paintings and two were commissioned. I've got to go down and sketch the horses again. And I don't want to go and leave the place empty yet. I've a man there now cleaning up, but I've got to get back.'

'Annie.' A girl came out of the tack-room, a bucket in her hand. 'Leave that and make Mrs Morland a sandwich, love. She hasn't yet lunched; and after having her place wrecked last night she won't eat unless we make her. Take her in, will you. I want to go on with this fellow for a bit longer; he's just settled in to his work after playing up like hell.'

Annie was a small dark girl with brilliant blue eyes that looked up at Rhea, before reflecting her smile.

'That was rotten luck. There's a mob of idiots in the town; we suffered here last year. They knifed one of the horses and slashed two blankets to ribbons and let Lucifer out of his stable, which was a big mistake.'

'What happened?'

'We aren't sure; he either kicked or bit; when he's upset he's likely to do either. The little mare turned so nervous we can't do much with her now. She's terrified of men. Not even Rory can go near her; she goes spare. We're having to work hard to make her feel secure again.'

The kitchen was warm and comfortable. Annie buttered bread and cut cold meat; and added lettuce. Rhea was hungrier than she had realised. She drank more coffee; it seemed to be a hazard of visiting.

Outside the window Lucifer was being put through his paces.

'He's not very far advanced,' Annie said, seeing that Rhea was watching. 'Rory wants to try him in three-day eventing.'

She forgot everything for the next few minutes as she watched Lucifer put through his paces by a master. Rory had been good when she first knew him; now he was very good indeed. She had not felt the old hunger to ride for years, but now it almost overwhelmed her.

She watched Rory dismount, and one of the girls rug the horse. She watched Lucifer walk away. She wanted to draw him again, draw him posing, in one of the movements, and wished he lived with her, to handle and to train. If only she were twenty again; if life had been different; if she had never married John . . . she wondered what would have happened in her life if Rory had stayed on and they had married. It was odd to think of a different path, a different world, and to wonder whether other events would have changed beyond her own life.

She would not have had those children; Elizabeth would not have been born and would never have died . . .

It was an unprofitable line of thought. She must be getting senile. She was thankful for the coffee and for the sandwich.

Rory walked into the room. He always seemed to fill a room; no one could ever ignore him.

'Much damage?' he asked, taking up the conversation where it had left off, as if they had never been interrupted. It was a trick that brought back memory again.

'All they could do. I'll have to leave the place empty and go south and draw one of the mares again, and I don't want to do that.'

'Who owns the mare?' Rory asked.

'A Mrs Panter. The mare's called Lilac Dream.'

'She's booked to Lucifer,' Rory said. 'Write and tell her what's happened and ask for time; and offer to draw the mare and foal when she comes here and give her the stud fee free. You can add it to the cost of the picture; she'll never know.'

'Oh, Rory,' Rhea said. 'When is she coming?'

He went to a big ledger that lay on the table and flipped through the pages.

'Foal's due second week in January. Not so long to wait. And you'll have a foal to paint as well. You always went for the foals. Remember Funny Filly?'

She had totally forgotten Funny Filly. The tiny foal had been a clown, posing and pirouetting, adoring an audience, kicking up gleeful heels.

'What happened to her?' she asked.

'She went into a circus. The audiences loved her; she was as good as any of the clowns and could be relied on to do something quite unpredictable. She lived to a good old age. I saw her when she was retired; she had a very good life that suited her perfectly.'

Lucky Funny Filly, Rhea thought. Life was so much easier for an animal. No foreknowledge of pain or death; no awareness of right or wrong; the ability to be yourself all the time, knowing people were invented entirely for your own benefit. In her next life she'd be a dog or a cat in a splendid home; or perhaps a horse learning dressage.

No worries about anything; people to produce food; no need for money, or clothes, but maybe it wasn't much fun standing out in the cold and the wet and always having to obey someone else.

'Getting you down?' Rory asked.

She came back to earth with a bump.

'In a way. I thought it would be peaceful here . . . and that people would be friendly. We've not moved for years; it's one thing to live in a place where everyone knows you and you belong. In a strange place you stick out, people notice you, they're wary, don't accept you . . . how long does it take to be part of a place?'

'For ever,' Rory said. 'You make your own life; no one makes it for you. And you have to work out who is right for you and who is wrong. Your kind of people are probably not mine. You won't find anyone to talk painting with here; and they won't trust your Alsatian; the press write them up all the time as dangerous and treacherous, so you're branded from the start as owning a dangerous dog.'

'And there's that silly story . . .'

'There will be a lot more silly stories, Rhea,' Rory said. Annie had gone outside and was hosing down the yard. Rory was sitting on the edge of the kitchen table, swinging his leg. He rubbed a hand over his chin. 'People have nothing to do; they hear half a story, and jump to conclusions. Some years ago I had a fall; not even a bad one, broke a collar bone . . .' he laughed. 'In no time at all the ambulance had been here, picked me up, rushed me to hospital where I lay in danger of death from breaking my spine; the horse had been shot and the place was up for sale. There wasn't a word of truth in any of it, but for months people rang me to know if I were OK, and what I was asking for the place . . . you get used to it. I invent my own rumours now.'

'Such as . . .' Rhea was curious.

'That you're buying half my stock; that you're painting my portrait, that I left you at the altar and have been breaking my heart ever since because I was crazy about you; but I suddenly couldn't face marrying for money . . .'

'Rory, you're outrageous.'

Rhea was so angry that she got up to go.

'Oh, sit down.' His voice was impatient. 'At least I've

shocked you out of misery. You can go back and fight now. Don't give in, Rhea. When you fall off you get on again. You remember.'

Rhea looked at him. He *had* shocked her out of her misery. No one was going to drive her away; not Thorpe or Wilde or the villagers; not Agnes Redpath and her nonsense. At least she knew where she was if anyone threatened to sue. John had taught her more about her legal rights than she had realised. Rory was talking again, talking to help her regain her self-control.

'Your husband came down here once to see a racehorse we had in briefly; she'd had her foal, and there was some talk of someone having switched her; so that the foal had a far better pedigree than was in fact the case. The mother was supposed to be out of a famous mare by an equally famous stallion, but when we checked on her and had blood tests done, she proved to be an unregistered mare from a stable no one had heard of, and her sire was a stallion that had got into the field by mistake off a neighbouring farm. They wanted five thousand guineas for the foal.'

'What did they get?' Rhea asked.

'Damn all. And I charged them double for daring to send her to me with false particulars. She didn't get covered by my stallion either. They timed it all wrong and your old man did a good job when he acted for the foal's future buyers. Funny case, as the mare was a dead spit of the one she was supposed to be, but that one was sitting quietly up at the other end of the country, having proved barren.'

'I never knew anything much about John's cases,' Rhea said. 'Only what I read afterwards – and by then he was already busy with the next one.'

'You'd never have stood his world or mine, love. You'd have felt you were hovering above quicksands all the time; you're too good to be true at times, Rhea. Do you still trust every person you meet, until he or she turns round and thumps you in the jaw or stabs you in the back, or steals from you?'

'I never learned not to trust,' Rhea said. 'You have to trust someone or you can't live . . .' She knew as she spoke that it was no longer true. The cottage and the studio would be a retreat into which few people were ever invited. She looked at people now and wondered.

'They want to know you for what they can get from you,' Rory said. 'I'll be bragging that Ray Morton owns one of my horses; not Rhea Morland. And they'll angle for invitations to meet you; maybe you'll paint one of their horses cheaply; maybe you can advertise a stallion by painting him and put his fee up. On yes, Ray Morton painted him; he's in the National Gallery; worth a fortune that painting is, and his fee is now five hundred pounds instead of fifty pounds.' He laughed at her expression. 'I'm only teasing.'

It hadn't felt like teasing. Ray longed for her anonymity again; no one had bothered overmuch about Rhea Morland; she was Roderick Morland's mother, and John Morland's wife; and she was also a mother-in-law and would soon be a grandmother.

Maybe Louise's baby would paint. Neither of her sons wanted to or understood why she wanted to. You couldn't explain a passion; something born into you, that was part of you, that had to be worked on, no matter how difficult, no matter how you had to fight.

She had fought all these years to preserve her talent; had developed it until it was something fine and special to her; and no way was it going to go.

She went outside into the yard to look at Lucifer.

He was rugged and in his stable, and came to her and reached out towards her. Next moment her coat button was in his mouth. She'd never remember. He had bitten the thread clean through.

'He's well practised,' Rory said. He was eyeing the horse as if he longed to be on his back again.

'Why do you want to train him?' Rhea asked.

'Because I should have been a centaur; I was born to ride,' Rory said. 'You were born to paint; the horses came second, always. Or you could never have left them. You'd have stayed till I came back and married you. I often thought about doing so – I never quite gave up regretting the way I chose.'

'You must be joking,' Rhea said, and, as she drove away, was irritated and puzzled by the laugh with which he had greeted the statement.

111

9

The mess had been cleaned up when she returned, but the major damage remained and had to remain until the insurance assessor had seen it. They promised to send a man soon.

Jim and Brian had brought things from their own homes for her and she was touched by their efforts, though it was hard to hide the total sense of outrage and deprivation that she felt. The things from the London studio flat had been precious; her own things carefully chosen, and had been the start and origin of her new life here.

The little collection of collectors' plates, each with a horse's head; the tiny statue she had made long ago, far from expert, but treasured because it had been the image of her own pony, now long dead. That lay in fragments on the table, swept up and kept as evidence. The police had been and fingerprinted the place; Dave had called briefly to tell Jim and Brian there was more work for them soon, as both Thorpe and Wilde needed their help. Seven sheep had been knifed on Wilde's farm and Wilde was blazing with rage, ready to shoot men as well as dogs. They had, with total coldblooded malevolence, singled out the best and left them damaged and suffering, but far from death. The hay in his barn had been fired. The firemen had only just managed to save the house.

It was senseless and pointless and Rhea felt sick.

She did not want to be alone; she did not want the men to go but she couldn't keep them. They had made her a small island of comfort – the fire was alight, wood logs blazing; Jim had provided a rug and a chair; Brian had brought a camp bed; Dave had left a pillow and a sleeping bag. She unloaded the food. Brian had also brought posters which he must have had in his own room. He had pinned them on the walls with blu-tack, livening up the squalor. Paint had been thrown all over the walls and floor. The wood needed cleaning, might need sanding down again. It had looked wonderful, only two days before; her new home, the start of a new life.

The slashed pictures mocked her. All that work for nothing.

She looked at the posters. A tiger leaped through an improbably green jungle; a panda looked out at her from a World Wildlife appeal poster; three Guide Dogs looked out from another. A chart of British birds. She wouldn't have thought it of Brian. She had imagined his interests would lie in the realms of bathing beauties and pop stars.

Witch was busy sniffing the unfamiliar objects, and Rhea wondered what she read in them. Had either of the men a dog or a cat? Witch would know – it must be odd to live through one's nose.

Jim came back to the window and beckoned her and she went to the door.

'Would you like my daughter for company tonight?' he asked. 'Liz is seventeen, and she wouldn't mind. She could bring her school books and work here as well as at home, and I can bring a mattress and sleeping bag for her when I bring her.'

It was a wonderful thought but she had to face life on her own. She thanked him. 'I've got to get used to it,' she said. 'It's like riding a horse; if you don't get straight on again you never ride again.'

He nodded.

Rhea listened to the sound of the engine, driving off into the night. She was alone with the whispering trees; with the creak of wood and the crack of sound from outside. She peopled the woods with men; alien, drunk, ready to set on her and torment her as they had tormented the sheep. She switched on the radio that Jim had brought over. The two of them had thought of everything and she was more than grateful.

Witch was whimpering for food. One of her ears was trying to stand erect, giving her a comical expression, and Rhea bent down and lifted the little animal and clutched her tightly, needing contact with something warm and alive.

The radio news was more depressing than the silence. Desolation flooded her. There was no point in going on. She was totally alone. The boys wouldn't miss her. None of her friends had written or phoned since she moved; not even Rachel. No one here would even notice if she died. She could die in the night and lie alone . . .

She took Witch out into the garden and almost jumped out of her skin. A man was standing by the gate.

The pup growled, a sound she hadn't made before and her ruff bristled on her back, baby fur fluffing up. She barked, a small high bark.

'It's all right, Ma'am,' a voice said and the man moved, 'I'm Jack Wilde. Bob Thorpe and I decided we'd patrol tonight and keep an eye on you. It can't be nice for a lady here on her own. I don't think there'll be any more trouble. There was a disco on in the district last night. We both had the same treatment as you; and we know how it feels. If you hear noises it's just the two of us. I wanted to knock but was a bit worried in case I frightened you, being it's night.'

'Would you like some coffee?' Rhea asked. The man seemed harmless enough. Maybe she was wrong to trust him. Maybe it was not Jack Wilde at all, but she no longer cared. She couldn't go through life being afraid of everyone, though here she felt as if she would never trust again.

He came in, and looked around him and made a face.

'Jim told me you had it fitted up real nice,' he said. 'I'd like to get my hands on the young devils. Lost all my winter hay and it's going to cost a fortune to replace.'

'Don't you insure?' Rhea asked.

'Not hay; have to carry a fortune in insurance if I insured everything I ought. Just insure my best ram; and luckily they didn't get him last night. We found him this morning.' He flicked his fingers at the pup.

'She might make you a good guard dog one day,' he said.

Rhea looked at him and he grinned.

'You've heard the tales,' he said. 'I do shoot dogs when they get in among my sheep, but only if they've killed. Stories grow round here. You don't want to believe half you hear. Thorpe now, he's not so black as they say, but he doesn't mind the stories round, as it keeps some of the lads from poaching. They're scared stiff he might shoot them.'

'He shot the pups,' Rhea said.

'He didn't know you were going to rescue them, did he? And the bitch had had three of my sheep before I got her; I saw her kill. Can't blame her, mind, when she's running wild and pups to feed, but it can't go on and if those pups had grown up, by five months they'd be killing too and it'll be lambing time and lambs, especially when newborn, are easy for them.'

Rhea poured water on to the powder, added milk and sugar for Jack Wilde and put another log on the fire. The pup stretched her tummy to the blaze and sighed deeply, and slept.

'Why did he hang the pups on my fence?' Rhea asked.

'I heard about that. It was right nasty and it wasn't Bob Thorpe. He was angry about it. He has his enemies too; and one of them probably had it in to make trouble for you both. And we've one or two round here that are only a penny in the pound as far as brains go. People don't travel to wed and you get bad bloodlines through inbreeding, just the way you do in a flock of sheep.'

Rhea was making sandwiches, using sliced ham and a sliced loaf. She hadn't the energy to think about cooking a meal. The mutilated studio was a new form of torment.

'You're lucky,' Jack Wilde said. 'They went through my place like a tornado; and Bob's, which is why it's as comfortable in the woods as at home tonight. I haven't got a thing left undamaged. Luckily that part is insured; but replacing things . . . it's never the same. Some of my grandmother's stuff there, and worth a mint if I wanted to sell it. Now it's not fit for matchwood. Makes you sick.' He drank the coffee. 'I'll leave you now.'

'Can you stay a bit longer?' Rhea asked. She didn't want to be alone. Her thoughts were unpleasant company. Jack Wilde was a young man; not yet thirty, small, neat, dark bearded, dressed in workmanlike thorn-proof trousers and a thick padded anorak. It was a frosty night.

'I'd like to. It's warm here. But I want to be sure there's no one near my sheep. You never know; I've a funny reputation with the way stories grow here and there may be someone who lost a dog, and has a grudge to work off. Injuries fester in a place like this.' He bent to pat Witch on the head. She opened her eyes and yawned, and for a brief moment wagged her small tail, but she was exhausted as only a puppy can be exhausted, living every moment of its waking life with all its energy, and she dropped back to sleep.

Rhea bolted the door. The windows were re-glassed and felt vulnerable. She thought about her visitor. She had, much to her own surprise, liked him and seen his viewpoint. There were always two sides and maybe both could be right depending on where you stood, she thought. If he shot Witch she would find him a villain, but if Witch had got free and killed his sheep . . . that put a different aspect on the story.

She was outside for the last time with the puppy on her leash when she heard footsteps again. They were heavier than Jack Wilde's. She lifted the pup and stood in the shadows. Moonlight speckled the woods. The man walking down the ride was carrying a gun.

She could hear her thudding heart.

Then she recognised him.

'Mr Thorpe?'

'Aye, it's me.' He came over to the gate. 'Nobody about tonight. You should sleep safe, and don't worry. Jack told me he had a word. I'd heard tales about you, which is why I wasn't too polite that day. And it wasn't me that hung them pups on the fence. I'd like to get my hands on the one that did. Dave told me the stories weren't true. I should have known; enough going round about me. You don't want to believe all you hear, Mrs Morland.'

'I'm sorry,' Rhea said. 'It's cold out here. Would you like some coffee?'

'I'd not say no, but I'll drink it out here. I'd like to be listening. Dave reckons that lot were from the disco and won't be back, and they've got a couple of them in the cells now. It doesn't bring things back though. Rare old mess they made at my place and Jack says yours is the same. Old lady down at the end of the village had her place messed up; she's in hospital; had a heart attack when she tried to clear up.'

'There's always someone worse than yourself,' Rhea said,

unable to make conversation at midnight and wishing the trite words unsaid.

'Aye,' Thorpe said. He had little use for words. People always heard them wrong or twisted them against you. Least said, the better.

Rhea slept at last, but her dreams were so vivid that, when she woke, she felt exhausted, having spent the night battling with terror.

Sunshine spilled across the doorway and brightened the room. She would start to paint the first picture again; she had her preliminary sketches for that. The vandals had missed them. She was busy at her easel, while the pup played end-lessly with a rolled-up sock, carrying it around, dropping it and lifting it again, rolling it with her paw, totally busy and absorbed in her tiny game.

The knock at the door startled her.

The pale-blue van was unfamiliar and at first she thought the man standing on her doorstep was a policeman. He was a huge man, his body too big for his clothes. He looked at her with unfriendly eyes. Not another, she thought wearily. What now?

'I'm from the RSPCA, ma'am,' he said. 'I have a report about a puppy. Can I see her, please?'

Rhea looked at him blankly.

'What kind of report?'

'Where is she, madam?'

'She's in here,' Rhea said. 'Come in.'

The man came in and stared about him.

'I had vandals,' Rhea said. 'I don't live like this normally. I'm waiting for the insurance assessor. I hoped that was him, I mean you were him . . .' her voice tailed off.

Witch trotted across the floor and laid her sock at Rhea's feet. Rhea bent down and lifted the puppy.

'I paid for her,' she said.

The man took the pup, and put her down on the floor. He threw the sock and she trotted off to fetch it, pounced on it, and brought it back, not to him, but to Rhea. She leaned against Rhea's legs.

The man looked baffled.

117

Rhea was no longer afraid of the people in the village. She was angry. More angry than she remembered ever having been in her life. She hated fuss and she hated arguments, but here she was going to have to learn to live with both or go under. And she wasn't running away.

She thought of Lucifer, standing proudly, moving beautifully and the picture she was going to paint of him; the picture that would be better than anything she had ever done before; the picture that would survive long after she were dead and that men in the far future would bargain for and covet; the picture of a lifetime, the best picture anyone ever painted of a horse. Far better than the picture she had done for Sadie.

It was her reason for living, for surviving, for going on when everything seemed hopeless and when she was lonelier than she had ever believed possible.

'I suppose you were told I killed four puppies and was torturing this one,' she said. 'This village has nastier people in it than any I have ever met in my life. Are you satisfied? If you aren't, go and see Dave Martin at the police kennels. He knows I'm not that sort of person.'

'I can see the pup's in fine shape,' the man said heavily. 'May I ask your name?'

'I'm Rhea Morland. My husband was John Morland. You might have heard of him.'

'I knew him,' the man said. 'We met on several occasions when he prosecuted people who had mistreated animals. I used to be in London. Came across him a lot. That wasn't the name I was given. I do have to check,' he added defensively.

'I know you do.' She would offer coffee as a compensation for his misery. He looked at her unhappily, not sure how she would react. She seemed to be offering coffee nonstop these days.

'You were told I was the woman John was about to prosecute when he died,' she said.

The man nodded.

Rhea filled the kettle and switched it on.

'Maybe in a year or two I'll think it funny,' she said. 'Just now I don't. I thought last night someone was punishing me for being someone I wasn't, but other people had their homes wrecked too, so that was just another senseless incident. There isn't much sense in the world, is there?'

'Not much sense, not much kindness and not much understanding,' the man agreed. 'I'm Peter Sendon,' he added. 'If there's anything I can do to help you with the puppy . . . she looks in pretty good shape considering her beginning.'

'Her mother apparently fed her on sheep,' Rhea said.

'So that's it,' the inspector stirred his coffee thoughtfully and added four lumps of sugar when Rhea passed him the packet. Her sugar bowl had also been smashed and her silver teapot, an heirloom from her grandmother, had been kicked in and badly dented.

'Mr Thorpe and Mr Wilde patrolled the woods last night,' Rhea said. 'I met them both.'

'You don't want to believe all you hear about either,' Peter Sendon stood up and walked to the window and looked out at the garden. The fence round the puppy's enclosure had also been smashed. 'They foster the stories; it helps keep dogs out of Wilde's sheep fields and poachers out of Bob's woods. He's not an easy man, but he's OK if you play fair with him. He probably wanted to put the fear of god in you so that you don't let that pup run wild near his pheasant pens.'

'It all depends on where you stand,' Rhea said. She was not thinking at that moment about dogs, but about painting. Evening light and morning light; the bright glare of the midday sun; shadows at dusk; the half-hinted half-imagined creatures of night, seen darkly, half guesses, half dreams.

'My viewpoint, your viewpoint, their viewpoint,' Peter Sendon said, as if echoing her thoughts, but his mind entirely on animals and his job. Sometimes he hated people enough to want to kill and the thought frightened him. That horse, the night before last . . . they had had to put it down. He wished the poor brute had trampled its tormentors and hoped at least it had kicked and struggled and hurt them while they were indulging their vicious nastiness. They wouldn't find out who. They never did, as that kind were apt to retaliate on anyone telling tales.

'I can see their viewpoint if they had the right woman,' Rhea said wearily. 'How do I convince them they're wrong?'

119

'Some won't listen. Some would rather pretend; it gives them power, especially if they know it hurts you. Unhappy people; a lot of them about. Happy people don't need to be jealous or unkind; but the unhappy ones never learn that, as their needs are different.'

'Happiness is transient,' Rhea said, looking back; to moments when she had adored the boys; to Elizabeth who had been total joy, an enchanting child. Those the gods love die young. Then there had been torment for years; was she to blame for the crash? She had been exonerated, but the doubt remained for ever, to come back when the nights were long. A doubt she had never shared with John who had behaved as if the child had never existed. His adored baby daughter.

That didn't help bring back happiness.

The pup was dragging a slipper across the floor, shaking it as if it were a rat. It was so easy, being an animal; no tomorrow ever, but maybe yesterday had held terror and was remembered. One never knew.

'You don't want to worry about me, Mrs Morland,' Peter said. 'I'll tell everyone who talks to me about you, of course, but most won't. They don't accept us or our jobs, I sometimes think. Troublemakers, like the police. But what would the world be like without the police or without us? Those who enjoy inflicting suffering would go on without ever being checked or punished and the nice people would turn their backs and pretend it wasn't happening because they didn't want to be involved.'

There was sudden bitterness in his voice.

'Your husband knew a lot about the worse side of people,' he said. 'He was a passionate man; I heard him several times in court; he said what he thought and he knew how to say it. He couldn't bear people who inflicted pain on the innocent . . . and he believed in justice, not law.'

'He never said that to me,' Rhea said. She had not ever thought about the difference. John at home talked trivia; rarely about his cases. Maybe he had needed to forget; to island himself with her, away from the real horrors that lurked outside in the jungle.

She shivered and looked through the window, at the deceptive innocence of trees, and sunlight, and leaves that moved in the breeze. Out there were hunting animals: rats and stoats and weasels; foxes and hawks; and out there were those like her, defenceless against ferocity, beating their wings or racing to hide in shelter. John had gone out into that world daily; and come home to a kind of peace.

Had she given him that? Had he appreciated it; appreciated her non-involvement in his world? She had been abstracted often, her mind busy with a shape, the way a head turned, an expression in the eyes of whichever horse she was painting.

'Don't let them get you down,' Peter Sendon stood up, putting his coffee cup neatly on the table. He walked to the door. 'It's lonely here.'

'It's odd,' she said, wanting to hold the man back, not wanting to be left alone with her thoughts. 'I tell the absolute truth and no one believes me; they look behind what I say for something that isn't there.'

'Maybe honesty is too unusual. A small lie to hide your age, a larger lie to hide a social gaffe, an inability to say look, I'm wrong, and I'm sorry – most people cover up.' He had heard it so often; the tales people told to cover neglect, or worse.

'I had a Quaker headmistress. If we lied, our mouths were washed out with soap and we had to learn a psalm every day and recite it to her. She was terrifying. If we got it wrong we had to learn it again and a second one besides. It taught you to tell the truth whatever the cost; it was much better to be punished by your form mistress than to stand and die daily on the hearthrug in Her Majesty's study, as she towered over you and glared at you. She was over six feet tall and a very big woman; even the staff were afraid of her.'

Peter Sendon laughed.

'Our head was five feet nothing and appeared to be nine feet high; it's a matter of personality.'

Personality. John had had that and had dominated her; she could never argue with him. But it had been his job to argue so maybe that wasn't so surprising.

Peter Sendon ducked his head under the lintel and walked out into the little garden. He lifted a hand as he drove away.

Silence settled behind him. The room was still. Witch had

curled to sleep, her head on the slipper she had been carrying. A tap dripped, a noisy insistent pit-pit-pit that was infuriating. There wasn't even a bird note to break the spell. She felt as if she had been bewitched; left alone with all the rest of the world gone in some terrible holocaust.

Loneliness was destroying her.

Rhea banged the kettle against the tap; stood watching it boil and made coffee. She was drinking endless cups of coffee, but it was something to do.

The postman knocked on the door and she jumped, startled by the unexpected sound. He held up two letters at the window and put them on the sill of the open window. It was out of his way to come down here and he was pushed for time. He waved, and she picked up the mail. Witch woke and greeted her and she took the pup outside.

One letter was from Louise. She recognised the childish, scrawling handwriting. It was full of small details, descriptions of the layette she was making for the baby. A grandchild. Rhea wondered if she would feel more when it was born; it seemed remote and absurd. She couldn't be old enough to be a grandmother. Where had all that time gone? It was a pity John wasn't there; he would have loved to have another little girl to cherish. If it were a girl they were going to call her Elizabeth.

The second letter was in unfamiliar writing with a local postmark.

She opened it without more than a passing wonder as to who could be writing to her here.

The words were printed; block capitals all through and the venom behind them sickened her so that she had to sit down. The start was innocuous enough; it was silly.

'WE KNOW WHO YOU ARE. YOU CAN'T HIDE FROM US: IF YOU DIDN'T MAKE US SICK YOU WOULD MAKE US LAUGH. PRETENDING TO BE THAT LAWYER'S WIFE – EVERYONE KNOWS SHE LIVES IN LONDON. PRETENDING TO BE THAT PAINTER, AS IF A PERSON LIKE YOU COULD PAINT. I SUPPOSE YOU BOUGHT THE PICTURE AND STAND THERE PRETENDING

TO WORK SO PEOPLE CAN SEE THROUGH THE
WINDOW.

'TROUBLE MAKING, SHOOTING PUPPIES;
TORTURING THEM, AND WE'LL GET THAT
ONE AWAY FROM YOU BEFORE YOU HARM HER
TOO. PRETENDING TO LOVE DOGS AND
RESCUE THAT ONE, DON'T THINK WE DON'T
KNOW WHAT YOU'RE UP TO, WE DO.'

It descended into obscenities.

Rhea stood looking at it, her hand shaking.

Her tongue felt rough and she tasted bile. Nobody could be
so cruel, surely; she would never get away from the stories,
never live down this beginning. She had hoped to make new
friends, imagining herself to be welcomed and accepted.

She couldn't have been more wrong.

She lifted Witch and went out to the car.

She returned twice to make sure she had locked up properly.
Suppose they came in her absence and set fire to the place, or
worse, suppose they set fire to it in the night when she was
there?

The road to the police kennels seemed endless. If only Dave
were there. Brian and Jim weren't coming; there was nobody
to talk to. Nobody at all.

The letter in the glove-box contaminated the car.

10

It was good to see people. Five vans were drawn up in the yard and the men were washing them with a hose. Their contents were stacked neatly out of reach of the water. They worked as a team, one hosing, three cleaning, while the fifth, a tall man with a saturnine expression, was schooling a young dog.

'Is Dave in?' Rhea asked one of the younger men and was just in time to dodge the hose as he turned towards her, caught out by the sound of an unexpected voice.

'I'm terribly sorry,' he said. 'I didn't hear you drive in. Dave's in the office. You aren't wet, are you?'

Rhea grinned. It was good to be among people again and she listened to the sounds of happy horseplay that went on as she left the men.

'Maybe Dodgelight will do it today . . . ran as if he had four left legs, last time out,' a voice said from somewhere behind her.

She knocked on the office door.

Dave opened it. 'Mrs Morland . . . is something wrong?'

She nodded.

'Sit down. Here, have a cigarette. I know you don't smoke, but you look as if you've had a shock. Nobody's been bothering you, or done any more damage, have they?'

'This isn't physical damage,' Rhea said. She inhaled the smoke gratefully and coughed. It was daft to start smoking again. Dave glanced at her and went out.

'Tom's bringing in coffee. What is it?'

She handed him the letter. His eyebrows lifted as he read it through.

'Nasty. But I think I know who wrote it; he's a strange old

man and fairly harmless; he jumps on to every bandwagon.'

'Suppose they get at Witch? I'm getting neurotic about her and can't let her out of my sight. I never imagined that anyone could live like this; there isn't a single person who believes I really am who I am. How do you defeat gossip?'

'You never do; it's like fire in dry forest that's never checked; it starts in one place as a tiny flicker; and then the wind fans it. It's trodden out, but a spark blows on the breeze and lands a few yards away and it starts up again. It's destructive as fire; and unless you can get words said in front of witnesses and take action, you don't ever check it; and even then you don't, as what can you do about a whisper in a room, a gossip session between two cronies. Mary told me . . . you won't tell anyone will you? Of course not, but they always do, Joan told me in confidence, do you think it's true . . . where there's smoke, there's fire. I know how it feels, believe me.'

His voice was suddenly bitter.

Tom came in, two mugs of coffee held in one hand and a dog's chain collar in the other.

'Sam's slip chain, back from the vet.' He banged the mugs down. 'I don't like losing a dog like that.'

The chain rattled on the desk, a fanfare for a departed hero, Rhea thought absurdly, noticing Dave's sombre face and Tom's misery for the first time. Tom went out and the door shut behind him was as pointed as a slam.

'What happened?' Rhea asked.

'There was a punch-up in town last night and someone stuck a knife in Sam. We got him to the vet about four this morning but nothing could be done for him; the knife had punctured his heart. Tom had to go and get his chain; we're short of them and they're not easy to get as we use special chains, different from the general public. Tom regards all the dogs as his. He's a damn good kennelman.'

He drank and lighted another cigarette from the stub of the first.

'He was one of our best dogs; it takes years to train a dog to Sam's standard. And he was all set to do well in the police trials at national level. We got the joker who did it, but that doesn't bring the dog back. That's why the men are skylarking; and that's why George is trying out the young dog; he'll be remembering Sam all the time he's working. And I'm not sure that Kaspar is bold enough for us; he's a bit timid, though that could change. Time you were starting on your baby, or you'll lose out; they need to learn in the first few weeks, and be taught the house rules. Or they take over and boss you and do as they choose and in this breed it isn't funny when they weigh over a hundred pounds and pack a hefty bite.'

He was talking for the sake of talking. Everyone had problems, Rhea thought; you thought you were the only one, but you weren't alone. She watched George with a more interested eye; the dog was wild and pulled him, and he checked him and praised him, and tried again.

The vans gleamed in the sun. Rhea wondered how often they were cleaned; was it a daily ritual or a weekly ritual? Her own car needed cleaning. She'd have to buy a hose; it made it so much easier. She was very ill equipped. She didn't seem to have had time to sort out what she needed and what she didn't. She had bolted from home; she should have stayed but it was too late now.

'I'd better be going. I'm delaying you,' she said.

Dave glanced at his watch. He pushed his hair back out of his eyes with a weary gesture.

'We're going down to the Jester and Bells for a bit of lunch. Join us. You need company after that. You can have something with chips or a beef buttie. It's good food; plain, but well done; and not expensive. We're tracking this afternoon for practice. Would you like to come and watch? You won't be in the way and you might try later with Witch. Susie would help you; she's a good little track-layer and Trot works as well as any of our green dogs. She's a lonely kid. Being a policeman's daughter isn't always good fun either; you'd do me a favour if you could spare her some time; if it wouldn't be a nuisance.' He didn't add that it might do Rhea good to spend time with the child, who had fallen in love with the puppy and liked its owner. Mair was busy with the babies and Heather, though kind, was far from stimulating company, concerned only with woolly vests and a good hot meal inside you, and not very happy about the mess that Trot made. He loved wallowing in mud whenever he could, and brought it into the house.

Rhea was introduced to the men.

'She's had a letter from the Old Goat, at least, I think it's him,' Dave said. 'A bit of company will do her the world of good.'

'One of his usual bits of nastiness?' George asked. He had put his dog in the kennel.

'A bit more so; he'd heard the gossip.'

'You don't want to take much notice of that, Mrs Morland,' Reg said. He was a comfortable-looking man, who in a few years would present a fatherly image to everyone, as well as his own two children. He sounded as if he was used to pacifying small quarrels and as if, when Rhea went to bed, a kiss would make it all better.

Only there was no one to kiss her now.

The thought was remembered desolation.

The Jester and Bells stood back from the road; a black and white timbered building that looked from the outside to be a total fake, but proved inside to be as old as it seemed. The warped beams were black and from them hung mugs and jugs of every sort, battered pewter, china, copper; a brightly decorated German Bierstein, a tankard that looked as if it had been dug up on some battlefield, a bullet hole in its side. The fire blazed on one side of the room; the bar was crowded with pushing men, and the two waitresses, dressed alike in blue jeans and a tee-shirt which had 'Jester and Bells' written across it in capital letters, tossed their pony tails as they trotted round with food, reminding Rhea of two ponies. They laughed and joked with the men.

'What'll you have?' Dave asked Rhea.

She settled for a lime and lager and a beef buttie. It looked an ample meal; the party of four on the next table were tucking into them. Thick rolls, huge chunks of meat, lettuce and tomato and onion rings on a side plate, and pickle, chutney or mustard.

'Betty bakes the bread,' George said. 'It's worth coming here just for that.' He was holding a pint of bitter as if it might take away memory. Grief hurt just as much even if it were only for a dog, and Dave had told Rhea on the way to the Jester and Bells that Sam had been seven years old and had lived with George and his wife as a pet. They had no children and Molly had her own dog and trained that for Working Trials, so that she and George spent a great deal of time together with their dogs.

'Molly's judging over at Welking next week,' George said. 'I'd promised to tracklay. . . .' he tailed off. No one had a reply.

'I've been thinking,' Reg said, as if it were an unfamiliar action. 'You know that burglary last week; we didn't catch up with Chummie; he got clean away, though we thought we knew who he was. He went off across Len's land . . .'

'The track ended the other side of the hedge,' George said. 'Didn't seem possible, just to peter out there . . .' He shook his head.

'I asked the farmer. They'd covered that field with liquid manure the day before; that stuff stinks to high heaven – it would get up the dog's nose – and Rex has been sneezing ever since. I wondered if it would affect him for long; and that could be why the track petered out.'

'Could be.' Dave bit into his buttie. 'Scent's a funny thing, though. Sam found a knife in a pig midden; so it doesn't follow.'

'Hero found cannabis in a sponge bag full of bottles of perfume,' Leigh, the drug doghandler said.

'Is Hero a German Shepherd?' Rhea asked. She felt slightly uneasy, among professionals, and out of place with them, though they accepted her without any sign that they thought she should not be there.

'He's a Labrador,' Dave said. 'He has a wonderful nose; it's easier to take a Labrador into a private home; somehow it doesn't seem like a police dog.'

'Time we were getting off,' Reg said. Rhea opened her purse to pay, but Dave forestalled her.

'Witch is in the back of my van,' he said. 'I forgot to tell you that Tom had put her there. You can have her out this afternoon and let her roam, where we're going.'

She had driven with Reg and thought Tom had put the puppy in a kennel. He had told her he'd take care of her, and had had her out briefly, playing with her, enjoying her small

128

importance as she frisked around him and sniffed his legs, reading the detailed information from his trousers of the dogs he had handled that morning.

Witch greeted her as if she had been away for a month. Her small nose butted against the wire grid behind the driver's seat and the dog in the second compartment barked briefly and was told to pack it in. He stood, his tail waving, watching the pup as if she amused him.

They drove fast down narrow winding lanes until they came to an old road that proved to lead to a disused aerodrome. The vast hangars stood bare to the sky, the roofs half fallen in. The wiry grass was brittle and the ditches, filled with frothy peaty water, crossed and criss-crossed the ground.

Witch, released from the van on her lead, sniffed the ground intently.

'Hey, you'll have to teach that to track,' Reg said, watching with interest. 'She's born to the job. Can't neglect a nose like that.'

The men were walking the dogs, letting them run and then simulating a chase, the 'victim' being one of themselves. The dogs screamed with excitement.

'We can't train young dogs near people. They think we're killing them,' Dave said, and pointed at Witch who was rushing excitedly round the ground yelling as loudly as the distant adult dogs.

'She doesn't know what she's doing but she's doing it,' he said with a grin.

'How did you lay that track? It looked most complicated,' Rhea said. She had been watching him pace out the ground.

'It wasn't; the first leg is about two hundred yards, and goes straight out to those two trees on the horizon. Then I came to a big clump of nettles and used that as my turning point; I marked the ground well there as these are young dogs just learning their job. I used the pylon and another tree behind it on the horizen as my next marker, and walked a leg of about a hundred yards towards that; the track turns slightly just before that second bramble bush and ends up halfway here. I used the vans as markers to keep me straight; it's easy to wander and that makes it hard for man and dog. Also you have to watch the wind. If you get two legs too close, the scent from one blows across to the other and can muddle the dog. It's not easy to lay a decent track. But if we aren't to mess up our dogs we have to get it right, and while it only means a civilian is losing marks at a Trial, with us, it may mean a crime that could have been solved goes undetected because the dog wasn't expert enough. A good tracking dog is worth any number of humans, because the human can't follow a trail.'

The men came back, dogs leashed, racing ahead of them. Reg was to work the track while George had laid a track for Morris further over the field. Leigh had a small piece of cannabis which he had hidden for his dog to find. Rhea shortened Witch's cord and brought her in close. The pup, exhausted by new experiences, curled up and went to sleep. She seemed able to sleep anywhere, exhausted by her own energy which only lasted for such brief spells.

'Funny how appealing a pup can be,' Dave observed, looking down in amusement at the tiny animal, so small beside the big police dogs. She was quite unafraid of them, and had gone happily to each and sniffed and been sniffed. She had rolled over for Leigh's dog, and he had looked down at her as if astounded that anything smelling of dog could be so small.

'He's never seen a pup before,' Leigh had explained, an amused smile on his face. He tickled the small tummy before moving off and Witch laughed up at him, mouth open, tongue lolling, eyes glinting, tail wagging. Her puppy coat was soft and dense and fluffy.

Reg's dog was harnessed; he pulled eagerly towards the post that marked the start of the track, knowing the routine well.

'Seeeek, good dog, seeeek.' The soft voice was encouraging, and the dog's head was already down, Reg standing holding the tracking line short, its length lying uncoiled behind him. The dog caught the scent and, concentrating completely, began to track, his tail moving very slowly from side to side.

'He's a good, steady, sober dog once he gets on a trail,' Dave said, watching closely. 'He may have trouble at the turn; he's not always very confident at bends; seems to expect it to go on straight for ever. A man running doesn't keep straight; he veers and dodges; so we have to lay more and more com-

130

plicated tracks as the dog gets more experienced. If we're lucky, though, we may get a nice straight easy one, along a road, from a man who trod in creosote or pig muck; things don't always work out easily though.'

The dog came to the turn; the man had stopped, intent on his animal. The dog was circling, and then once again he caught the scent and started off in the right direction. Reg turned his head briefly and Dave signalled, his thumb up.

'Doesn't do to let the dog make a mistake at this stage,' he explained. 'It'll put him off; he's got to be keen, or he won't go on. He'll give up.'

The second turn presented no problems whatever. The dog came down towards them at a cracking speed, like a horse that has smelled his stable and knows that the end of the ride is near and food ahead.

The dog bent his head and picked up something from the ground. Reg removed the harness and threw the object; Rhea could now see that it was a battered leather glove. The romp with the glove lasted for nearly five minutes before the dog was called in and arrived prancing and eager, his tail going, full of his own importance.

'He's improving,' Dave said. 'The first turn foxed him for a moment, but he did that second turn well.'

'He's getting the idea,' Reg said.

He turned to Rhea.

'Suppose we set a baby track for your little one?'

'Isn't she too young?' Rhea asked.

'She could track her mother at four weeks old, I'll bet,' Dave said. 'Have you anything on you that she could play with when she's found it?'

Rhea had her own gloves in her pocket.

'Hold the puppy,' Dave said.

He backed away from her, scuffing the grass hard, never lifting his feet, and called to the pup at every third step.

'Hey, Witch, little Witch, what's this then?'

He dragged the glove, flicked the glove, and finally put it down about ten yards from Rhea.

'When I come back to you, let her go,' he said. 'Keep behind her and whatever you do, don't pull on the lead.'

Witch was dancing in eagerness, sure that this was a lovely new game invented entirely for her benefit. Dave circled to break the trail and came back.

'Now', he said and the pup was off and away, her small nose against the ground. She reached the glove. She lifted it and ran on.

'Call her in and throw it for her,' Dave said.

Rhea called, and clicked a finger.

The pup turned and raced at her, and offered her the glove. This was a wonderful game that was improved immensely in the next few minutes by having the glove thrown for her to bring back.

'That's the age to teach them,' Dave said.

It was time to go back. The sky was grey, a thin rain now falling and the place was barren and desolate, a gruesome place where a thousand crimes might be committed and no one ever know. Rhea, whose imagination seemed to be working overtime, could imagine a rape victim brought here; or a black-mailer making an assignation with his victim; the fruits of a dozen bank robberies buried under the dilapidated hangars. But the dogs would find anything that was hidden here; she had had proof of the efficiency of Hero's nose, as he sought his trophy in all sorts of unlikely places.

She would teach Witch to track. It would give her another occupation; it was becoming very plain that she needed to trust to her own company as she seemed unlikely to find friends here, except perhaps for Dave and he was very busy.

'Go to the dog club with Susie this evening,' Dave said. 'I'll drive past your place and make sure it's all right, during the evening.'

It was an idea. Maybe other dog people would understand her and welcome her. Maybe they hadn't heard the rumours about her; maybe they would know the truth, and she would at least find other people to talk with. It would be company and a change from the lonely evenings in the studio, with the only voice that on the radio or the television set.

Maybe there should be a ban on all bad news. Had there ever been a time without it, she wondered. She was glad to relax and listen to Susie, talking about school and about Trot, making a fuss of Witch, telling Rhea solemnly how to lay a track, and how to make sure the wind was right and not too blustery for a young dog, blowing the scent everywhere.

'I talk too much to her about technicalities of track-laying,' Dave said, half ruefully, as they ate scrambled eggs and bacon and tomatoes and an apple pie that Heather had made and left for them.

Rhea liked ten-year-olds; they had not yet learned total disrespect of their elders, or the cynicism that started young with the debunking of every kind of authority by pundits on the box. Susie was not a pretty child but she had lovely thick shining hair and brilliant eyes, very like her father's, and an attractiveness about her that had nothing to do with beauty. One day she would be a striking adult, and she plainly had a mind of her own.

Driving through the town at Susie's direction, Rhea was aware of uneasiness. She wondered if she would ever face people again without the fear that under the geniality and behind the mask, they were filled with hatred for her, accusing her or criticising her, and she wondered how it was that all her life she had taken people at face value, accepting the self they presented to the world, unaware of hypocrisy.

It was a horrifying thought, and she swallowed and brought her mind back both to her driving and to Susie who was telling a long and involved story about a girl called Fiona and a sandwich. Rhea hadn't heard the beginning and the ending remained mysterious for ever as she didn't like to tell the child she hadn't been listening, or to ask why on earth a ham sandwich should have been put in the Geography book cupboard before they went home. It seemed to be a funny story, so she laughed dutifully, and then drew up at the edge of a large car park beside a lighted hall.

She lifted Witch out, and Susie leashed Trot and waited as Rhea locked the car.

The hall was remarkably scruffy, dust on the three pianos lying thick. It seemed to be in the middle of some kind of alterations as the enormous windows were masked with hardboard that had warped and let in cold air. The dusty floor looked as if it had never known water. Chairs were ranged at

133

one end, and a slight woman sat at a table on which was a large ledger, a small card-index file, a notice which said that there was no training the following week owing to the alterations, and a box containing money. Behind her on another table were various items of equipment and of dog food.

Rhea gave her name and that of her dog and paid two pounds, of which most was a membership fee. The woman gave her a curious look but said nothing except to ask questions. Name, address, phone number, dog's name and sex.

Was Witch likely to be a dog and not a bitch, Rhea wondered, and went to sit down. Susie walked on to the floor with Trot and joined a group of people already working.

People sat in small groups, dogs at their feet. A rough-haired terrier kept up a constant irritating barking, the owner occasionally twitching the lead and saying, 'No, darling, be a good boy then, don't bark.' The comments, made in a very soft gentle voice, seemed only to increase the dog's noise, and his tail wagged frenziedly every time she spoke. Rhea wondered if it wouldn't do more good to use a scolding voice on the dog, whose owner seemed to her to be praising him for barking, but she had no one to ask.

Since no one seemed to be inclined to talk to her, she watched the dogs on the floor. There were two other girls a little older than Susie, a slender tall girl with a little black dog that never stopped wagging his tail and appeared to enjoy every minute of his work, and a smaller girl with dark hair and remarkable brown eyes, with a black Labrador that she handled like an expert. Beyond her a man in a camouflage jacket with long dark hair and a long dark beard was working a collie that was smaller than Trot, a smaller bearded man marched as if he were an army officer beside a large German Shepherd, and a woman with dark red hair that leaped in uncurbed ringlets round her shoulders, was working a German pointer.

Rhea watched in admiration as they walked together in line; left their dogs sitting alone and walked round the room, spent a short time doing a complex step routine, during which each dog circled its owner and each owner circled the dog, and then were left lying in a row while the owners went out into the car park and stayed there for ten minutes. It seemed a remarkably long time. One dog moved its head, another twisted its body from one hip to the other, but no dog broke from its position.

A few minutes after they returned, an alarm-clock bell rang and the dogs and owners left the floor.

'That's our top class,' Susie said.

'You look very good to me,' said Rhea.

'Your turn now. Go and stand over there so that you can hear; it's very difficult to hear properly, especially now with no windows,' Susie said.

Rhea stood up, feeling conspicuous. Witch had no desire to walk beside her; she danced out at the end of the lead, and tried to play with the dog next to her, an elderly Labrador that growled suddenly and savagely. The owner ignored the noise. Witch retreated to lean against Rhea's legs, a worried expression on her face.

'Move your puppy over here,' the man in the centre said. He was an odd-looking man with a lined face and dark grey hair that came down his forehead in a widow's peak, as if it had been cut in that way, and was not natural. He looked at Rhea.

'Get your pup's attention. And keep it,' he said. Rhea wondered if her expression was as blank as she felt it must be. She looked at Susie, who had her hankie out of her pocket and was shaking it above Trot's nose. Trot was looking at it as if nothing else existed. She felt in her sleeve; no hankie. She felt in her pocket; no hankie. She was wearing a tiny scarf, however, knotted at her throat, and she took it off and teased it above Witch's head. The response was magical; the pup was entranced.

'That's very good,' the instructor said, in so astounded a voice that Rhea wondered if any owner had had such a response before. The dogs around her were doing anything but paying attention. She was delighted with the result. Witch walked beside her, looking up.

'That's enough for the moment; puppies can't concentrate for long,' the man said. He smiled at Rhea. 'Practise that all you can, every moment you have time; you've got a promising pup there.'

Rhea looked at Susie who patted the seat beside her. The group of people Rhea had just left were now trying to get their dogs to lie down; one dog had its head down and its tail in the air; a big Samoyed was lying on his back, bicycling, much to his owner's embarrassment, a golden retriever appeared to be trying to mate the dog next to it, which was reacting by barking and growling, so that the instructor had to stride across, grab the retriever's lead, and snatch him away from his victim. The owner, her face bright red, stood against the wall, apparently hating her dog. An Afghan stood as if turned to stone, refusing to listen or move, though a second Afghan was lying quietly at his owner's side as if nothing in the world would induce it to move.

The door opened and a woman came in, towed by an enormous German Shepherd dog. There was something about her that was familiar and as Rhea looked, she recognised the thin spiteful face, and the long black hair. It was Agnes Redpath. She saw Rhea and glared.

Rhea lifted Witch on to her lap and held her as if afraid the pup would be taken away. Susie's whispered, 'Oh glory,' did nothing to help.

Agnes came across the room and stood in front of them.

'I said you weren't fit to have a dog,' the woman said, her voice raised so that all the room could hear. 'Look at that puppy; there's nothing of her; she's just skin and bones. You won't come to me for food, so you feed her on rubbish; table leavings, I suppose . . .'

Rhea sat as if paralysed.

'She's far too small for her age; just look at that puppy over there; the same breed and twice the size. And his coat shines and his eyes are bright; your pup's eyes are dull; the coat's staring and she's obviously full of worms. I sent the RSPCA inspector to you this morning; he told me nothing was wrong. How much did you pay him?'

Rhea couldn't answer. She couldn't believe that this was happening, that the thin voice was accusing her of such idiotic things, in public. People were looking away, embarrassed, except for one dark-haired woman whose eyes were amused, and who looked as if she were enjoying a first-class film at the cinema.

Rhea could think of nothing to say. Her voice had dried up and the familiar, miserable sick feeling came back. She felt as outraged as she had when she had reached home and found all her possessions ruined. She felt like a hooked fish, unable to escape. Every time she thought she was free, as the line had run out, the hook caught once more and she was reeled in, and her hard-won and fragile sense of security was breached again.

John had protected her from people like this. He had known them, but his home had been his sanctuary and hers. A place where he could shut the door and forget the world outside; a base to work from; a tranquil island; and she with her almost total lack of curiosity had helped him beyond measure. She suddenly realised that now.

'Of course we all know that people like you know nothing of reality,' the voice went on. 'You probably don't feed yourself properly either; painters live in an imaginary world, and have very strange ideas about life. We know all about them; some of them were shut up in asylums, weren't they, and that's where they all ought to be, not outside among decent people allowed to have animals. Poor little mite; what a life for her.'

The woman put down a hand to Witch, who bared her teeth and growled.

'There, you're even bringing her up to be vicious. The puppies I breed are never vicious.'

The class on the floor behind her was functioning as if nothing was happening. People were drinking tea. A small girl in a corner was trying to make a very young puppy sit. The world was going on, but Rhea was marooned in her corner, and nobody spoke. Nobody looked except for the woman who was enjoying every moment, as if it were an entertainment laid on especially for her.

Rhea could think of nothing to say. She turned her head and saw Susie walking towards her carrying two cups of tea, biscuits in the saucers. She turned away, leaving Agnes Redpath talking to nobody, and walked with Susie over to the far corner of the room and sat down, afraid the child might notice her shaking legs.

137

Trot was lying quietly in a corner, watching every movement that Susie made. She walked over and untied his lead and brought him back.

'Dad or one of the others will be here in a few minutes,' Susie said. 'I've got homework to do, so I never stay very long. Our class is always first so that we can get home; there are five others from my school, but they aren't here tonight. They've got an exam in the morning. They're a form above me.'

She chattered on, and Rhea half listened, longing for the sight of one of the men in the doorway to release her, and then suddenly realised absurdly that they had come in her own car.

'We came in my car,' she reminded Susie, who began to laugh. Rhea, suddenly feeling hysterical, began to laugh too. Eyes watched the pair of them as they walked to the door, leaving those behind them wondering what the joke could be.

Outside, the night was bright with stars. A crescent moon hung, uncaring, above the chimneys. Rhea stood beside the dustbins for a moment, and looked up. The dark was healing.

A man touched her on the shoulder and she jumped.

'Don't worry, Mrs Morland,' he said. 'We all know Agnes here. Some of us have also had trouble with her. I own the puppy she was talking about. Dogs are always bigger than bitches and he's twice as old as yours. Witch looks fine. Try and ignore her. I know it's difficult, but she has very few friends here. Come back next week. That's a cracking little pup.'

He went inside again.

'Did Mrs Redpath have another go at you?' Susie asked. She had gone to get tea, not knowing what to do about the encounter.

'She tried,' Rhea said. She was feeling too vulnerable, too raw, too easily bruised. John had only been dead two months and she had already lived through a lifetime since then. If he had been alive would she have told him about her adventures, she wondered, and then realised that if he had been alive they could never have happened at all. She would be safely in a London mews house, living as they always lived, with Ray Morton still painting and living her secret life and Rhea Morland always at home in the evening, in a house filled with

138

flowers, with large solemn furniture, with velvet curtains that shut out noise and darkness, and that enclosed them in a cocoon of unreality.

Susie was tired and sat quietly, Trot between her legs and Witch on her lap. Trot nosed the puppy, who licked his face. The evening had been strenuous for her and she settled to sleep.

The bright headlights picked out the hedges and trees in the silent lanes that led back to the police houses. A fox slipped out of the hedgerow and Susie pointed to him; he stood, poised for a moment, posing in the headlights, and was gone. He was old and rather mangy, but for a brief moment he had looked beautiful.

Dave had bought food from the Chinese takeaway, and was putting it out on three plates when Rhea walked into the house with Susie. Trot and Witch had been left in the wired-in garden and were chasing one another.

'Trot loves your puppy,' Susie said. 'A chinky . . . oh good. Did you get sweet-and-sour pork, Daddy?'

'I got a whole mixture; there's sweet-and-sour pork and pancakes and chop suey; I thought Mrs Morland could do with something to eat before she went home. I've got to drive down that way later, so I'll follow you when you go, and maybe you can give me a coffee before I drive on. Mair says if you want to sleep in their room tonight instead of here, you can, Susie love.'

'I don't mind being here,' Susie said. 'I can hear Mair and Reg anyway; and hear the babies when they cry. It's not like being alone at all. And Trot's by me. He's good company all the time.'

She called the dogs in and they raced in together, tails banging against the furniture. Witch settled down on the hearthrug, gazing into the fire, and rolled on her side, spreading her tummy to the warmth. Trot curled up by Susie's chair.

'We'll eat on our knees,' Dave said. 'I want to look at the news.'

It was good to be part of a group again; part of a family. Dave and Susie got on well together, and Dave, Rhea suddenly

139

thought, laughed far more than any man she had ever known. Rod seldom smiled; his face always said that life was grim; Mark invariably looked bewildered, perhaps inheriting that from her. At least she had the stallion – pride of possession awakened again. He was magnificent and the pictures she would paint would more than earn his price. Rod had made her feel guilty.

The pup came to lean against her legs.

'She's not nearly as wild as I thought she might be,' Dave said, watching his visitors. The pup turned her head to look at the man. Her ears were not yet fully pricked and as she sat, one ear fell rakishly over one eye and she pushed at it impatiently with her paw, an amazed expression on her face. She tried to roll her eyes upwards and look at her ears, reducing the three watchers to laughter. Trot came over to see what was happening but could not understand, so gave a deep sigh and curled up on the hearthrug.

'I hardly ever got the chance to have Chinese food,' Rhea said. 'John hated it; he preferred Italian or French cooking, or sometimes we went to a little Greek restaurant. Their food was gorgeous.'

'I'd like to live in London,' Susie said. 'Then I could go to the zoo and the Tower of London and see the Crown Jewels and go to the Planetarium and the Natural History Museum and go to all the exhibitions like the Tutankhamen exhibition. Nothing ever happens here, and the only zoo is Chester and that's too far to get to easily. Daddy's going to take me to stay in London, one day.'

One day never comes, Rhea thought and wondered where she had heard that, then had a vision of herself as a small girl, listening to her grandfather. He had also loved saying jam tomorrow and jam yesterday but never jam today; and also, tomorrow never comes.

She looked around the room. A photograph of a woman remarkably like Susan stood on the mantelpiece; a quiet grave face, with only a hint of smile. Rhea wondered how she had died. Dave never spoke of her.

The room was warm and comfortable and lived in; the settee needed re-covering, but the covers were clean, and the crochet-covered cushions were an unexpected shout of colour in the room. Dave saw her glance at them and laughed.

'Heather adores crochet,' he said. 'She also likes bright colours and buys remnants of wool in the market. So she makes us new cushion covers for presents every year. Neither Susie nor I exactly admire her colour schemes but we wouldn't hurt her for the world.'

Susie laughed.

'I've got a bedspread that Heather crocheted for me; it's purple and orange and green squares. My curtains are red. But there's nothing I can do about it, except dormouse.'

'Dormouse?' Rhea looked at her, puzzled.

'Didn't you read your children about the dormouse and the doctor?' Dave asked.

Rhea laughed. She had totally forgotten the poem. The dormouse had liked geraniums, but the doctor had ordered him delphiniums, so he had lain there with his paws to his eyes and imagined himself back among the flowers he liked. Or had she got it wrong? She couldn't remember, couldn't even remember who had written it, thought she felt it had to be A.A. Milne.

The ringing phone interrupted her thoughts.

'Trouble,' Dave said with a sigh, as he put the receiver down. 'I still have to drive your way. I'll have to go without that coffee, but at least I can see you safely home.'

He put a small parcel into her hands.

'Sorry about that; no time for afters, which is what that is. It's your share. Eat it when you get in. I'm taking mine in the van. Yours is on the draining-board, Susie love. Get to bed in good time, there's a good girl. I'll be late, I expect.'

The night was still star bright, without a hint of cloud. Rhea lifted Witch and walked to her car. She wouldn't be able to lift the pup for much longer; she'd have to teach her to behave, or she'd waste an awful lot of time. And she mustn't ever run off. Thorpe and Wilde might be more friendly to her now through common experiences, but neither would tolerate the dog out near sheep or pheasants, and both always carried guns.

'I'll lead,' Dave said. 'I know a couple of short cuts and I'm in a hurry. Just follow me.'

That was easier said than done as Dave drove fast and knew the lanes well. They twisted and turned, not always in the direction Rhea expected. They came to her cottage sooner than she had imagined possible.

'I'll show you that route one day when I have time. There's a near riot at one of the pubs. I sometimes wonder if one night I won't come back, and what will happen to Susie then . . . doesn't do to wonder.'

Rhea had her key in the door and had opened it. Dave checked quickly to make sure all was well, and she stood in the doorway and watched his rear lights vanish.

Darkness swept back.

The little packet contained an apple, a banana, a doughnut and a small bar of chocolate. He had obviously been shopping with Susie in mind. It was the sort of food she would have loved at that age.

Sitting eating it, the electric fire switched on, relaxing in the armchair that had been loaned to her, she felt exhausted, as if she had lived through several days instead of one. She had to take the puppy outside before bed, and outside was suddenly frightening. The darkness was so absolute and the wood so wild. The wind was stirring and the soft noise of the rustling branches of the winter trees caused the pup to sit, ears alert, and growl softly.

Was there someone about?

Was that a footstep? Were there intruders in the night? Would she ever feel safe again?

There was nothing outside, but she couldn't rid herself of the feeling of uneasiness. It persisted even when she came in. It continued as she got ready for bed, and it was not allayed in the least when she went to put her keys away in her handbag and could not find the bag. The keys had been in her pocket.

It was not in the car.

It was not in the house.

She must have left it at the dog club. She couldn't remember picking it up from the chair she had first been sitting on when Agnes Redpath accosted her. She had totally forgotten it. Her purse was in it; and her cheque book; and her credit card. Also the ring that John had given her on their Paris holiday. She wore it now daily, to remind her of him; it was the last present he had ever given her and the one she had liked the most. She had not wanted to wear it while she was training her pup.

Sleep was a very long time coming, and when at last it came she had continuous nightmares, so that at five in the morning she was glad to dress and take the pup outside, and then settle down to sketch the woods.

She remembered Rachel's fairy tales, and sketched in giants and trolls; gruesome half-hidden terrifying creatures, stretching their arms out of the shadows. It filled in the time till she could drive into town and find out if anyone had found her bag. She would have to go to the bank first and cancel her cheque card, just in case.

She was tired of grief and she was tired of fear and she was tired of worry. She fell asleep again, sitting by the window in the armchair, and the puppy curled up beside her and slept too.

11

She seemed doomed to be wakened by heavy knocking.

Rhea found herself momentarily unable to get out of her chair and answer the door. There were so many people she almost feared, and her horror of the pup's breeder was now so great that the mere thought of the woman made her feel sick.

'Is anyone there?'

The voice was that of a stranger. Rhea pulled herself together and opened the door.

The dark woman who had looked so amused the night before stood on the doorstep, holding out her handbag.

'I saw it almost as soon as you had gone,' she said. 'I did come by last night, but you were out and I didn't like to leave it anywhere outside. I had nothing to write a note with. You must have been worried. I would have been.'

Rhea grinned at her in wholehearted relief.

'I can eat my breakfast now. I don't know how to thank you. Would you care for a coffee?'

'I wouldn't mind breakfast. I overslept and had to drive my younger son to school. His foot's in plaster. The silly kid jumped off a stool and broke his ankle. He's the same age as Susie. He ought to have been there last night but he can only just hobble. What it is to be young!'

'I've bacon and egg and tomato and bread,' Rhea said. 'I'm not very well stocked.'

'You had vandals. So did my next-door neighbour. Trouble is we were out, but we'd left lights on. We always do. She's had a heart attack, poor old thing. She's nearly eighty and it was one hell of a shock.'

'I don't know your name.' Rhea had disliked the woman last night, but now began to like her.

'Meg Williams. I'm half Welsh and half Scots. I did enjoy your set-to with the Harpy last night. No one else has ever stood up to her. I hope it did her good.'

'Stood up to her? My knees were knocking, I felt sick and I didn't say a word because I was too terrified; I've never met anyone like her.' Rhea, frying bacon, had turned to look in astonishment at her visitor.

'That wasn't the impression we got. We thought you were facing her with absolute dignity, refusing to be drawn into an argument. The rest of us would have flapped and fluffed and floundered. You just stood there in icy calm and then walked away from her, leaving her mouthing nonsense to thin air. It was hilarious. She was completely flummoxed.' Meg had been looking round the room.

'This place did take a pasting. I can imagine you haven't had time or energy to do anything about it. When my first husband died it took me about two years to get over it; I never thought I would. But I did, and now I'm married again, and it's hard to remember those ghastly months. It's absolutely vital to make plans and stick to them; little goals. Like getting this place straight again quickly, before it gets you down or you run away and hide. Look, I know what the village said; and don't worry about our Agnes. Everyone calls her the Harpy; not even her husband liked her. He had a nice little bit going on the side, a much kinder person. Agnes would turn the milk sour in a Jersey cow. My father had a herd, and I miss them; I ought to have married a farmer, but my first husband was a sailor and my second is a builder, so if you want any help here, yell at us. I had a bit of trouble with our Agnes myself, because I hunt, and she and some of her cronies damaged our horses with their wicked goings-on.'

Rhea was a little dazed. She ate in silence, listening.

Meg Williams saw her expression and laughed.

'I was born with the gift of tongues,' she said. 'I never get the chance to use them. My husband's a strong silent man, and never replies when I talk, and the boys never listen. I've three sons; two from my first marriage, both grown up now, and this young hellion. I would have managed him a bit better ten years ago. Motherhood begins to pall after nearly thirty years and poor little Simon came very late in my life. Luckily my second son is still at home and has enough energy for both of us. Bill's even older than I am; never been married before and he finds fatherhood a bit daunting at times. I used to want to be free; but after two years on my own and then a couple of years more with Bill in the offing and not able to make up my mind, I value what I've got now.'

Rhea, cutting bread for toast, discovered she was so used to silence that she found it hard to answer. Being alone was very bad indeed. She didn't want to talk about John to a total stranger, and she didn't quite know what else to talk about.

If only she could talk about painting.

Megan Williams, who seemed possessed of a vast curiosity that she didn't trouble to hide, was walking about the room, looking at the books that lay on the window sills, and at the sketch pad that Rhea had thrown down.

She picked it up. Rhea had drawn the woods, drawn the twisted trunks close and thick and secret, gnarled and distorted, the leering faces in the background taunting and dissolute. One of the trolls, his body grotesque, his mouth enlarged, his hair cascading round his shoulders, glared out with inimical eyes.

'Your vision of the dog club,' Megan said, rather surprisingly. She pointed to the leering troll. 'And there is our Fury. Did you know you've caricatured us all? It's wonderful.' She laughed.

Rhea stared at her.

Megan laughed again.

'I do things like that. When life gets me down I draw all kinds of things and I get very good at finding out what triggered them off. But if I drew last night's meeting I'd draw you as the Ice Queen, silent and dignified, with long flowing draperies and beautiful blonde hair and eyes shining with courage and indignation, and I'd draw our Anges as a rather mean little terrier with a shaggy coat trying to tear the clothes off you. Like this.'

She flipped over the sketch pad and produced a picture with

146

lightning swift strokes. It was a caricature, and yet it showed exactly what she had said she would draw.

'That's very good,' Rhea said.

Megan laughed.

'I've a confession to make. I hid your bag; I've been dying to meet you. I saw the picture of that little mare of Joe Nathan's over at Hartley, and fell in love with it. I can't ever afford a Ray Morton, but the man I work with produces limited edition prints for me. Would you consider having some of your pictures printed? Hal's very very good, and also he's a good business man. I do things for the Nature Conservancy Board; bird and animal pictures, very stylised, nothing like yours. I'm extremely competent but I'm not talented; I thought that if I had a good excuse I could sound you out; and own up if it worked out right. There are several galleries all round the country that would take the prints, and as Hal only does two hundred and fifty and it's always a signed limited edition, they usually increase in value and get your name known, not that you need that.'

'I thought of doing pictures of Witch,' Rhea said. 'Perhaps ten or twelve different poses in an oval, round a poem. I haven't found a poem I want to use yet. It has to be either original or out of copyright.'

'Try John Clare,' Megan said. 'Maybe he wrote about a sheepdog; and Witch is a German Shepherd; they use them for herding in Germany. It's a great idea. I'll keep you to it, and call again if I may. And do get this place sorted out before it gets to be such a nightmare you can't face it at all. Believe me, I went through it, and I do know what it's like; no one else can even guess. And don't let the village get you down. We aren't all like the Harpy. She doesn't seem so awful if you call her that; I suppose the poor thing can't help it. She's either got some twisted mental kink or she's so desperately miserable that she takes it out on all the world. She's a very mixed-up person.'

Rhea watched the little Fiat drive away with regret. Meg Williams had left a note with her name and address on it, and the visit had given her something else to think about. Her handbag safe, she could turn her attention to other things and began to clear up the studio with far more enthusiasm than she had the day before. By midday it looked habitable again and almost comfortable. She would need to buy more furniture. She sat and looked at the room, wondering what she would get. It was so large that she could turn one end of it into a sitting-room; there was a stove at the far end which she could replace with one of the Norwegian wood-burning stoves. Wood was here for the taking. The rides were full of kindling blown down from the trees and she could bring in sacks of pine needles.

Autumn colours: bright yellow and scarlet and auburn; rich reddish browns and perhaps green to offset the tawny shades. She would print her own curtains and make them; buy a sewing machine; match cushion covers. She wondered if perhaps she might get to know Heather and persuade her to let her make cushion covers for a change for Dave's sitting-room; a beautiful misty mauvey blue was what it needed to complement the curtains and the carpet. And maybe Susie and she could re-do Susie's room.

It was pie in the sky and castles in the air and whistling in the dark, and she mustn't interfere, but dreams were nice to have and there was no harm in them, so long as they were kept secret.

Megan's brisk company had done her good, so that when, just as she had finished her after-lunch coffee, a red Ford drew up, she found herself able to watch the man getting out without any worry at all.

'I'm from Worldwide Insurance,' he said.

He looked at the cottage; the windows had been replaced but the swept-up glass was outside, safely covered, so that Witch couldn't hurt herself; the damaged furniture was still in the garden, obviously unusable; the paintings lay on top.

'That must have hurt,' the man said.

Rhea nodded.

'It's never the same the second time round,' she said.

'There won't be any problems about getting the money. Carry on and replace it all and get everything in order. Lightning never strikes twice in my experience,' he said, after a brief exploration.

'Never?' Rhea asked.

'Never,' he assured her.

He was a big solid man, moving heavily, his face absorbed as he added up sums of money on his notebook. Rhea made more coffee and brought out a cake that she had discovered in a tin on the windowsill. Megan must have brought it with her. It was a rich cherry cake, that looked good enough to paint.

'Would you do me a favour?' the insurance assessor asked, as he finished his coffee, and ate the last crumbs of the cake. 'This is a good cake.'

He hesitated.

'If I can,' Rhea said, wondering what he was about to ask.

'My daughter's a Ray Morton fan. One of your pictures was reproduced as a centre spread in *Pony* some months ago. It's pinned on her bedroom wall. Could she have your autograph? She's thirteen . . .'

Rhea laughed.

'I've never been asked for that before.'

'There's always a first time. Theresa would treasure it.'

Rhea looked about her for a piece of paper that would be good enough to use. A scrap seemed to be almost an insult to the child. There was only her sketch book, with some of her poses for the picture she wanted to build round Witch.

She tore the page out and signed it.

'She'll love that.' He looked at it, and stroked the puppy, who had come to him and was investigating his trouser legs with a slowly moving inquisitive nose. 'We've got a rabbit, a hamster, a very elderly poodle that was left us when my mother-in-law died, and a young spaniel bitch,' the man said. 'She knows, doesn't she? Are you sure you can spare this?'

'I have plenty of time to do more,' Rhea said. She regretted the words as soon as she said them, as the assessor gave her a sympathetic look that almost reduced her to tears. Don't pity me, please, she said inside her head, fiercely. Never pity me. It won't do.

She rang Jim and Brian to tell them that the cottage could now be finished and the studio also restored to its earlier splendour, and decided to spend the afternoon shopping for furniture. The phone had been installed two days before. She needed to think and to plan and maybe to hunt around. She had her own ideas about colour schemes and would probably never find what she wanted for the cottage windows either.

As she drove to town she felt, for the first time since she moved, a sense of purpose. If the picture with the puppy poses worked, and also sold, and she sold the prints, maybe she could do the same thing with Lucifer, using a poém about a horse as the centrepiece with pictures of him in different poses all around it.

Almost without thinking, the design for her curtains came to her; tawny gold and brown, with the silhouettes of horses in lines across the pattern; with horse pictures on the walls; nothing but horses.

She would get the cottage furnished within the next month; she had Witch to train and maybe Susie would show her how to teach the pup to track, as Witch seemed to know already that the ground held wonderful scents, and when she was off lead, which was very rarely, she followed intently. Rhea found it difficult to keep her head off the ground when they walked together.

The pup nosed her hand and she reached across and patted her, and as she parked the car and left the windows an inch open all round, and walked into the shop that sold all the materials she needed for her painting, she felt a small glow of satisfaction, a prick of interest, an urgent desire to start life again, a feeling that the storm clouds were lifting and that better times lay ahead.

She left the art shop and walked into the book shop, looking for a copy of John Clare's poems.

She found it, and leafed through it, not finding what she wanted, but enraptured by words that would turn into pictures.

'There's Bucket's Hill a place of furze and clouds,
Which evening in a golden blaze enshrouds.'

She could see the hill rising to the sky and the sunset beyond the peak, the light flooding grass and gorse and wild flowers; and rabbits playing. She bought the book, even though it did not have what she wanted, and nor it seemed did any other books of collected poems. Surely there were dog poems.

She racked her memory, trying to remember poems about dogs. Mad dogs and Englishmen; the little dog died when he'd had his day. Neither offered the right image for her.

She suddenly remembered that long ago she had collected a series of poems published in a magazine; cut them out and pasted them in a book. The scrap book must be in one of the unpacked boxes. Fired by enthusiasm, longing to put her vision on to paper, she drove home and began to burrow in the stack of boxes waiting to be sorted. She needed bookshelves; she needed so many things, and everything took such a time to buy. It was never in stock; or what was in stock was the wrong size or the wrong shape.

She had not even realised that she had lacked all enthusiasm for weeks. Everything had seemed dreadful, perhaps out of all proportion to the real magnitude. Little disasters overwhelmed her as they never had before. Maybe, she thought, sitting back on her heels, looking at the wedding picture she had not been able to put out, grief attacks people in different ways. It's reduced me to an idiot. I'm not like this at all.

The box contained so much of her past. Photographs of the boys when they were babies. Had Mark really been as beautiful as that? Where had that lovely little boy gone? Would her grandchild bring back those memories, kindle a new feeling in her heart? At the moment the baby seemed unreal; impossible to think the years had gone by and somehow she was old enough to be a grandmother; a great aunt; it sounded as old as history.

She turned over the pages.

Herself as a child riding her pony. Blaze. She had forgotten about Blaze. How old had she been then? Three, perhaps. The solemn little girl, pigtails in ribbons, stared at her from the faded picture, nothing to do with her at all. She couldn't even remember how that child had felt.

A family photograph album. The pup nudged her, bored, and she threw the old slipper across the room for her to fetch, continuing the game absentmindedly. Witch seemed to have retriever instincts in her and loved carrying things, and Dave had told Rhea to encourage it as a major asset. The pup was content to trot round the room, head held high, eyes bright with interest, so long as Rhea said 'Clever girl' now and then.

The scrap book at last.

All sorts of rhymes cut from all sorts of places; things that had appealed to her once.

'So stick to the fight. When you're hardest hit,
It's when things seem worst that you must not quit.'

She would letter that, all of it, as there was much more in the same vein and stick it up above her dressing-table mirror where it would catch her eye each day. Some of her own early drawings; treasured for a long time by her father and found in his desk when he died; he had kept all of them. He never knew about Ray Morton; her career was only beginning and she had kept it quiet. She wished, suddenly and achingly, that he was there to tell; he would have shared her pleasure, would have loved to own one of her paintings, and would have been so proud. He had died a very poor man – life changed for everyone. She missed him desperately.

The loss was momentarily more intense than her grief for her husband. She and her father had shared so much.

Irene McLeod's *Lone Dog*. That wasn't quite what she wanted now, but she had a sudden vision of a picture of a lean dog running, the wind blowing his fur, keen faced, sharp featured, the hunter after his kill. Bleak moorland and high peaks; barren ground but it wasn't what she wanted. She wanted something gentler; with more line and movement.

She could see the picture, but as yet what she had wasn't right.

Pictures of horses. A shire-horse stud card; she had painted that horse for his owner; he had been magnificent. Power in every line of him. She had fallen in love with him as she painted, always enraptured by horses, unable to explain the passion they roused in her, the need to get that shape down on paper; sometimes the need to get the shape under her hands and sculpt it, her fingers itching with desire.

How did you share such feelings, she wondered desolately. John would never have understood; her sons didn't understand. Only Rachel had understood. Rachel with her dark intense face, with her own passion for flowers, so that she painted flowers that danced off the paper, elegant, dainty, thin stems and butterfly-bright petals. Her pictures were in great demand, and she only had to see a flower in a garden and she was seized with the same urge that seized Rhea when she saw a horse that was eminently paintable.

That little grey last week that was being schooled on a lunge line as she passed the stables. She had stopped the car and watched him. Perfection of movement; that was what she needed to paint now. Needed to paint so desperately that she could barely wait to get to work and yet the form eluded her. Surely somewhere . . .

And there it was. She had remembered it all these years, but not in detail.

It was exactly what she wanted and she didn't even know if it was in copyright.

She read it through again. The picture took shape as she read, and she was glad when Witch tired of exercise and came to lie against her, stretched out in a deep puppy sleep that would last for an hour or more.

She began to think about the shape of the picture and the lettering.

The poem was by Dale and entitled *The Greyhound*. Who was Dale, she wondered?

Gracefully coursing the level ground,
She stretches her limbs to the final bound;
Effortless movement, perfection in speed,
And elegant power are the greyhound's creed.

She is Ariel's hound, a gift from the Gods,
Surpassing in flight all mortal dogs –
No lurcher or longdog could ever outpace
This celestial messenger's easy haste.
Or is she a phantom, a child of our minds,
Epitomised fleetness, outstripping the wind.
Will we dream of her galloping, reaching her soul,
To achieve some impelling yet secret goal?
So swift is her passage, so regal her air,
Can but language encompass the beauty there?

She is gone in a glance – just a shadow remains,
Where the Greyhound has fled to fairer domains.

Rhea began to block in the words on her sketch pad, very roughly, and then to build the design round them; the greyhound running; beauty, strength, power, in every line, stretched out, and then curved, as she fled down the long trail, the shadows sketched lightly. She needed to find someone who owned a greyhound and go and watch; to take some photographs of the movement; and maybe if she did that and it went well and sold, she might find a poem about a racehorse and paint the racing movements, one horse after another in a different position round the words.

She drew on, oblivious of time, totally absorbed, remembering nothing. Slowly, peace came back; the fears and terrors of the past weeks slipped away, so that there was only the moving pencil, the ticking of a clock and Witch's soft breathing as she slept.

Somehow through the picture came a feeling of tranquillity, of deep satisfaction, of fulfilment, as it took shape; it would need a lot of work. She would ring Rachel, having at last something worth saying; but first she would get the pattern right; get the idea crystallised; get the feeling that she needed, so that the final painting said all she wanted it to say.

Effortless movement, perfection in speed . . .

How did you show people how it felt to watch a horse galloping; mane and tail tossing in the wind; to watch a dog racing, full pelt, every muscle moving perfectly; to build the animal by exercise to attain perfect balance; the shape of it just as you had dreamed, taking an untried animal and making it into something that even nature hadn't thought of, not by breeding, but by training?

Up to the jumps and over . . . round the track lightning fast; flowing into a hurdle and flowing away, watching dogs in the breed-ring moving to perfection, though that was so rare. Movement . . . how many people walked beautifully instead of lumping along in miserable huddled bundles? She had once watched a girl striding free, unaware of her own beauty; not the stilted walk of mannequins; not the jaded walk of the overburdened, but a gay carefree walk, of a young creature that had not yet learned that life could be unhappy, instead of a realisation of something wonderful.

Rhea yawned and stretched. It was long past her time to eat. Witch woke and also stretched and shook herself and went to the door. Outside, a grey rain was falling and dusk had come without being noticed. The tranquillity remained. It stayed with her while she fed the dog and cooked for herself; it stayed with her as she eyed what she had done and knew that it was good; it stayed with her when she went to bed and went to sleep, forgetting the last few weeks, wanting only to wake in the morning and start the picture again, life returning to numbed senses and anticipation and, above all, hope, a feeling she hadn't had since she was a child.

Tomorrow was a new adventure, not a day to be endured. Anything might happen in the morning. She slept, with Witch curled against her, and dreamed of greyhounds.

12

It became increasingly plain in the next few weeks that plans were made only to be brought to nothing. Rhea had planned to paint her stallion, but he was never ready for her when she got there; he was always out in the field, or covered in mud, or being trained. Rory had little time for her; the girls were busy and she felt rather like a ghost haunting the stables, so that she took to driving further and further afield, trying to find horses she could paint.

She trained Witch daily, teaching her to track. Whenever Dave was free he came to help, running down the lane holding her toy denim mouse in his hand, calling back to Witch.

'Find it girl, find it, where is it then,' and then hiding it in the grass at the verge, so that it was all Rhea could do to hold her before she galloped off, nose down on his track to find her toy and be rewarded by the game she loved, of having it thrown further and further away into long grass and finding it again.

She remembered herself long ago schooling one of the ponies. Slow gradual improvements daily, taking each step carefully, desperately anxious not to ruin what she was doing by being too impulsive. She remembered her father's voice.

'Easy lad, easy, good lad then. Easy lad, easy, good lad then. Walk on. Good lad.'

Soothe and reassure, teaching all the time without the animal even being aware that it was being coaxed into learning. Dave had the same approach with a dog. Each exercise was built on the one before; go slowly. How do you train a good dog? Slowly. So many people took short cuts and ruined the dog and never knew they had. They blamed the dog but they hadn't taught it the right way. A before B and then B before C, until the slow teaching made the dog quite certain of the ABC and then you could progress. No use giving a five-year-old the Bible; yet people did the equivalent time after time with their dogs. Stupid dog, won't learn.

Witch had hang-ups at times, and stood puzzled. What do you mean? What are you trying to make me do? Rhea learned to think about herself. Did I do something wrong? Have I taken her too fast today? Am I expecting too much?

She began to re-read her old horse-training books; the dog books didn't explain the same way and half the time the writers didn't seem to know the purpose of the training. It was so like training a horse. The aids for the horse were the reins, the body, and the voice. You kept in touch with the horse through the bit and the hands and through your legs against him, telling him what to do with his hindlegs.

The aids with the dog were the lead, the slipchain, the voice and the body, only instead of using pressure on the dog's body, you taught the dog to watch you for signals. Unrealised by the handler half the time, Dave said. Always scratch your head when your dog barks and one day you scratch your head and the dog barks, sure that's what scratching your head means. You may never know why the dog barked then.

Always drink your coffee before going out in the afternoon and as soon as that cup goes down on the table the dog is at the door.

Change your shoes; it is a signal to your dog.

Pick up the lead; it means out.

Pick up your coat; it means out.

Pick up the tracking harness and Witch would go crazy, tearing round the room. Going to track, going to track, going to track. Slowly her confidence grew; and the lessons got harder, but if too hard Rhea always went back two steps to make sure that that fragile confidence was never destroyed.

She became as enthralled as she had when schooling her horses.

It was different; yet the principles were the same. She wished she could find somewhere to ride again. She didn't want to go back and ride with Rory. Every time she saw him

157

brought back the past. She was nineteen again and betrayed by his defection. She could never trust him a second time. But the old attraction was there.

When he chose he could charm a nightingale out of its nest.

She didn't want to be with him too much. She didn't want to visit too often and she wished in some ways she hadn't bought the stallion. She would paint him; and make all the money she had invested in him repay her in good measure. It had been a mistake to try and renew past friendship. She should have known better. Her feelings towards him were very mixed indeed. The wariness she had felt when first meeting him was there all the time.

She had once been ready to marry Rory; and then he had left her and she had gone through hell; and that was what she would need to remember. People didn't really change.

She had just settled to giving Witch a training session when there was the sound of a car drawing up outside, and a hammering on the door. She didn't want any more visitors, and since half her encounters with people here seemed to be totally irrational, she felt very uneasy as she went to the door.

Rory stood there, and she bit back an impulse to say 'talk of the devil' as she stood looking up at him.

'I had to pass, so thought I'd come and look you up and see where you'd hidden yourself,' Rory said.

'I'm waiting for carpets and furniture.' Rhea felt defensive. The critical eyes were laughing at her now. He walked over to the easel.

'You've come a long way since the days you drew ponies all over the stable records and made your father mad,' Rory said.

'A lifetime away. I've been married, had children and I'm about to be a grandmother,' Rhea answered, wanting to put as great a distance between him and her as possible.

'It suits you,' Rory was grinning now, the attractive eyes crinkling. 'I still think you and I could make a go of it . . .'

'And I don't,' Rhea said. 'I value my freedom. I can do as I choose, go where I choose, and for the first time in my life, make my own decisions.'

'Was your marriage happy?'

'It lasted over thirty years,' Rhea said, resenting the

question. She did not want to talk about John to Rory. She wondered what John would have made of Rory. He would not have said; he never discussed people, not even his own children. She had known very little about his private thoughts. He had been a very private man. All those shared years, yet she knew little about his inner self. Or even what he had felt about her.

Rory laughed and caught her hand.

'Rhea, you can't fool me. He was never exciting, was he? A dull man, a dull life, no spice, no fun. So you bought the stallion. To get back in touch with me again . . . do you think I don't know that? It was a good excuse, but it won't wash; it's an insane sort of investment for a sensible widow woman.'

'Is it?' Rhea drew her hand away and crossed to the other side of the room. The pup sensed her anger and bristled and growled, the hackles on her back rising; Rory laughed.

'She's as effectively angry as you are. All show and no reality. A stallion . . . you can't ride him, or manage him, or help with him; what sense is there to having him?'

'Firstly, I presume you do intend to have mares for him? I'm going to get some benefit from that. Secondly, I have access to him whenever I want as he's mine and I want to draw him; I can't go to any stud whenever I choose and ask for the stallion to come out; I can come to yours at reasonable times, and look at him, photograph him, sketch him.'

'With me thrown in.'

'I don't want you thrown in. I wasn't even thinking about you. I felt that you know how to handle horses; I know all about your horsemanship and about the way you feel for them; I knew he'd live like a king, be fed royally,' she said. 'I saw your advertisement – and I knew when we met that you didn't really want to part with him – he means a lot to you.'

'He could have meant a fortune,' Rory said, mystifying her.

Rhea looked at him, considering him. He was flamboyantly dressed in dark blue trousers and a perfectly matching shirt and tie, with a cream jacket over them. The outfit looked wrong, although it fitted him perfectly. The dark hair still curled thickly but was turning grey. He was tanned and fit and had an air of gallantry about him, a swashbuckling style that had attracted her at nineteen. Now it faintly repelled her.

'Come to town with me and I'll take you out to lunch,' Rory said.

'I'm waiting for a delivery of furniture.' Rhea was reluctant to spend more time with him.

'I could do with coffee before I go.' He flicked his fingers at Witch.

Rhea spooned instant coffee from the tin into two mugs, and added water and milk.

'Sugar?'

'Three spoonfuls,' Rory said. He walked to the window. 'You could make a very attractive garden out there; I always wanted to garden, but never have time.'

It seemed an unlikely ambition, Rhea thought, as she sipped the hot coffee.

'I know a chap who would landscape it all for you,' Rory added.

'At an astronomical price and you'd get commission, I suppose,' Rhea said.

'You have learned a lot,' Rory laughed as he put down the cup. 'You won't change your mind about lunch?'

'Not lunch and not anything else,' Rhea said.

Rory went to the door and opened it. His shadow spread across the path.

'Arrivederci,' he said, and pulled the door shut behind him. Rhea watched him stride down the path, a powerful active man, a very attractive man, a man who still had the ridiculous power to make her feel nineteen again. She'd been a fool to get involved with him; but she had thought herself immune after all these years.

She ought to sell the stallion, but no way was she going to change her mind. The boys would tell her they had always known she was wrong; and she'd lose Sadie's respect, which was something she valued.

She settled in her chair with the pup sitting in front of her, and picked up the toy mouse that Susie had made for the little bitch. She flicked the long leather tail.

'One of the Metpol inspectors makes them and uses them to train dogs,' Dave had told her, 'and what's good enough for

160

the Metpol is good enough for us; though our dogs are far better trained of course,' he added with a laugh.

Training, Rhea was discovering, was far from easy. She wiggled the tail again.

'Watch, Witch, watch,' she said and thought that she had picked on a very awkward name. She changed the command. 'Witch, *look!*'

There was nothing else in the world but her and the pup and time went by, and she relaxed, entering a simpler easier world. At the end of the lesson the pup settled to sleep and she went to the easel and began to draw wtih swift sure strokes, and as she drew, her spirits rose until excitement mastered her and she knew that what she was doing was good.

She stopped for a quick snack lunch and then took out the pictures she had taken of the stallion. She wanted to sculpt him as well as paint him; she could feel the lines taking shape under her hands; the itch in her fingers to model each muscle, to capture the regal pose, the arch of his neck, the shape of his head, the uplifted curled foreleg, the neat beautifully formed hoof; the flare of his nostrils.

The power was returning.

The excitement of creation was there, rising to the surface, and she knew that within a few days she would start again to live, and that her work would be better than it had ever been before.

That evening she began on the sketches of Witch in different poses.

It was late that night that, unable to sleep, she picked up her book of Kipling poems, which was always guaranteed to bring pleasure, even though most of her friends laughed at her liking for him.

The obvious poet, Rachel had named him.

But the book fell open at *The Power of the Dog*, and as she read it she found the words she wanted to put in the centre of her picture of puppies. She had the poses she needed: Witch sitting; Witch curled up asleep; Witch scratching busily; Witch investigating a molehill, nose down, fascinated; Witch prancing on a ball; Witch feeding.

She read the poem again. The second verse was what she needed.

Buy a pup and your money will buy
Love unflinching that cannot lie –
Perfect passion and worship fed
By a kick on the ribs or a pat on the head.
Nevertheless it is hardly fair
To risk your heart to a dog to tear.

Witch curled up at her feet. The brown eyes looked at her, the small head lifted, and Rhea looked back.

I've done it now, it's too late, she thought, just before she drifted into sleep.

The warmth at her feet was very comforting; the sound of soft breathing was company in the night, and for a brief moment she felt a small desolation knowing that this pup would not be there in a few years' time. But that was in the future and the present had to be lived, and life was short and sometimes very unrewarding and if you ran away from feeling, then life had no meaning left.

It was a small price to pay for ten years or more of perfect passion and worship, and all that the dog asked was a hand on the head.

Love unflinching that cannot lie.

She thought of Rory and knew that she was wise never to trust him. She could never be sure that he wouldn't run off and leave her a second time. He was nothing like John.

13

With painting came peace of mind. Rhea could lose herself on the canvas. Slowly, again and again, the shape appeared; the idea took form, the picture developed, and her post began to contain requests for paintings of other horses. Ray Morton was becoming more widely known.

Rachel had a hand in that, she knew. Now there was no need to hide herself behind a pseudonym, now she could reveal her double identity, old friends were impressed. She could imagine them talking. 'Did you know Rhea Morland was really Ray Morton?' – or was it the other way round? Old clients of John's wrote to her asking for a picture and one morning, when Witch was lying stretched in the sun, her adolescent body lanky and long and out of all proportion, there came an imperious rat-tat-tat on the door.

Knocks on the door were no longer frightening. Rhea had no idea whether the gossip had died, but at least most of the dog club seemed to realise who she actually was, and not who she was supposed to be. The woman she was thought to be had now come up for trial, been banned from owning a dog for life, and a few of those who had believed Agnes were making amends. Rhea found that talk could no longer distress her; though she preferred not to know what was said.

Dave and Susie had become part of her life. Sometimes Susie came to stay the night, if Dave were out on duty and Reg were also out, as another baby was almost due, and Mair tired easily. The baby was due at almost the same time as Rhea's own grandchild.

Rhea opened the door.

She grinned at the man who stood there. He and John had

163

often worked together and she knew Derek Lacey very well.

'What on earth are you doing here?' she asked.

'I was in town on business and got your address from Mark. I thought I'd stay an extra day and look you up. Take you out for a meal.' He looked curiously round him, and petted Witch who had come to sniff his trouser leg.

'She can smell our cat,' he said, looking at the easel and the half-finished picture. 'Funny to think you are Ray Morton. Why did you keep it so dark?'

Now, almost six months after her husband had died, Rhea herself was wondering.

'That's a good question,' she said, busy with the kettle. 'I honestly don't know now; it seemed a good idea at the time. Somehow, John and I never talked. Just "pass the salt", and "are you in for dinner tonight", and "which shirts do you want packed".'

'He always said you were very relaxing to live with; no demands that he couldn't comply with; you never resented his work or his dedication, you never asked him awkward questions that he couldn't answer because of confidential knowledge; he thought you were the perfect wife for him. You were his sheet anchor to go back to and the home you made for him was his refuge.'

'He said all that to you?' Rhea asked in astonishment. 'Why never to me?'

'Perhaps he felt you knew and he didn't need to. I don't say much to Betty, but I often wish I could. Things that matter aren't easy to put into words and often it's easier to talk to a stranger.' He sighed and then laughed. 'Betty is more subtle perhaps than you were, or maybe less so. Recently she has been playing, over and over, that song "You never buy me flowers any more." A large hint!'

'Did you buy her flowers?' Rhea asked, intrigued.

'I keep meaning to, but I'm late home and the shops are shut or I know she won't be in . . . and time goes by and you regret it more and more and never do a thing about it.'

'And then one day it's too late,' Rhea said. She turned to face Derek and perched on the edge of the table. She was wearing fawn trousers and a dark blue shirt with a creamy-coloured scarf tucked neatly into the throat. He thought she had never looked better.

'Derek, what would John have thought if he'd known how I spent my time? I never did know; I never dared tell him. I was so afraid he might ask me to stop because his career came first; or he might be jealous when he found out how much I was earning. He thought my mother had left me the money. Rachel organised it to come via her solicitor. She's my agent. We never saved much; everything seemed to cost so much and when we entertained we had to do it properly – flowers in every room, perfectly arranged; the best food and the best wine; the best of everything. It mattered enormously to John.'

'A symbol of success. The best clothes too. That's something Betty has refused to do. We entertain in a small restaurant where she can wear her ordinary clothes; she won't buy grand-occasion clothes. But then she's half Scots and they are always very good managers.'

Rhea liked and trusted Betty. She was plain, capable, down to earth and a staunch friend. She had come round as soon as she heard of John's death and had been more help than all the family put together. Yet they had rarely met other than on business occasions. Friends who Rhea had thought would come had written little polite notes of sympathy and avoided her. People were very odd and totally unexpected, Rhea thought as she spooned coffee into the two hand-thrown mugs.

The studio was as she wanted it now; one end carpeted and furnished with deep armchairs, close to the fire; a low table that was always bare because Witch's tail had a habit of sweeping it clean. The rest of the room was also bare, so that she had room for her easel, room to move around, to stand back; uncluttered space for thinking.

She glanced at the picture on the stand now. She had spent three afternoons over at the stables in Rory's absence, preferring to avoid him. He had a new beauty, a little Arab filly just beginning to show her adult quality. She had been running free, mane blowing in the wind, head held high, nostrils flared, her lovely tail arched and held high, gaiety in every movement. Rhea had sat entranced, watching the youngster race against the wind, dance against her shadow, powerful muscles thrusting her body forwards. Once she stopped and kicked up her heels, frisking for the sheer pleasure of living and Witch, lying at Rhea's feet, had looked up at her as if wanting to join in the game.

Rhea had been painting the tail, painting every individual hair, seeking to put the flow and the shape on the paper, to put into it all the passionate pleasure she had felt, sitting watching.

Derek stood, considering it.

'Horses do something to you,' he said.

Rhea laughed. 'I don't know what; I can watch them for hours. Watch the foals, watch the mares; I can watch dogs too; greyhounds running. There's nothing like it for sheer perfection of movement. You can't paint movement, only suggest it; I always feel so frustrated. You crystallise an instant but what you need is to get every pose, to get the rhythm and the animal's glory in being alive. Humans never glory like that. We only half live.'

'Or less than half. Will this monster behave in my car or will she eat it?' He threw Witch's slipper and she pounced on it, delighted to be noticed. She brought it back, her small eager body full of pride, her head lifted, her tail waving.

'She'll behave,' Rhea said. 'I go to the dog club and train her and I know the local police sergeant and his little daughter. He's showing me how to teach Witch to search and track. It's terrific.'

'You have changed,' Derek said.

Rhea shook her head.

'No. I've become myself again. All those years I tried to be what John wanted, and perhaps that was why I never told him about my other self. I needed to keep that private, away from the family; family criticism can be so destructive. This was something of my own to reassure myself with when I was being John's wife and the boys' mother; and then a mother-in-law; and soon a grandmother. It's too many roles and you can't always be good at all of them but you always can be good at being the person you really are, if that person is the right kind of person.' She stopped, thinking of Agnes and her accusations.

'I'm not at all sure that John might not have found Ray

Morton more exciting than Rhea Morland,' Derek said, as they closed the door behind them, and then, seeing Rhea's expression, wished he hadn't spoken.

Rhea, sinking into luxurious upholstery, listening to the engine as the very expensive limousine whispered along, thought how her life had changed. Once she would have taken this for granted; John had always liked exotic cars. She had often felt they couldn't afford them, couldn't afford any of the luxury with which he surrounded them, and that life would have been happier with less expense. Life was simpler now; she knew exactly what she wanted and it wasn't luxury. Enough comfort and enough food; a few good friends and a little time for talk, but above all she had time for her own real passion; to spend her hours painting, striving with every brush stroke to get down exactly how she saw the horse, exactly how she felt about horses, so that when she had finished the picture was alive, the animal leaping out of the canvas, every muscle saying, 'Look at me.'

She hadn't yet done that with her own stallion, although she had painted him a number of times. His essence eluded her. Perhaps because of Rory. He wasn't entirely hers; she owned him but he didn't belong to her; she didn't tend him, didn't ride him. Nor did she ride this filly she was painting, but that had worked. Anyone looking at that painting would know just how she felt and how the filly felt, that it was wonderful to be so beautiful, so vital, to move against the wind, to gallop in the sunshine, to feel full of health and strength. The future mother of great foals; the future winner of many shows; all her potential in the painting.

'I thought you were wrong to move,' Derek said. 'I think now you were right. Had you stayed the boys would have absorbed you into their lives; or Louise would. She would never have learned to stand on her own feet or to cope; she'd have rung you whenever life treated her badly.'

'You knew her as a little girl?' Rhea thought she remembered the two families had been close friends. Louise was almost the same age as Derek's younger daughter.

'Very well. She worshipped Anna. You know how positive Anna is about anything; full of self confidence all the time.

Louise followed her like a little dog, and whenever she needed a champion to fight for her, Anna was elected and somehow Anna adopted the role of protector. Louise was always too spoiled, she had all she wanted and more, and her mother never expected her to face reality. She sheltered her from living.'

'And now?' Rhea wondered what life held in store for Louise, who seemed to run away whenever things went wrong and never face them.

'I don't know. Anna has her own life and rarely sees her now; she's going to be very good at her job and she's very busy, even if she has taken up a very obscure sort of profession.' Anna, much to everyone's surprise, had become a pilot and was flying for a charter firm that was widely known all over the world. She was, when she chose, extremely feminine, but she rarely chose. Her work was important to her, and that always came first.

Rhea looked up at the sky. A foam of soft cloud obscured the blue. It must be very peaceful up there, high above the earth away from all the pettiness, soaring like a bird. She wondered briefly about the world of the eagle and a picture took shape in her mind; the soaring eagle and the mountains below and horses racing across the moors. In a moment she had forgotten the world about her, trying to think in terms of shape and colour, to plan the way it would look when finished, and Derek, realising she had lost herself in a reverie, drove on, saying nothing.

They left the town behind and were up among the hills. Fields, patched with hedges, rose towards the sky. They stopped where heather and bracken met the road, and let Witch gallop down towards the rocky river, where she drank.

'Lunch,' Derek said. 'Here. I'm tired of cities; for just one day I'm going back to nature, too. I think perhaps I envy you, Rhea.'

She wondered if he would envy her if he knew of the past months and the misery she had lived through, but the past was past and not to be brooded over. Maybe too she had over-reacted; grief did odd things and though she hadn't realised it, her misery had been very deep and there was no one at all to talk to about John. No one who had known him; no one who would understand.

'John hated picnics,' Rhea said, watching Derek as he brought out a basket from the back of the car.

'I know. We love them and Betty remembered how much you enjoyed one picnic you and she took the children on, long ago. She suggested it. She knows people well and always said you would have preferred a much simpler life-style. John loved success and all it brought him.'

'I think maybe it was his rebellion against his puritan upbringing,' Rhea said, calling Witch to lie beside her, panting with her exercise. She took a smoked-salmon sandwich. 'Who made these?'

'It's what the hotel call an executive lunch pack,' Derek said. 'I hoped your desire for the simple life wouldn't extend to food. There's a bottle of wine as well; not a great vintage. Betty's orange wine. Do you remember?'

Rhea laughed, suddenly feeling as if she were fifteen again and all the years were rolling away. Betty and she had shared a bottle of orange wine on one dreadful night when Betty's youngest son had been rushed to hospital for an emergency appendix removal. The two husbands had come in to find their wives rather the worse for wear, giggling over nothing as they prepared baked beans on toast for the children. Derek had fetched another bottle and joined them, but John had sat stiffly disapproving, and had been very cool for more than a week. Anger always made him silent. Rhea felt she had let him down badly, and always, when entertaining, made her one glass of wine last the whole evening, afraid to relax.

It was peaceful sitting on the rug in the heather, the dog lying beside her. She offered Witch a tiny morsel of her sandwich. The world was remote and they were beyond it, nothing mattering. Derek, lying back against a rock, watching water ripple over rock, watching a hovering kestrel, thought lazily of his own wife. Betty would love this; he must bring her here one day.

Rhea was absorbed in the scene. Dark hills in the distance, the fresh green of young bracken, the springing branches of the heather, the white of distant sheep, roaming freely; the shape of bushes against the skyline. Her fingers itched to be drawing. She wanted to draw the river, the sparkle on the water when the sun came out, the shape of the flower at her feet, a tiny yellow flower on a slender stem. She was in unknown country for the first time. She had not explored beyond the town, and she wished she had her sketch book with her. She must come out here. She could draw and lay a track for Witch and fill her pocket with tiny objects that the bitch, now almost eight months old, could search for. She loved hunting for hidden toys.

'I know quite a few people in the horse world,' Derek said. 'Has your stallion any progeny yet?'

'I never asked,' Rhea said. 'It would be nice to have news of his sons and daughters. He's eight now; he must have sired some in his life. I didn't ask Rory.'

'Why did you buy him?'

'Rory needed to sell him. I needed to have something I'd lost; to re-capture my girlhood; to have a stake in horses again. My father owned a stud. My grandfather owned a stud. My great-grandfather bred Shires. The family history is all round horses and all I could do was to paint them. I never had the money to buy them; and now I need to paint and I haven't the time to care for them. It's a silly world, isn't it?'

The orange wine brought back memories and she laughed as she sipped.

'John was so angry,' she said. 'Getting tight on orange wine.'

'John never really outgrew his puritan upbringing,' Derek said. 'He was often very disapproving. He was also very intense and he cared passionately about his work and always did more than his best. He was very reliable.'

'He almost never laughed,' Rhea said, and for some reason that eluded her, it was suddenly more than she could bear, and she jumped to her feet and whistled to Witch and walked until the tears had stopped falling.

Behind her, Derek packed the basket, and wondered if the picnic had really been all that good an idea.

14

That night, Rhea knew the picnic had, in some ways, been a mistake. Memory returned and with it grieving. Derek had been a major part of their lives, and she could see both men vividly; Derek tall and thin and almost violent in his ways, his now grey hair then red, a flaming thatch that went with his temperament.

He was often angry, often forceful, often dramatic, mounting passion ruling his head, and sometimes his extravagant language infuriated John. John beside him was a slender man, a very elegant man, cool, always in full control of his temper, using his tongue to hurt, capable of biting sarcasm that was far more painful than any physical demonstration of anger.

Somehow, seeing Derek had brought back the bad times instead of the good. All triggered by a glass of orange wine. The nights she had sat alone, agonising because one of the boys was ill when they were small; the nights she had waited up, knowing that one of her sons was out and was driving. Both of them seemed to be fast and reckless for some years, one car after another being written off. They came home with hair-raising descriptions of near misses, of how they had been almost killed.

In time she learned to discount it; to isolate herself from them, to armour herself against worry by her painting. Witch came to lie at her feet and to look up adoringly into her face, willing Rhea to notice her, but all she received was an absent-minded stroke on the head. Yet her presence was comforting. Without her this place would be dead, Rhea thought. Nobody moving except me; no sound unless I turn on the radio, nothing to listen to except the clock ticking away the remaining minutes of my life.

No one beside me in the dark. No breathing in the room, no hand to hold as an anchor against fear, against age, against loneliness. And when I am old, what then? Who will care?

She made herself a small meal and could not eat it. She drank coffee and knew she would regret it as she would now be unable to sleep. She drew the curtains against the threatening dark. Out there were the lonely woods and the foxes slinking. An owl cried, a mourning keen that made her shiver, and that sent Witch to the window barking. Who stalked out there in the night? Why had she moved to such an isolated place? What had she been thinking about? Yet it had seemed so peaceful; no close neighbours, no prying eyes. No one to intrude.

She had not cried when John died. Today she had felt tears too near the surface, and now, suddenly, months of misery released themselves and she was unable to stop. Witch, disturbed, came to her and pawed her and she took the dog in her arms and lay on the floor beside her, wishing that life could end. No one could feel like this and live.

She longed for someone to call; for the phone to ring, for the heavy bang on the knocker that would bring her company, but nothing moved except the wind in the trees. Far away a fox yelped. Far away a train went through the tunnel, its hooter sounding, one-two, a train with people aboard, speeding to home, people who had families to return to, who had husbands to greet them, who had a life that was full of interest.

All she had was the bitch that licked her face desperately, trying to shake her out of the depression that had seized her. She wished Derek had never called. He had meant it kindly but she wasn't ready yet to come to terms with the past. She saw herself as a failure; a wife who wanted her own life and maybe neglected her husband; would John have preferred Ray Morton? Was Ray Morton a different person? She knew now that she was; she was more alive, more intense, more open to the world outside than she had ever been before. It had been hard to be wife and mother and also try to paint; and she had needed to paint so desperately.

Did all women feel like this?

Singers, writers, dancers, actresses? Was it wrong to be born with a talent that set you apart? Was it wrong to aspire to the stars? To want to leave something behind in the world that others might cherish? To improve on craftsmanship?

How did you combine two worlds, two lives – maybe more than two as whatever a woman did, wherever she worked, even if she were holding high office, at the end of the day she was still a woman and on her devolved all the household chores: the laundry and the shopping; the meal planning and the cooking; the organisation of the family. It was a full-time job in itself, yet so many women did two jobs. Diplomat, keeping rival sons from major jealousies; juggler, trying to keep a husband's affection when too tired to want anything but to sleep for a week on end; always manager, somehow making every penny do the work of two as no matter how much a man earned, it never seemed enough. Hostess, dressing for his friends; trying always to do him credit. Now she had no need to try any more and yet it was not a pleasure. She had to learn to be alone. She thought she had succeeded until today, when she had discovered that all she had done was push her feelings down, never allowing them to erupt, keeping herself calm and sensible when it might have been better to explode, to yell and to throw things.

The little French clock struck one.

Rhea sat up. Witch was pawing her, needing to go outside, and she went out with her into the windy dark, leaving the door ajar and the light flinging a wide lance across the lawn. Thorpe and Wilde between them had fenced her garden. She watched Witch roam, sniffing at first one patch of grass and then another; once she pounced, as if on a mouse, but there was nothing there. She returned to Rhea, tail waving, her body ecstatic, loving the night and the dark, the scents on the ground and the whole wild world that was her heritage and which she would only know in brief moments, living a life as alien as was human life.

That was an odd thought. Rhea pondered it, looking up at the starry dark. The little garden was shaping now, and she loved working in it; she had planted roses and lavender and thyme, remembering her grandmother's garden. She hadn't thought of her grandmother in years, but she saw her now, small, determined, white haired, resolutely attacking the weeds as if they were personal enemies. She had had a beautiful garden; smooth lawns, herb gardens and rose beds, and had been famous for winning almost every flower award at every show. She had loved flower arranging, and, looking back, Rhea knew that she had been an artist in her own way.

She had specialised in exquisite miniatures, egg-cup small, each tiny flower carefully chosen, the colours perfect. Perhaps Rhea could remember some of the arrangements and reproduce them and copy them. Rachel had always said that flower pictures sold well.

Slowly, peace returned. Looking up at the stars brought life into perspective again. Those pinpoints of glittering light would shine there in years to come when earth was only a memory in time: when there was no one and nothing left, only a burned-out ball, perhaps as dead as the moon, whirling through infinity. Did human affairs matter so much?

She watched Witch, full of self-importance, bristle with anger and growl softly. There were footsteps in the night. She took hold of the bitch's collar and stood, wary, about to run indoors and slam the bolts.

A voice called out and Witch barked.

'It's all right, Mrs Morland. It's only me.' Thorpe was on his last patrol. 'You're late up,' he said.

'I couldn't sleep. Would you like to come in and have a coffee? I'm lonely tonight.' She regretted the words almost as soon as she said them.

'Happens to us all at times,' Thorpe said matter-of-factly. He followed her indoors, standing the unloaded gun in the corner. 'I usually pass by, just to make sure. It's isolated here.'

Rhea, busy with the kettle, suddenly remembered the pointer that always accompanied him.

'Where's Blue?'

'Lying at the gate till I want him. He knows the drill,' Thorpe said. 'It's just a matter of doing the same thing the same way so the dog learns to live with you and do just what you want. Your bitch is coming on. I've seen you training her. I thought . . .'

His voice trailed off as he realised the words might be better unsaid. Rhea's eyes were still red; grief took a long time to ease, as he knew only too well and for a moment an old memory returned to plague him, so that he frowned angrily, trying to shake it off.

'You thought I would never train her and she'd cause trouble,' Rhea said.

'Something like that.'

The coffee was hot and strong, just as he liked it. Rhea, as she handed it to him, turned to the mirror and saw her own face, bearing only too plainly the signs of misery. She looked a mess. Too late now to do anything about it. It would make it even more obvious.

She had made herself cocoa. She sat, sipping it.

'A friend of my husband's called today,' she said. 'It brought back . . . memory.'

'You never know when it will hit,' Thorpe said. 'I was married once. She loved winter jasmine; I can't bear the stuff now.'

They sat in silence, both remembering. Thorpe hadn't talked of Jenny in years; Jenny with her bright face and laughing eyes; Jenny with the baby inside her, fainting, the doctor said, at the top of the stairs, and falling, with no one in the house to help her; there had been poachers that night. Five of them, after the salmon. It had taken half the night to catch up with them, and then he had to make a statement to the police. When he got back to Jenny it was too late for both her and the baby.

'My wife fell downstairs when I was out at night; chasing poachers,' Thorpe said. 'She had no one to help her and she bled to death. The baby came too soon.'

He hadn't said the words before, ever; hadn't admitted even to himself that it had happened like that; now he felt as if he had eased his soul. Maybe that was why Roman Catholics went to confession.

'It makes a man bitter, a thing like that,' Thorpe said.

Rhea nodded. She could not think of anything to say; no words could bring comfort, no trite phrases of sympathy. Nobody would understand the yawning gulf between those who had suffered and those who had not, she thought. Or the darkness of despair that waited in the depths of the night when you wondered how you had failed those you had loved. Nothing could make up to them for past slights and past miseries.

'I wish sometimes I could live those years again,' Rhea said, and then thought that even that was the wrong thing to say, as she had had years of marriage and he had had so little.

Thorpe drained his mug and walked over to the easel. He looked at the mare, dancing in the sunlight, joy in every stroke of the brush.

'You've put life on paper,' he said. 'That's a gift to treasure; life . . . you see it, out there. I hate destroying the foxes. There's nothing like a dogfox and vixen courting, playing together, enjoying one another's company, loving one another in a wild animal way. People say animals don't love; but you watch a bull seal court a female; a mare running with a stallion, the two of them old friends, even before they were put together, knowing one another from their youth; see a wise dog court a young inexperienced bitch; see a vixen with her cubs, and see the pups come to their dam and lift their noses. It makes you wonder.'

'Living for the moment,' Rhea said, wondering how it felt to be young again, with the wild wonder of newness on everything; the first time you went to the zoo; the first date; the first dance; the first day at school. Some of it was terrifying in retrospect; some of it had an air about it that was difficult to recall. She had broken her wrist the day she was to play in the first eleven for the first time. Her family had laughed at her agony; she had been sixteen and life then was all black and white. Politicians had been heroes then, men of stature to be revered; now they were tired and seedy and sometimes corrupt and the press gloried in revealing their deficiencies. There were no heroes left; her childhood men were tainted by the truths that now were told and she thought of Chesterton writing of Fleet Street:

'All the truths men talk in hell
And all the lies they write . . .'

176

'I never can put down what I really want to put down,' she said now, as Thorpe went on looking at the filly, revelling in the picture, admiration in his eyes.

'I want to grab people by the hand, say look, look, look. Watch her run, watch her mane fly and her tail lift, watch the pride of her, and the confidence and the beauty; look at the ripple of muscles under her hide; look at the shine on her skin; look at her eyes. I want to get their attention, make them stop and think and see what's there. So many live in cages, live in traps . . .'

'You belong here,' Thorpe said.

It was the biggest compliment he could have paid her.

He lifted his gun, and went out into the darkness and whistled his dog. She heard a soft whimper from Blue, and then watched as the moonlight showed the man and the dog striding out without a backward look. A strange life, she thought as she went in, alone for ever at night, patrolling to keep the wild birds safe for men to shoot. How idiotic could life get?

Sleep was as far away as ever.

She did not want to work on the mare. Instead she took her sketch book and began to sketch a man, small as an ant, a dog behind him, walking through a world of mountains and towering crags, of threatening clouds and huge trees, trees that twisted inimically towards him, thrusting contorted branches; the dog was part of him, almost growing out of his leg, and somehow she wanted to make it the man's protector. But the picture wouldn't say what she wanted.

She drew on till dawn lightened the sky, let Witch out and then went wearily to bed, feeling as if she had lived through twelve months since the day before. She was not destined to sleep long. There was a knock on the door just after eight and she woke and went to open it, knotting the girdle of her towelling robe around her.

Dave stood there.

'I'm sorry; I didn't mean to get you up. Are you busy?'

'I'm not awake,' Rhea said. 'Is something wrong?'

'Reg's little Maxie's vanished; we don't know when,' Dave said unhappily. 'They're searching now. I wondered if we could try Witch; she's able to track Susie; she might just manage. We haven't enough dogs . . . Rand has had a lump on his leg removed and is lame. Trojan's got a throat infection; and one of my best dogs has just been retired and he really isn't up to having a day's work. I've sent for him, but they're fifty miles away, and I'm feeling frustrated and helpless. I thought you might like to help; there are civilians searching too; she's so little – she's a monkey, so we hope she's safe.'

'Make me a coffee and I'll come,' Rhea said. She went off to dress fast, dragging on blouse and trousers, lacing her shoes, fingers all thumbs, finding Witch's tracking harness. The bitch raced at her, seeing it, knowing they were going to work.

Dave did not wait to boil the kettle. Impatience mastered him. He wanted to be off; wanted every available dog hunting. Susie was out with her collie, desperate to find the little girl. She was almost five. No one had seen her vanish; one moment she had been there and the next gone and at first the hunt had been round the houses and kennels, thinking she might have wandered off and fallen asleep somewhere.

Minutes lengthened to hours and fear grew.

Fear.

It was always there. Dave had seen too much; knew too much; had found too many victims of other people's madness. He feared for Susie; he feared for every child that wandered on its own. And this time he could not summon his professional armour because it wasn't just another child; it was the little girl who came to tea; the little girl playing round the kennels making them all laugh as she tried to master the big dogs.

'Trojan heel.' 'Trojan sit.'

And the big dog obeyed her and the men grinned at one another and prophesied a great future as a dog-handler for Maxie, who revelled in their approval. The small girl played with Susie endlessly, loving her, following her, wanting to be big like Susie, to have her own dog like Susie.

He watched Rhea drink the coffee down. He had made her a marmalade sandwich, which she found utterly revolting but it was better to eat. He checked the windows and doors, checked that she had her key and hurried her unceremoniously to the van. His own dog was inside and Witch, who had travelled there often before, jumped happily into the other compartment, her tail wagging furiously, knowing only that they were off for fun.

'If only we could care as little as the dogs,' Dave said and started the van with a scream of tyres, driving fast down the ride towards the road. Rhea said nothing; there wasn't anything to say. She thought of the child, somewhere out there on her own. The sky had clouded and rain was beginning. She would be drenched; she would be frightened; she would be hungry.

The police kennels were transformed; there seemed to be policemen everywhere; inside the office someone had a map and was pinpointing places to search.

'She couldn't have gone far,' Rhea said and then realised as the men turned to look to her that she might have been picked up by a car, might have been taken anywhere, might have had unspeakable things done to her, and she felt sick.

'There's a field beyond the houses where the children sometimes play,' Dave said. 'No one has searched it yet; if you take one side and I take the other we'll cover the ground in half the time. You just let Witch seek out whatever is there; you never know, we might be lucky.'

They drove off again, down the road, parking by the fence. The field was enormous, a rough area of ground with hiding places that children might well love; places for dens; places to play houses; places in which a small girl might lie dead, unseen, for days. Rhea shivered. Her own troubles seemed remote as she thought of Reg and his wife.

'Is Reg searching too?' she asked.

'Yes. But not well ... Heather's over with Mair. She's always a tower of strength,' Dave said and wondered why when people were upset they always talked in clichés.

He showed Rhea where to start. This was something she had never done; the bitch had always had a laid pattern to follow. Now they were hunting for real; and there were rabbits here, and partridges too, as one flew up suddenly from beside her, and flew off, its wings whirring.

Dave was gone, his walk purposeful.

She was on her own and was struck for a moment by absurdity

as she wasn't up to this sort of work and nor was Witch, but at least they were trying; they were doing something that might be useful. She let out the tracking line, and watched the little bitch begin to hunt for a trail to follow. She was baffled; there was nothing there; nothing that was recognisable. She turned to look at Rhea, who moved on.

A moment later Witch had put her head down and was moving determinedly. She was on some track, but heaven knew what. She lost the track and came back to Rhea who stood still and encouraged her. 'Good girl, seek.' If only she knew what they were following.

The bitch put her nose down again. There was something on the ground. A piece of paper, part of a Mars bar. It couldn't be of any value, but Rhea picked it up, as Witch was determined that her find should not be overlooked. She felt a sudden surge of feeling for Louise's baby, so soon to be born. Suppose this were her grandchild?

The ground was rough and very uneven. She twisted her ankle in a small scrape that was possibly done by a fox, seeking to bury his food after killing. She paused to allow time to recover and went on as Witch pulled her. The bitch was tracking now, and tracking determinedly.

Dave had turned his head and was watching her.

The trail led through a bramble bush which was painful, and also it was unlikely any child had come this way. It led through deep grass and through a wet boggy patch where Rhea sank ankle deep in black mud and cursed, because she had not worn Wellingtons. Uncomfortable, her shoes squelching, she plodded on, the line taut, the bitch pulling excitedly. Something was there.

There was a faint noise from a bush. The bitch raced across to it, and into it, and re-appeared, carrying some object in her mouth. She came to Rhea and Rhea took her burden gently. It was a kitten, perhaps two months old, soaked and pathetic, half starved, ribs plainly visible under the draggled fur, but very much alive and mewing in desperate hunger.

Dave came across.

'That's all we need,' he said. 'I'd hoped . . .'

180

He had no need to voice his hope. He ducked into the bushes.

'There's nothing else here.'

They went back to the van, the kitten tucked into Rhea's coat to warm it. It purred; someone must have dumped it. It was far from wild; or maybe it too had wandered away.

'We'd better get Heather to feed it and dry it and hand it over to the RSPCA.' Dave's mind was only half on the kitten. He was reviewing the neighbourhood, trying to think of places that might attract a small girl.

'Maxie's so little,' Susie said forlornly. She had taken Trot's harness off and one of the men had insisted she sit down and drink coffee and eat a sandwich. Her small face was white and her eyes were shadowed.

'She's too young for this,' Rhea thought and then wondered how much the child heard about what went on; she would hear the men talking; she would perhaps know when her father was out on a serious case; she would read the papers. Children were no longer protected and innocent; they saw men die on the news bulletins as the television camera zoomed in on the bodies. How was it the media were there, Rhea wondered, in at the kill, filming life as if it were another form of entertainment; did they care, these young men with their eagerness for red-hot news, did they realise these were people, with feelings, people whose relatives could be hurt, people who were entitled to privacy but who died as red-hot news and whose dead bodies were shown to millions all over the world, before they were given the decency and dignity of oblivion.

There was a TV camera in the yard now, and an interviewer talking to the Inspector, who listened with weary patience, anxious to get on with the job. This child meant more to the men in some ways than a child they'd never met, yet they could do no more for her than for any child; it just made it worse, knowing her. Reg had come in and smoked two cigarettes in quick succession, downed a cup of coffee, gone in to see his wife and driven off again with his dog. He had more chance than any as the dog knew the child so well.

Vans drove in and out.

There had to be a plan but Rhea couldn't see one; she was

181

feeling slightly sick after her hasty breakfast. What had made the child wander? Or had someone passed and picked her up? Suppose it was an attempt at ransom, hitting at the police themselves, asking perhaps for a notorious criminal to be released in exchange?

She was perverted by the media; too many TV serials; too many police films; too much crime. As if there were nothing else. Drama, for everyone; even when she came here they had invented drama. People lived such dull lives; they needed more interest and could only get it by peeking in on others.

It was so much more interesting to be a famous film star. Or was it, when in the end you grew old and had nothing to do but see the re-runs of the days when you were a beauty? That must be hell, Rhea thought wearily.

She looked at her watch. It was just after eleven. Witch was lying asleep at her feet. How lucky dogs were.

Heather came in, carrying a tray full of steaming cornish pasties. Heather's thoughts in emergencies always turned to food. Feed them and they could stand anything, was her motto, more than obvious by her own very ample form.

'Eat,' she said. 'Wars aren't fought on empty stomachs and you'll be no good if you don't. Doctor's been and Mair's had a sedative and she's asleep. Come on, Susie love, no use sitting there looking like a wet weekend; keep your pecker up, and you, Mrs Morland too; you look as if you need feeding; like a drink of water, you are to look at. No body at all. Not like me. Look at her, lads; and then look at me; make two of her, wouldn't I?'

She was trying her best, Rhea thought, but somehow the cheerfulness grated. It was no use glooming, but it was impossible to avoid doing so.

The pasty was hot and was delicious. Heather was a first-class cook and the food heartened all of them. Maybe hunger did make you glum; maybe Heather owed her ability to cheer up any situation to her plumpness and her ability to eat no matter what went wrong in her life.

Heather had gone and returned with a plate full of scones. Plainly no one was going to starve while she was around. They were hot from the oven and lavishly covered in butter. She had shut the door firmly, excluding the people from the TV networks. There seemed to be more of them now, and a couple more men who must be reporters.

There were civilians congregating in the yard and one of the local radio men had offered to help with the search. Dave was studying the map morosely, wondering if there were any hideouts they hadn't covered; wondering if there was any news of a car cruising in the area picking up a tiny girl.

'Report from a woman down the road that her small son's tricycle's been pinched,' one of them said 'As if we hadn't enough to worry about.'

'Keep your eye out for it,' Dave said wearily. 'Anything else that could tie in?'

'Mrs Grundy has seen a Martian come down and pick up a little girl with red hair; the Martian was in a flying saucer. It had huge yellow eyes.'

'I wish they'd put her in a flying saucer,' somebody said. 'She's always the first on the blower.'

'She's harmless so long as she sticks to seeing Martians,' Dave said. 'Nothing else?'

'Not a whisper. A lost purse; a lost dog . . .' he paused.

'No lost kitten?' Rhea asked. The tiny ginger mite had been taken off by Heather, who was clucking loudly over it and would doubtless be busy with towel and heater and a drink of milk. Heather couldn't help mothering everything and everyone.

The phone rang.

There was instant silence, and everyone turned to look at it as if it were a personal enemy. It could be bringing good news; or bad news; or no news. Dave found himself picking it up with dread, clutching the receiver tightly, willing the voice at the other end to bring the kind of news he needed to hear and not the news he was afraid it might give him.

Rhea was aware that the men were watching as intently as she. Susie had paused, one hand halfway to her mouth, forgetting the scone she held. The butter dripped from it, unnoticed, on to the table. The men had put down their cups. Witch, alerted by the tension in the room, was growling softly, and Rhea quieted her, praying so hard that it hurt.

183

Please God, not bad news. Please God, not bad news.

Once as a little girl she had made a bargain with God. Please don't let it happen. I'll be good for ever.

One of the penalties of growing up was that you knew there was never any chance of a bargain. What was to be would be. Would Dave never speak into that phone?

He was speaking now.

'Police dog kennels. Sergeant Martin speaking.'

The room was so silent that Rhea could hear the ticking clock, and far away a car that revved its engine noisily and then hooted. A dog in a van outside started a frenzied barking as one of the TV camera men came too near the van. The door opened and Heather came in again, and stood staring at Dave, who was standing holding the phone as if it were glued to him, listening intently.

Please God, no, Rhea whispered, and looked at Heather who was crying silently, large tears rolling down her cheeks, showing at last that all the cheerfulness had been only a veneer and that the day's events had taken too much toll. She put her arms around the older woman and they stood together, waiting to hear what message had been relayed, sharing terror.

15

Susie was standing close to Rhea, waiting, watching her father. Dave spoke briefly, and then, incredibly, began to smile. In a moment he was laughing and his thumb went up. Relief lightened the room at once, and Reg went over to stand by the phone.

'I'll send her dad. Little monkey!' Dave said, and put the receiver down.

'She's OK. She was found sound asleep in a garage on a pile of old carpet they had put out for the dust collection, with the tricycle beside her, about three miles from here.'

'A tricycle?' Reg looked bewildered.

'Must be the one that got pinched; your small daughter's going to need sorting out,' Dave said, and everyone grinned at the thought.

'What was she doing?' Reg asked, shrugging on his coat. 'And where is she? Heather, go and tell everyone it's OK.' Heather was already out of the room, and Rhea stood feeling as if someone had just relieved her of immense pressure.

'She was going to London to see the Queen,' Dave said. 'Funny; kids do the oddest things.'

There was a wail from Susie and she rushed out of the room, leaving the men staring after her.

'I'll see what's wrong,' Rhea said, as Dave was obviously going to be busy for some time, with calls to relay to the searchers still out, and the address to give to Reg, and a number of other things to do to complete the morning's work and report a successful ending.

'We'll be lunching in the Jester and Bells to celebrate,' Dave called after her. 'Join us.'

There was a babble of laughter and chatter from the men. Rhea, listening, thought how quickly moods changed; they had all been expecting disaster and now relief had made them almost drunk. Reg was already on his way, his little van driving swiftly out of the entrance and turning into the lane. Children, Rhea thought as she went indoors and found Susie clutching Trot and sobbing desperately.

'She's safe, love,' she said, sitting down to offer comfort and a shoulder to cry on.

'It was my fault,' Susie wailed.

'How could it be your fault?' Rhea was mystified.

Susie sat up and wiped her eyes. She tried very hard to control herself. 'I told her a story about a little girl who had a red tricycle and went up to London to see the Queen and the Queen gave her strawberry pancakes for tea.'

Rhea restrained a desperate desire to laugh. 'And you probably told her stories about little girls and boys who threw kittens in wells, and stole pigs, and blew their horns and little girls who lost sheep and sat on tuffets,' Rhea said. 'We all do. You can't see into a little child's mind; she must have caught sight of the red tricycle outside the garden gate and it put it into her mind; there's no harm done now. One of my boys tried to fly after seeing Peter Pan and fell off the settee and hurt himself very badly, and lots of children fall over and hurt themselves whizzing round like Wonder Woman. One little girl I know fell against a fence doing it and cut her head. You can't ever think of everything a child will do . . . or a dog either.'

Trot was pushing his head against Susie's knee.

'Go and wash,' Rhea said. Dave was walking across the yard. She went out to tell him why Susie was so upset and he grinned ruefully.

'Kids. Tell her we're all going out to lunch; it's a nice day and we can sit outside and she can help celebrate. She loves Maggie's beef butties. She'll feel better if she knows that's ahead of her.' He went back to the office as the telephone began to ring. Rhea went next door to see Heather and to make sure that Reg's wife was feeling happier. She found a small party in progress and was offered a glass of sherry to celebrate.

Everyone was laughing and talking at once. Three of the men who had been off duty, but had come to help in the search, had come in and seemed to fill the little sitting room.

By lunchtime Maxie was tucked up in bed, sound asleep, and though Reg elected to stay with his wife, everyone else piled in to vans and drove off to the Jester and Bells, where Dave had ordered already. Rhea, squashed against a very large police dog-handler, almost on his lap, Witch behind her in the van, felt suddenly accepted and belonging. Everyone had come to talk to her and Reg had thanked her for troubling to help in the search, so that even though she and Witch had only played a tiny part, merely by being there, she was aware of rising happiness and a genuine interest in living that had been lacking ever since John had died.

The euphoria lasted through lunch. There were ten of them in the party besides Rhea and Susie. Susie sat quiet, listening, once or twice answering when somebody teased her. She reached under the table for Rhea's hand and squeezed it. Inside the inn a juke box played noisy music, but outside the sun shone warm, the small tables were gay with bright red and white umbrellas, and the neat flowerbeds brilliant with massed flowers. Nothing seemed quite real.

The men were soon discussing tracks and searches; two in the corner speculated on the winner of that afternoon's major race; Rhea sat back, feeling the sun on her face, glad to be part of a group for once, instead of by herself, aware that she now had a slightly different status.

'Need to give that pup of yours a track she can do,' Dave said as they got up to go. 'She'll only remember failure. Let's get back and get her out and she can track for a piece of tripe.'

'I gave Trot his sweetener,' Susie said and her father grinned at her.

'Big professional words now, is it?' he said. He pulled her ear gently. 'We'll make an expert out of you yet.'

Rhea grinned. Every dog that worked without success was given a track with a certain reward at the end.

Susie came to watch the track being laid for Witch. It was very simple, only a few yards long, with Dave giving her the scent of the stinking tripe. Rhea loathed undressed tripes but the dogs always adored them. Witch caught the scent and stood screaming with excitement, eager to be off.

A moment later the tripe was on the ground and Rhea was almost flat on her face as the bitch leaped into action, pulling frantically along the ground, nose down until she found her trophy and gobbled it fast.

'She'll remember that next time out,' Dave said, with satisfaction. 'It never does to let them fail. Remember to go back and do something easy for a change; if they have a hard time, they're like us. Nobody approves of us and we turn crochety; be part of everything and life has a new savour. That's why I like my work so much; we're a good team here. Have our moments, but who doesn't?'

It was time for work; time for Rhea to go. She put Witch into her car, and was about to start the engine, when Reg tapped on the window. Tony was beside him.

'He's made you a present as a thank you for finding his sister,' he said.

'I didn't find her,' Rhea said in surprise.

'No, but he adores your little bitch and is sure Witch really found her; it isn't much,' Reg said.

The small boy was looking at Rhea with solemn eyes. Blond hair floated in the wind.

He handed Rhea a lump of plasticine that looked rather more like a dinosaur than anything else.

'It's a horse,' he said. 'Daddy says you paint horses so I thought you could paint him.'

Rhea looked at Reg whose eyes were alight with amusement, but his face was as solemn as hers. She got out of the car and knelt and kissed Tony, surprised at the slight feel of the tiny body against her. It was so long since she had hugged a little child. In a few days she would be a grandmother. She leaned back on her heels and took the model.

'I will paint him for you to hang in your bedroom,' she promised. 'He's lovely. Has he a name?'

'Yes. He's called Tapioca Blancmange,' the small voice said and once more the two adults had to control their lips. Rhea kissed him again.

'I must go home and do all the things I haven't done,' she said.

The small boy nodded.

'Ladies always have a lot to do; washing and cooking. Have you any babies?'

'Not now. I did have, and I'm going to be a grannie soon. Have you a grannie?'

The solemn nod came again.

'Two grannies. You can be my fifth.'

'He's only three,' Reg said, as Tony ran into the lane.

'He's a darling.' Rhea's voice was warm, and she laughed as she put the misshapen little lump of plasticine on the passenger seat.

'I'll keep it on the mantelpiece; it will cheer me up when I feel bleak,' Rhea said.

'Come and see us if you feel bleak. Don't sit alone,' Reg said. He waved as Rhea started the car and she drove off down the lane, feeling totally lighthearted. It was seven months to the day since John had died. So much had happened since then, and there had been so much to hate, but she felt today as if she had been re-born. Nothing could go wrong on a day like this.

Home was welcoming; the garden taking shape, the cottage now furnished as she wanted it; and inviting. She made herself a cup of coffee and sat down to think over her future work. Megan had asked if she could do some black and white pictures of ponies, for prints; they would sell well to teenagers, who were often horse crazy, as she had been. She had two pictures in mind; one of a Shetland pony she had seen on her way home; and another of three horses running, the wind in their manes, ecstasy in every movement.

Maybe she could find a horse poem to go with the greyhound poem; and if she drew the greyhounds, in every pose she could think of, running round the outside of the poem, that too might make a seller. Even a best seller, as the words were lovely.

She did not realise that this was the first time she had made plans, and not drifted from moment to moment. She sat, revelling in the sunshine that flooded the room, in the bitch lying at her feet, head against her ankle, occasionally turning so that

189

deep brown eyes gazed up at Rhea, adoring her. She put down her hand, full of affection, and Witch sat up, and put both paws on Rhea's knees and looked deep into her eyes.

They held totally silent and complete communion.

The spell was broken by the ringing phone. As Rhea went to answer it, she wondered what the bitch had been trying to say; there was an attempt at communication that couldn't be ignored. All her body was eloquent, but her eyes spoke.

'Rory?'

Her voice held disbelief.

'Is it that important?'

She put the receiver down, looking at it, puzzled. What on earth could Rory have to say that couldn't be said on the phone and why such urgency? She felt her previous mood of content shatter and turn to worry. She wished she hadn't acted on impulse and bought the stallion, yet the stallion had helped her regain her own sanity. He had been something to own, to revel in, to plan around; when life held very little indeed.

Driving into the stable yard took her back as it always did to her childhood and their own stables. Rory had used the same plan, building round three sides of a square. The schooling field was beyond the loose boxes. Heads looked at her, and in the box in the far corner, Lucifer whinnied as she came in, now knowing her and sure she would have a carrot for him. She had forgotten, but one of the girls came forward and gave her one.

'Rory's indoors waiting for you,' she said.

'It's all very mysterious,' Rhea said.

'It's been like that for nearly a week,' the girl said, grinning. 'Just like the films.'

Rhea looked at her, and went indoors.

'This is Mrs Morland . . . Ray Morton in disguise,' Rory said. He glanced at her, and she looked back, trying to read his expression, but it told her nothing.

'I've two propositions to put to you,' the man who was standing in the window said to her. 'I'm Richard Narin . . . you won't know me, and Rory as usual forgot half the introduction.'

'Sorry,' Rory said. 'I was wondering what Rhea will say.'

'I'll have to hear them first,' Rhea said.

'I've an Arab stud in the south. I want pictures by Ray Morton of my three mares, of two foals, and of my best stallion. He's a world beater. Name your own price; I can meet it.'

'Then I'll ask ten million pounds,' Rhea said absurdly, and was rewarded by laughter.

'You accept?'

'I accept, but it'll take time; and I'll need to visit.'

'That's soon arranged. There's a cottage you can have and you can bring your bitch; no problem at all. I'll see you have household help and nothing to do but paint, and you'll eat with us . . . a very important visitor.'

Rhea was slightly dazed.

'Originals only; no copies ever.'

She nodded.

Rory handed her a glass of sherry. It seemed to be a day for celebration.

'And the second thing?'

'Would you sell me your stallion? I want him, badly. And I'm prepared to pay for him, too.'

'Is he that good?' Rhea asked.

'He's had a good year,' Rory said. 'I didn't know how to ask you; and I haven't yet told you, but the Derby winner is his son, out of a thoroughbred mare, and the filly that won the Oaks is his daughter; and there are four more of his sons beginning to make their mark in racing. It's only happened since you bought him; I've rather regretted selling him. You stand to make the most enormous profit.'

Rhea swallowed her sherry and held out the glass for more, then changed her mind.

'I can't take it in,' she said.

'You'll both stay for a meal?' Rory said.

Richard Narin shook his head.

'I have to get back. Will you sell?'

'The price?' Rhea asked. She had paid Rory ten thousand pounds and had since thought how crazy she had been.

'We thought two hundred thousand pounds,' Richard said.

Rhea looked down at her hands. She had misheard. No horse was worth that.

'You're joking.'

'No. There's money in his foals now; money in his stud fees. Rory has another young stallion coming on; and he thought maybe you could use the money.'

'You can buy another horse; a dozen horses; you can keep a mare here and start riding again,' Rory said. 'I'd make on the deal that way.'

'You agree?' Richard was insistent.

Rhea nodded.

The conversation floated past her head, and she had to rouse herself from a state of total unbelief to shake hands and say goodbye. All she could think of was her son's faces when she told them of the profit she'd made. She didn't need Lucifer now – life had begun again.

Rory came in, and looked at her.

'I think you have your revenge,' he said. 'I've been kicking myself for a total nut ever since I realised what was beginning to happen. He's sired a good number of foals in the years he's been at stud. Incidentally I owe you two more stud fees.'

'I'll go halves with you,' Rhea said. 'I can't take all that money; honestly, Rory, I'd no idea he was as valuable as that. Why did you sell him to me so cheaply?'

'I didn't know then,' Rory said. 'Things change fast. The Derby hadn't been run – nor the Oaks.'

'You've known how long?' Rhea asked.

'About ten weeks; that's for sure; I had an inkling before, when I began to check up. I just hadn't had time to think about it. We've been pushed for everything this year and life's been just this side of hell.'

'Pushed for money,' Rhea said. 'I'll have the money from the commissions. Would you like to buy him back and give me a small profit?'

'We share,' Rory said. 'Maybe I shouldn't even do that; I caught myself out; but I was pushed for cash at the time and that ten thousand made a hell of a lot of difference at the time.'

'Two hundred thousand?' Rhea asked. 'Are you sure he's worth that?'

Rory shrugged.

'One of the Olympic riders got eighty thousand pounds as

half share in a horse,' Rory said. 'You want to study the Newmarket prices. There's money in top-quality horseflesh. Not much down at the other end of the market.

'I nearly tried to buy him back two weeks ago; you'd never have known,' Rory said.

Rhea looked back at two weeks ago; she grinned and Rory, turning, caught her expression. 'I also thought I might marry you for all that money.'

'But you couldn't bear the thought,' Rhea said, half amused and half offended.

'It would never have worked; it wouldn't have worked before, would it? Be fair now. You were nineteen and an idealist; I was twenty-five and had no desire to settle down; oddly, all I really want in my life is horses. Women have a very second place; maybe it's twenty second, after every mare and every foal and every stallion. I'm not sure it's good to be born with a passion.'

'My father had it too,' Rhea said.

'And your mother . . . what life did she have?'

Rhea looked back into the past and was shocked to find that her mother was an almost forgotten figure; she had been around; she had been there; but they had never been close. And it was almost thirty years since she had died.

'Your mother loathed the horses and tried once to kill herself,' Rory said.

'I didn't know.' How could she not have known, she wondered.

'You were on holiday at your grandmother's. I found her. It was all hushed up. I think your mother had a very unhappy life, Rhea.'

He looked out of the window.

'My wife did too. But she got up and left me. Your mother could never stand alone; yet she had no one to lean against, ever. Your father barely knew she was there, I sometimes thought.'

Rhea thought back, remembering her father's long nights with foaling mares; sleeping in the foaling annexe night after night, never trusting even the head lad. He always had to be there, and he never went away. The horses came first;

speech days, sports days, her parents never came. It was a wonder he had even come to her wedding, she thought suddenly.

'Life's odd,' Rhea said. 'You never think about people; your parents . . . all the time they're there, through your childhood, yet you live your own life, intensely; they're on the outside, sometimes interfering, sometimes reprimanding, but somehow, you aren't aware of them as real people. I don't even know what my mother's hobbies were.'

'Crying,' Rory said, suddenly impatient. 'She was a very feeble person and your father despised her, I think. He made sure you were nothing like her.'

'Was he a kind man?' Rhea asked.

'To you, yes. He adored you. Besides, you were a very good rider. Your mother was afraid of horses. To other people, no. The horses were all important and if anyone did their work badly, he was cruel and ruthless with his tongue. We weren't allowed to be human; he wanted gods working for him, and do you know, most of the time he got them. I'm not sure that men like him aren't needed now; the young need driving and they don't know they need driving. And today few people drive them. Your father slept with his foaling mares because he never trusted anyone else; I sleep with them because my lads won't do overtime; and even the girls jib at it.'

He turned away from the window.

'I'm picking you up later in a taxi, and we're going out for a meal and we're going to have champagne; celebrate that sale. Do you mind very much losing him, Rhea? What did he mean to you?'

'Something vital and alive with a future; something outside myself, perhaps a bit of my past; perhaps a new meaning to a life that had lost its meaning. He was a symbol, I suppose. And a way of getting away from the family; they were threatening to swamp me in their lives and after being married for so long, always needing to be there for somebody else, never with needs of my own and with a growing feeling of selfishness because I did go off and paint, it was a way of finding out if I could stand alone.'

'You can. I think maybe you had a good marriage, Rhea. I'll

194

be over in three hours' time. Be ready. Will that animal of yours stay on her own?'

'She'll guard the house,' Rhea said.

She drove home, still bemused.

The phone was ringing as she opened the front door.

She ran to it, and picked up the receiver.

'Mother? It's a boy.' Mark's voice was elated, his excitement coming down the wire.

'Louise, is she all right?'

'She's splendid; she sends her love and says come and see your grandson soon. I can't stop, I'm at the office, and there's a crisis on; there would be, but I had to tell you as soon as I knew. I haven't seen her yet but I spoke to her on the phone.'

'Take her a dozen red roses from me,' Rhea said. 'I'll be over as soon as I can make it. I've a whole load of new commissions.'

'How's the stallion?'

'I sold him today,' Rhea said. 'I made a killing.'

'Mother, are you tight?' her son demanded, and she laughed.

'No, Mark, only happy . . . I'll see you soon.'

She rang off, and went into the garden and threw a quoit for Witch. Life was beginning to take shape again. Indoors, an hour late, she put the tiny plasticine model on the mantelpiece, resisting a desire to shape it anew. It had been made for her with love. One day her grandson would make her plasticine models too.

The phone rang again.

'Mother? I forgot. We're naming him John after Father.'

She managed to reply, and hide the fact that tears were falling. It had caught her unawares. She went to the cupboard and brought out the photograph she had been unable to face all these months because it hurt too much to remember.

Now she could remember without grief. The well-known face looked at her, the eyes a little remote, the mouth severe. She had not known till he died how much he had protected her; how much he had sheltered her; perhaps not wisely, but meaning so well.

Life could never be the same again, but now she had a future; she had work piling up and she had made friends. She had Megan as a partner; she would visit her grandchild and visit Rachel; she could go back without regrets and return home with pleasure. There was Dave, and Susie, and Reg and his family; and Heather. There was the dog club and she would train her dog and try and compete against the police; she would paint as she had never painted before.

She turned to look at the photograph again.

'We had a good marriage, John,' she told the pictured face. 'I think perhaps after all you prepared me for this.'

The doorbell rang, and she went to open it.

Rory stood there, a beautifully boxed orchid in his hand.

She pinned the delicate flower to her dress.

'Tonight we'll put the clock back and play Let's Pretend,' Rory said. 'The youngsters don't know how to do things in style, so let's show them. Madam, your equipage is waiting.'

She laughed as she went out to the waiting car, and stared at it.

'Rory, a Rolls. You're mad.'

He shook his head.

'I owe you an evening out. I know your coming here has changed your life, but oddly, it's changed mine too. I hadn't got many friends. I hope I can count on you; a man needs friends as he gets older, and someone who shared the past makes the best companion of all. I've a mare lined up for you. Will you ride again? I'm giving her to you if you'll take her, as an apology for long ago – I never realised till years later how badly I treated you.'

Rhea stepped into the Rolls and sank back into luxury. Witch was watching her through the window.

'I'd like that, Rory,' she said. 'And I need friends too. Thank you.'

There was, after that, only the silence of a companionship she had forgotten; someone with whom she had no need to pretend. Beyond the windows, the wind whispered in the trees, and as they got out of the Rolls, on reaching the restaurant, Rory looked up at the sky.

'A new moon. Turn your money and wish.'

'I've a new grandson to wish for,' Rhea said, and closed her eyes and wished for a good life for the baby, and freedom from fear.

'Then it's a double celebration,' Rory said. 'A day to remember, when life gets back again, as it will.'

She followed him inside.

Later, sitting over coffee he looked at her.

'The Valley of the Shadow of Death . . . have you ever thought about it?'

She shook her head.

'I had a son once; for two whole days. He was born with a heart defect. That was when our marriage began to go very wrong. And that was when I learned about that Valley and what those words really meant. The Shadow of Death; it's cast all round you and all over you. I'd set my heart on a son; to teach to love horses, to inherit all I'd worked for. Your father had too; and he had no son. I think that cast a shadow all his life. I lost my son . . . before I ever knew him. It's hard to understand when a baby dies; what's the point of it all? And then one day the shadows begin to lift. I think that today marks the end of your shadows . . . I wanted to help, Rhea, but nobody can. Shall we drink to the future; yours and mine?'

Rhea looked at him, and thought that one never really knew a person at all. Rory had not surprised her. He had astounded her. He understood far more than she had realised. She had been in the shadows, but the sun was breaking through and she wss suddenly filled with excitement at the thought of the Arab horses she was about to paint.

'To Ray Morton,' Rory said, and lifted his glass.

Light glittered on the champagne, which sparkled like sunlight on clear water.

'To the future,' Rhea said, 'and to Baby John.'

'I have another gift for you,' Rory said. 'I can't say thank you for my half share; words won't convey my feelings. I brought this as a thank you and hope you will accept it entirely as I mean it.'

He handed her a parcel.

She unwrapped it, and looked at the tissue inside.

Nestling against it, pefect in every detail, was a model of Lucifer.

'I know someone who sculpts,' Rory said. 'I had it made for myself, but I would like you to keep it, to remind you of months that you might prefer to forget. That is for a new beginning.'

Rhea found she couldn't speak, but her expression was enough.

That night, before going to bed, she looked at the plasticine model and the tiny perfect stallion, head arched, tail held high, an ever present reminder of what had been the unhappiest time in her life, yet a symbol of a future as yet unwritten, but that held excitement.

She switched off the light and looked out of the window. Thorpe was walking down the ride, on his patrol. Safeguarding her as well as his birds. The moon was high, a slender crescent, and the wind moved the branches of the trees, a soft whisper, that reminded Rhea of a murmuring sea.

The woods that once seemed so inimical now held peace.

This was her home.

She turned to go to bed, and as she passed the photograph, touched it gently.

'Goodnight, John,' she said softly.

Witch wagged an uncertain tail, and outside an owl hooted mournfully as he flew past on silent wings. The night surrounded Rhea, and her last thought as she fell asleep was of a small grandson lying in his cot, unaware of any future at all. Tomorrow waited for her, full of interest. She was alive again.

16

John had been dead for exactly a year. Rhea sat looking at her post. Sadie had sent her a photograph of the dress-rehearsal of the latest musical she had designed for. The brilliant colours swirled in a mazy pattern on the stage as the dancers obviously worked in an intricate maze. Sadie had had it blown up to giant size, a thought that Rhea appreciated. Her letter said nothing about John, or the anniversary, but Sadie rarely wrote and had taken care that this arrived on the right day, to remind her mother-in-law that she was thinking of her.

Louise had written too, sending an enlarged photograph of the baby. He laughed at the camera, totally adorable. Rhea had seen him twice in the past few months; she must go and visit them again. Motherhood had been very good for Louise, and it had been a good move to leave the district. There was no one to turn to, and Louise had come to grips at last with reality. Mark was much happier too. Rhea had enjoyed her visit, and as a bonus Witch had behaved beautifully and had fallen in love with the baby, fascinated by every move he made and very gentle when he was around.

Witch was almost ten months old; her training was progressing, and Rhea, whistling to her, thought how much her own life had changed during the year. This was now home. Thorpe and Wilde, whom she had feared, had become, not friends, but at least friendly acquaintances, accepting her and her dog, knowing now that she would take the greatest care not to let the bitch out of her sight, or cause either of them problems. They called on her with cuttings for her garden, with eggs from Wilde's hens, with a brace of pheasants which Thorpe plucked and brought her when he learned from the postman that it was her birthday.

Agnes Redpath had left the dog club and given up dogs, much to everyone's relief. She was part of the past, remembered ruefully, but now almost with laughter. The whole episode seemed so absurd. Rhea wondered why it had upset her so much. Grief did odd things, she supposed.

Lucifer had been sold but she had been down twice to visit him, and was now painting him again for his new owner. He had played a major part in helping her come to terms with her new life, and she was still amused when she remembered Rod's amazement when she told him the price he had fetched. Her older son had always thought her incapable of coping on her own and was rapidly learning that his mother was far more capable than he had ever realised; in fact as capable as he of managing her own life and in this instance far more capable of realising where profit lay. Rhea hid the fact that the profit had been accidental and nothing to do with her acumen. It wouldn't hurt Rod to remain ignorant of the facts.

The cottage and studio were exactly as she had dreamed. The door stood wide, inviting the sunlight that lay across the floor. Witch, basking in the warmth, was lying on her back, juggling with a bone held between her front paws, stretched out, blissful.

Rhea's order book was full; she had work enough to last her for over a year, and she had spent some of the money that Lucifer had earned her on a gelding that she could ride. Both that and the brood mare were kept with Rory, with whom she had slipped into an easy undemanding friendship. He was there if she wanted to talk; sometimes he dropped in, to discuss the mare, who was to be covered by Lucifer when it was time; she had been offered a free covering. She would have something of the stallion to own, as she intended to keep the foal. She would school it herself and maybe ride it; if it were a filly she might have two brood mares. The mare was the same colour as the stallion; a bright chestnut, the colour of sunlight, and she was beautiful, only a youngster now, but with a future if nothing went wrong.

There was interest in every day; plans to make and work to

do. A foal looked out at her from the canvas on the easel; an enchanting little filly foal, with a white blaze down her face, with four white socks, standing looking at the world with astounded eyes. She had been very new when Rhea saw her, and the amazed expression on her face was perfectly depicted. Her painting was improving all the time; there was room for more improvement, but the old skill was returning. She had been unable to paint well for months after John had died.

The foal was posed in front of a rustic fence; behind it were winter trees. There was very little left to do. In a few days she would be able to take the picture over to the foal's owners; she had been invited to lunch when she went.

She glanced at the rest of her mail. Ray Morton and Rhea Morland were now inextricably mixed and she used both names, and sometimes wondered who she was. Her two identities had long ago merged, and most people now called her Ray, which she preferred to Rhea. She thought of her grandfather and laughed. She had once asked him about deer in a letter, and he had solemnly sent her a list of butchers stocking venison. Why, she had never made out. He lived in a world of his own, his head in the trees with the birds, and he seldom came out of it. He was part of her past; never to be recaptured. Too many people were now part of that past.

It was one of the penalties of age.

'Hi.'

She hadn't heard the van, but Witch had and was standing with bristling ruff. She recognised Dave and launched herself at him, adoring him. He was part of her life, as now Rhea often went tracking with the dog-handlers, and had learned to lay tracks for them as well. She loved the off-duty days when they all went out together, into the woods or fields or over downland, and watched the dogs working. She had learned a great deal in the past year, in areas of experience she had never even dreamed existed before.

'We're having a party tonight,' Dave said. 'We've things to celebrate; Reg's new baby; four dogs that have passed their tests with flying colours, and Susie's Christmas exam marks; she was fifth in her class and as she was about fifth from the bottom last year that is something to celebrate. And also I'm making plans for you and Witch; how would you like to come with us in the summer when we go to the civilian Working Trials? Think you can get her up to scratch and try it?'

'I hadn't thought of doing it,' Rhea said.

'Why not? She can jump as well as our dogs; track as well, and her search is good; your heelwork needs working on and so does her sendaway; she hasn't cottoned on yet to running out a hundred yards, but we can work on that too; you need a new interest. You'll have paint coming out of your ears.'

Rhea laughed.

'Mostly it does,' she said. 'Are you off duty, on duty, or going on duty?'

'I've just dropped Susie at school; whole day to myself. I could do with some breakfast.'

He had glanced at the calendar and seen the ring round the date.

'You're all right?'

Anniversaries could be hell, he thought, memory suddenly bitter.

'I'm all right,' Rhea said. 'I was just thinking how much had changed; it seems like another life, another existence; a lot of it seems unreal, like Lucifer and the fairy gold he brought me. That will melt away; I still don't believe it. Or my mare and my new horse; Rory picked me a beauty; it's like riding in an armchair.'

'Rory knows his horses,' Dave said. He watched Rhea frying bacon and eggs, making toast, almost as at home here as in his own home. She was easy company, asking little, fitting in. Susie adored her, and she had been a godsend, helping the child choose her clothes with much more flair than Heather, who went for stout sensible things that Susie would grow into, so she had always looked a bit of a freak and Dave had never known why and the child had been miserable.

Rhea managed to find things that were cheap and pretty and fitted, and made Susie feel like a million dollars. She was growing fast; it would be good to have Rhea here to visit and help when teenage problems started. It was like having an older sister, a luxury Dave often wished had been his.

'The end of a year,' Rhea said, sitting with a cup of coffee, watching Dave eat.

'No, it's the start of a new one,' Dave said. He glanced out of the window. Witch was playing with Venn, the pair of them romping in the garden, now fenced all the way round and entirely dogproof. Both Thorpe and Wilde had helped her with that.

'The people I thought bad turned out fine after all,' Rhea said. 'It's funny . . . It's been a very odd year . . .'

I'm changed, she thought, watching the dogs; maybe that's all that's happened. I've come out into the world, instead of being sheltered; I've learned to stand up for myself, instead of never facing what lay outside the house; I've had to cope, without John doing it for me. I never even realised that he did.

There were two photographs on the mantelpiece now. She had snapped Lucifer, the last time she visited him, wanting a memory of an animal that had somehow never been part of her life, yet had given her a feeling of being able to go on; had given her hope instead of despair; had brought her opportunities that she had never dreamed existed.

At the other end of the mantelpiece was a photograph of Witch, taken when she was a pup, symbolising yet another change of direction.

She picked up the photograph of her husband, and put it on the table in front of them.

'I wonder if those who are dead know what happens to those of us that remain,' she said. 'I wonder what John would make of my life now . . . I don't think he'd recognise the woman he married.'

Dave, looking back for almost the whole of his daughter's life, found his own memories were blurred almost beyond recall. Donna had been gentle and had laughed and had died, and their marriage had been all too brief.

'Maybe we learn,' he said. 'If Donna had lived, Susie and I would be different people; you've grown up since your husband died . . . you've changed a lot, become stronger, and wiser, and less vulnerable.'

The dogs raced in, tails waving, and charged into the kitchen where they both drank from the same bowl, with a great deal of splashing and pushing and noise. Witch had recently been spayed, and was tired. She came to lie down with her head on Rhea's foot. Venn stretched out beside her, his eyes on his master.

Outside, the woods were bathed in sunlight.

'It's peaceful here,' Dave said. 'I hated you for a few weeks for buying my dream cottage; and now I can tell you how glad I am that you did.'

He stretched and flicked his finger to Venn.

'I must go back. Don't forget; eight o'clock tonight and wear a party dress; we're going to have a real slap-up do. We've hired the best room at the Jester and Bells and the landlord's laying on a really good spread.'

Rhea watched the van drive away.

Peace returned.

A heron flew over, towards the water, which lay beyond the trees. He sailed slowly, unbelievably large, and she watched him till he was out of sight.

She picked up her paint brush.

Witch curled up nose to tail and sighed deeply. It was going to be another boring day.

The phone rang and Witch leaped up.

Rhea sighed and put down the brush.

'Rhea, it's Rachel. Are you OK?'

'Very OK,' Rhea said. 'I was just finishing the picture of the Eldon foal.'

'Good,' said the deep lazy voice at the other end of the line. 'There's an American firm wants a whole collection of Ray Morton horse pictures; and a French paperback firm want you to illustrate a story written around a foal, and I've a client with an Arab mare that's just won one of the top awards, and wants her portrait. Shall I say yes to them all?'

'Yes,' Rhea said, and put down the phone and went back to pick up her brush. Dave had been right; it was not the end of a year; it was the beginning of a totally new life, with a fascinating future that beckoned to her excitingly, with the prospect of something worthwhile to fill every day, with the chance to paint as she had never painted before.

She looked at the foal.

It was good, very good, but the next picture would be even better.

John would have been very proud.

She knew that now.

It was too late; but 'if only' were the saddest words there were and regrets were useless. She had the future to think of and plans to make, and she would live life day by day as fully as she could; without that there was no point to living.

She switched on the radio and a deep voice filled the room.

'Mine is the sunlight, mine is the morning . . .'

She added her own words.

'Mine is the painting, all's right with my world.'

There was not enough colour on the foal's head; she filled her brush and within moments was once more totally absorbed. The bitch slept, and beyond the window Thorpe paused and looked at her, and smiled, and walked on, flicking his finger to Blue, knowing that Rhea was lost in a world of her own, as private and intense as his own world in the woods, and that she would not welcome interruption. He had known this was an anniversary and had wondered how she would fare. Now he knew he had no further worries, and within seconds had forgotten her and was as intent on his own business as Rhea was on hers.

She didn't move until lunchtime, when she turned and found Susie sitting watching her.

'I came to lunch,' she said. She went to Rhea, and leaned against her briefly. 'It's just like being at home when I come here.'

She went out into the kitchen to look in the cupboard and Rhea smiled at the small intent back. It was all she needed to make the day perfect.

THE END

THE MONASTERY CAT AND OTHER ANIMALS
by Joyce Stranger

Here, from Joyce Stranger, Britain's best-loved writer of animal stories, are all the animals that she understands and describes so well . . . pedigree cats and barnyard strays, working dogs and family pets, wild horses and untamed animals from the sea and the jungle . . .

Joyce Stranger can write about animals as no other writer – and make you love them . . .

0 552 12044 8   £1.50

THE CURSE OF SEAL VALLEY
by Joyce Stranger

"Death to the seal woman – death to her seal pup!" So ring out the wild curses of Gwyn, the lone madman.

Sula, washed ashore with an injured seal pup, storm-wrecked and covered with oil, has never harmed anyone – yet fear feeds the superstitious belief of the villagers.

When a run of misfortune strikes the community, they are easily infected with Gwyn's black hatred; with his tales of seal women and unnatural bewitchment; Sula is the imagined curse of Seal Valley – Sula and her seals must be driven out or destroyed . . .

0 552 52207 4   95p